VEGAS RAIN

By
RICK MURCER

PUBLISHED BY:

Murcer Press, LLC

Edited by
Jan Green-thewordverve.com

Interior book design by
Bob Houston eBook Formatting

Vegas Rain © 2013 Rick Murcer
All rights reserved
www.rickmurcer.com

ISBN:0615952216

For JC, who loves me and keeps me on the path, eternally.

For all of the wonderful readers I've met along this journey.

You are ALL special to me.

Thanks to my wife, Carrie. There is truly no one like you.

VEGAS RAIN

A Novel

By

RICK MURCER

CHAPTER-1

The roar of the large, yellow backhoe caught his attention. FBI Special Agent Manny Williams stared as the monstrosity turned the corner of the gravelly trail running through the middle of the cemetery and headed directly toward him. It swung to the left, barely avoiding a one-hundred-year-old tombstone, zigged back into position and was on track again, sprinting at him with the menace of a T-Rex. He reached inside his coat and placed his hand on the cold steel of his Glock 19.

A few seconds later, as the lumbering machine drew closer, he got a better glimpse of the driver and passenger. He pulled his hand from the gun and smiled.

Josh Corner, the leader of the FBI's Behavioral Analysis Unit, and Alex Downs, Manny's longtime friend and the most talented CSI he'd ever worked with, were crowded side by side on the bench seat, Josh driving, Alex giving animated directions with his hands. Manny's smile widened. He'd remember this one. It was like a Laurel and Hardy skit from the golden age of black-and-white television.

Wheeling up close, maybe fifteen feet, the smell of spent diesel fuel dancing amidst the crisp Michigan air, the backhoe rumbled to a jerky stop.

A moment later, Josh jumped out and Alex followed suit, shaking his head and clutching his chest.

"I got to get one of these," said Josh. "That was more fun than riding with Sophie when she's got a wild hair."

"Yeah. You need to go to backhoe driving school first. You only have to learn how to start one, drive it, and control the front loader and the backhoe. Other than that, you're good to go," said Alex, pulling his black-rimmed glasses from his round face and wiping them against his fleece jacket.

Josh shrugged, running his hand over his almost-shaved head, his cobalt-blue eyes sparkling. "Not bad for a city boy." Then he cocked his head toward Manny. "They have classes for that?"

"Man, I hope so. But you did okay. I only reached for my gun once."

Josh's eyes sparkled even more. "I'll take that as an endorsement then."

"Amazing how we hear only what we want to hear," said Alex.

Another roar of a high-powered engine caused the three men to turn in the opposite direction and focus on a black FBI SUV as it banked around the corner of the gravel road.

Stones and dirt flew like a mini snowstorm as the vehicle fishtailed to the left, then the right. Five seconds later, it came to an even stop, engine revving, smoke rising slowly from the exhaust.

Before the wheels had even stopped rolling, both doors flew open and the last two members of the BAU came walking in their direction, not appearing to be in any great hurry.

Sophie Lee, his attractive, diminutive Chinese-American ex-partner from his time with the Lansing Police Department, who had joined him at the Bureau, was a few feet ahead of the taller, bearded Dean Mikus, the other forensic expert of the BAU. Dean's face was flushed as he held tight to a red paisley driver's cap that matched his shirt.

Manny shook his head. The man had a fashion sense, if you could call it that, all his own. Just like his taste in women. Dean was partial to independent Asian ladies and none he'd ever met matched his partiality more than Sophie. That was probably an understatement.

Dean had been smitten by Sophie the second he'd laid eyes on her in Puerto Rico some five months ago. He'd even gotten down on one knee, called her princess, and kissed her hand. It may have been the only time in their respective careers that the collective BAU was rendered speechless.

It hadn't happened often in the nine years Manny and Sophie worked together, but she'd been totally shocked by Dean's confession of adoration, for a few seconds at least. And now, after all of these months, she was warming up to Dean, but was taking her time. Manny thought that kind of patience a great choice. She'd been through enough hell in her personal life over the last few years, including two divorces, so to dive in the deep end of the pool again wasn't wise. He liked that she understood that.

Sophie looped her arm under Manny's, then gave him a kiss on the cheek. "This better be good, Williams. You got my ass out of bed way too early for a weekend. Just because you gave up any hope of a real life now that you're married, doesn't mean I did. The nightlife in Lansing needs me. I'm in demand."

Patting Sophie's arm, Manny grinned. No matter the circumstance, and what was coming next was as unreal as he could imagine, she held an innate ability to make him do just that: smile.

"Hey. This is what you get when you sign up to protect your country and join the FBI. Besides, you know the BAU never gets any sleep. It's in the job description," Manny answered.

"Whatever. You dragged me to a cemetery on top of getting me out of bed? You sure know how to show a woman a good time, Williams. My public needs to see me looking my best."

"Public? Rumor has it that you were home and in bed, and alone, by eleven."

Sophie shot Manny a look and then turned an icy stare toward Dean. He shifted his feet, glancing down at his steel-toed boots. The newest member of the BAU was still a bit uncomfortable when the attention focused on him. That was okay. This unit had enough type A personalities.

Dean exhaled and scanned the group before his soft gaze settled on Sophie. Again, Manny wondered just what he and Sophie had going. Maybe the two of them hadn't a clue either.

"Hey, Princess. I can't lie to him. He called to make sure we were ready this morning. I told him you were tired and I dropped you off at your apartment at ten-thirty."

"Great. Makes me look like I'm forty or something. Traitor."

He shook his head. "No. I was tired too. But I watched you turn out your lights before I went to the hotel."

"You watched me turn off the lights? Normally I'd think that's creepy, even for me, but coming from you, that's kind of cool. Did you see anything? You know, like, was I naked and silhouetted against the curtain? That kind of stuff?"

Dean's face turned a bright scarlet. "Well, I didn't exactly, you know, see . . . "

"Okay. Let's stay on task. You two can talk about this on your own time."

Rolling her eyes, Sophie grabbed Manny's arm. "See what I mean, Williams? You're letting the air out of your marriage already. You need to do things like that to keep your sex life rolling, ya know? You're still hot, but man, you gotta keep things hopping. Chloe will think you've turned old. Hell, you know, like fifty."

"Chloe and I are just fine." His eyes narrowed. "You aren't allowed to talk to her about our personal life, got it?"

"Yeah, I got it, but what you don't know won't hurt you," said Sophie, her smile as incorrigible as ever. "And, well, women talk."

It was Manny's turn to roll his eyes. "I thought we were out of high school and college."

"Never. Anyway, what's going on here? You said something about Argyle's grave being empty?" asked Sophie, her voice growing softer.

For a numberless time, he tried to get his mind around what Sophie had asked. How Dr. Argyle's body wound up missing was the least of his concerns; the why held a much more pointed, unsettling overtone.

Manny had put the brilliant, but totally demented killer in the ground with a bullet to the head in Galway, Ireland a year ago. Even though the Good Doctor had cultivated some over-zealous groupies, the act of robbing his grave was almost beyond comprehension, even if any of his warped followers might still be around.

Running his hand through his hair, Manny spoke. "I had Alex get an exhumation order while we were coming back from North Carolina after we found out that Max Tucker had been killed."

"You didn't say why you wanted to do it exactly," said Josh.

"I'm not sure why . . . it was a gut feeling, I guess. It simply seemed odd to me that Max was murdered when he was a certified disciple of

Argyle. I mean what was gained by that? Toss in the circumstances involving the murder of Garity a few weeks after he stabbed me in San Juan and, well, it made me wonder, just for a moment, if I'd really put Argyle away."

"You know, that's a few times you've mentioned that. You blew his freaking head off, remember?" said Sophie, her voice rising.

"I know how crazy that sounds, but did I really? I mean, I was looking at his face, his eyes, and I'm still pretty sure it was him, sort of. But think about it, about him, and how he did what he did from the very beginning. He always had an escape, a way out, right? He'd never exposed himself to the remotest chance of dying. He had the money, the time, that brain-washing charm, everything he'd need to create a perfect doppelganger," said Manny.

Josh shifted his weight, obviously uncomfortable. "I don't question your instincts any more, especially when you trance, but like I said initially when you mentioned all this, you need to give yourself more credit. We beat him at his own game. He never saw us coming."

Manny nodded. "I keep thinking that, but I need to . . . no, *we all* need to make sure. I wanted Alex to do a DNA analysis of his body to help me rest easier."

He glance around his unit. "Anyone else think that my concerns could have a little substance?"

No one answered.

"That's what I thought."

Taking a few steps toward the open grave some twenty feet away, Manny turned back to the others.

"Now we get this—an empty grave without a clue of where the body might be. Does anyone else want to chime in with an explanation?"

"Not yet," said Dean. "Do we have any idea how this might have happened? It could lead to the why and where, maybe?"

"The how is simple. The man working the third shift at the cemetery dug the casket up sometime last week," said Manny.

"Why would he do that? And how do you know?" asked Sophie, shaking her head.

"I think we can figure those questions out. After Alex called last night, I had him do background checks on anyone who might have had access to this cemetery and the backhoe."

"Good place to start," said Josh.

"We thought so. At any rate, this guy was a City of Lansing employee, and he was also a patient of Doctor Fredrick Argyle five years ago. He was sent in for counseling after he'd lost his son to a drunk-driving accident."

"Shit, is there anyone that guy didn't treat in this damn city?" said Sophie.

Manny shrugged. "Dr. Argyle held the contract for city and county employees, so you can guess at the opportunities he had to spread his distorted gospel."

"Should we check out the rest of the people he had contact with over that time period?" asked Josh.

"We should. Although I suspect he only targeted people he could manipulate. I've talked to my old boss, Commissioner Gavin Crosby, and he's going to work on creating a list of names of employees who may have talked with Argyle."

More silence. Phenomenal how it could be so deafening.

The early spring morning accepted the uneasy stillness even if the crew in the cemetery wasn't sure how to handle it.

Manny knew that the talented group of FBI agents, and close friends, were trying to get their minds around what he'd already accepted.

Argyle could be alive.

CHAPTER-2

"Don't never matter anyway. I got shit for luck and *misery's my best frriieenndd.*"

Alonzo Smith stopped sifting among the green garbage bins located behind the Egyptian Casino just off from Las Vegas Avenue. He put his hand on his chest, one dirty foot on an old cardboard box, Sinatra-like, then sang the last phrase, again, of his newest lyrics. He listened intently as the melody echoed throughout the small, hot alley. His smile evolved into something more, and he laughed.

"I still got it, baby, still got it," he said out loud, bowing to an unseen crowd who didn't seem to mind the stench—his and the alley's.

Removing his foot from the box, he moved slowly to the next bin. His voice had changed over the last few years, but he knew good music when he heard it, whether he was drunk, stoned, or otherwise. He could still carry a tune better than most and, back in his day, during his fifteen minutes of fame, no one had written better lyrics. He wrote those moving love songs with sexy, steamy, get-laid lyrics that made peoples' temperatures rise as their imaginations took over.

Once, all of those years ago, he'd had the gold records to prove it. Motown. LA. New York. You name the city; they'd all been his oyster. And he could write the other stuff too. He'd written so many jingles that he'd forgotten the exact amount. Never mind a couple of those movie themes.

"You were the best, baby, the best," he whispered.

Looking down at his dirty hands and tattered clothing, he slowly waggled his head. That wasn't all he'd forgotten was it? She wasn't easy to erase from his tortured mind. Never would be.

It didn't happen often these days. The lucid, introspective moments of recollection reared ugly heads when their ghosts wanted to remind him of his sins.

He felt his angst rise.

These unexpected spells cast a peek into the past that was bittersweet. His successes, the money, the cars, the houses—those were pleasant things. Nothing matched her, however. How she cared. How she loved. How she lived. Then she was gone. All because of him.

His heart pounded in his chest.

All because of him.

Well, that was the true apparition that sent him back to his own tiny world, wasn't it?

He closed his eyes and waited for the page to turn so that he could go back to the world that always gave him sanctuary. He opened his eyes. Alonzo was still in the wrong reality.

Then he hit himself in the head with a quick right. Nothing. He was still of sound mind, her lovely face dancing in his brain so vividly that the tears came, again. His quiet cry turned into sobs. She was so beautiful, so trusting, then she was gone, and all because he wouldn't play ball with a couple of Vegas hoods.

Quickly fumbling through his deep pockets, he found his remedy of choice and drank a fourth of the pint of whisky in one gulp. Sniffing the bottle, he repeated the long swig. The smell and the incessant burn combined to form his version of comfort food. It worked.

A few moments later, the real world again a distant shadow, he rummaged around the remaining garbage bins, impervious to the increasing stench that would have driven most others to a safer haven. Any thoughts of his past life were finally and completely obliterated.

After tossing away a large section of cardboard, he stopped, tilted his head, and grinned. A shoe. Not just any shoe but a black, patent-leather, designer shoe was sticking straight up, looking like his size, at least close enough, and waiting for him to pluck it from its dicey prison. He bent closer and felt his pulse shift to fourth gear. The mate for his new treasure was right next to it, albeit buried a little deeper.

"Score! It's my lucky day, and I gotta say, *I did it my waayy*," he crooned, laughing at his good fortune.

Clutching the first shoe, he yanked, fully expecting it to come free. It didn't. He scowled and then gave it another yank. It moved sideways, not up, and he fell back, catching himself with his hands.

"You som'bitches are coming with me, like it or not," he yelled.

Alonzo spit on his hands, grabbed the shoe again, and yanked with all of his might. Again he ended up on his backside, but, this time, the black treasure came free. He stared at the shoe in his grasp, but that wasn't the only thing that came out from the rubble in the bin.

At first, he believed the leg belonged to a mannequin, but the dried blood and the rancid odor emanating from the human foot still wedged within the shoe told him otherwise.

The dark hairs standing straight out from the foot, just under the straight cut that had separated it from the man's leg, held Alonzo paralyzed.

But only for a small morsel of time.

What was left of his sanity demanded a whole new reaction.

Tossing the limb from hell aside, he scrambled out of the bin.

Alonzo Smith reached the hot asphalt and tore his shirt with both hands, screaming for Satan to leave him alone.

CHAPTER-3

After brewing another decaf mocha latte, Chloe Williams set the cup on the kitchen table and sat down. Ten seconds later, she stood, far too nervous to stay in one spot for very long.

Reaching for her cell, she turned it over in her hands and then, for the fiftieth time, checked to see if Manny had texted or called and wondered if, for some ungodly reason, the phone hadn't let her know.

She was quickly struck with the notion that she'd lived just fine for the first twenty-five years of her life without a cell phone. Now she spent more time paying attention to the damn thing than Manny. Well, not quite, but it was close.

She smiled. She'd have to fix that, particularly considering the events of the last five months. She'd found love. True love. Gotten married to the hottest FBI agent in the Bureau and was now pregnant with his child. Pretty cool.

Her smile faded. It hadn't been that simple.

Marriage to death-watch, and the eventual miracle-like resurrection of her new husband, wasn't exactly what she'd envisioned when she and Manny had gotten married in San Juan. She had gone from experiencing a special wedding night with the most intriguing man on the planet to utter hell for a full six weeks.

She'd never forget watching him in that hospital room the day they let him come home— putting on his shoes and then doing his version of the happy dance when he thought was alone.

The smile returned.

The only thing moving faster than his feet had been the beating of her heart. Never before had she believed relief and love so closely related.

There were times she suspected that God had a sense of humor she failed to understand. Giving her Manny, then almost taking him away with a blade to the chest, then bringing him back to her had almost driven her crazy. But maybe the idea was to appreciate him more. She hadn't believed that possible, but like her mom, Haley Rose Franson, had always said, you don't know about the fruit until you taste it.

"Enough of that fruit," she murmured.

She stared at the phone again, slowly moving her head. Earlier that morning, Manny had talked to her concerning the fact that Argyle's grave had been tampered with and his body was now missing. She'd moved closer to him as they lay in bed, resting her head on his thick chest, listening to his strong heart. Manny's heartbeat always helped to calm her, and she had done her best to ensure her dread hadn't given her away as they talked regarding the potential reasons that the psychopath's body was AWOL. Some of those possibilities, no matter how unlikely, terrified her.

She sipped from her cup. Trying to hide emotions from a man like Manny was like the sun not rising each morning. Her blond-haired, blue-eyed husband was without doubt the most gifted profiler she'd seen. His innate ability to see what others couldn't was the reason they'd cornered Argyle in her hometown of Galway, Ireland, in the first place.

Doctor Fredrick Argyle.

Had there ever been a man that fit the term "demonic evil" better than he? It hadn't been just his sick, yet brilliant mind; it was also his charm that had draped even her mother under his spell. Argyle's power to manipulate others to do his bidding was uncanny.

His training as a psychologist had given him incredible insight to the human condition, even a degree of mind control, and he'd used it. That's what Manny had suspected had happened at the grave site.

Argyle must have recruited a lackey with untold loyalty to mind-screw the Feds, and Manny, one last time. And why not? The Good Doctor hadn't left a detail unconsidered while he was alive. Her husband and she had agreed that he hadn't in death either. Manny had smiled at her, given her one of those long kisses that pulled her feet from the ground, and said this had to be Argyle's final trick. What could be left?

Then he went out the front door to meet the rest of the BAU unit at the cemetery.

Chloe twirled her red hair in her finger as she recalled her husband's exit. The problem was that Manny wasn't the only profiler in the house. The look in his eyes and the way he'd moved his hands told her that he wasn't convinced in the least that this was Argyle's last stunt. She wasn't at all sure she knew what the hell that meant.

She tried to sit down again. Got up, again, and then entered the foyer with the full-length mirror. She touched her belly, and the grin returned.

Moving to the front of the mirror, she lifted up her blouse past her breasts and looked at her profile. She'd always been busty, but now the soft, white flesh was falling out of her bra like never before. But that wasn't her focus. The small bump in her usually flat stomach was where her eyes rested. The idea of being almost ten weeks pregnant with the next member of the Williams family and her own Celtic Franson clan made her hold her breath. Giving birth to a baby changed everything, or so she'd heard. And this one belonged to her and Manny. And in a real way, only to her.

Questioning God about circumstances in her life had been a regular practice for Chloe, but not this time. The gift of this child was beyond questioning.

To say she was overwhelmed with the prospect of bringing this little one into the world was an understatement. She'd been entrusted with the most noble of vocations: motherhood.

She now knew what women meant when they said they'd protect their children even at the risk of death. That was now a given. And Manny felt the same way. All one had to do was see the way he looked at his daughter Jennifer.

Slowly dropping her shirt, she rubbed the baby bump again. She'd thought it inconceivable to love anyone more than Manny, yet she saw the possibility of that truth changing.

"Lucky wee one, you are," she whispered.

The phone began to play an old Celtic love song, the ringtone that alerted her to an inbound text. She hurried to the kitchen and picked up the phone, eagerly searching the screen for Manny's first contact of the morning. She was hoping to read that they'd solved the mystery of Argyle's missing body.

That's not what she got.

She frowned.

The number where the text originated from wasn't familiar. It came from an out-of-state area code. She couldn't put a finger on why, but her angst jumped. She was still an FBI special agent, and Chloe's training took over. She studied the number, memorized it, then taking a deep breath, she opened the text and read.

As the words tumbled down the screen, Chloe felt her knees grow weak.

Congratulations on your pregnancy, Agent Williams. The Good Doctor is so looking forward to meeting the newest member of your family, up close and personal.

CHAPTER-4

Kicking a clay-covered pebble into the hole that once housed Argyle's body, maybe, Sophie then glanced at the other members of the BAU. They'd formed a rough semicircle around the empty grave site. Each member of the BAU wore a different expression of what-the-hell-is-going-on, except Manny. Her eyes settled on him. Dean, Alex, and Josh had done the same thing.

It would seem that after ten years of working with, and hanging out with, this man, and after seeing what he was capable of in so many ways, she would be beyond surprised with how his brilliant mind worked.

Guess not.

Sophie crossed her arms. "Okay Williams. I get how this is kind of weird, the whole damn casket being gone and all, and at least we know how. I also get why you might think we need to be here in the first place. Crazy as it seems, you make a point. But what I really want to know is—"

What's the point of taking the body?" Manny completed her thought.

"Yeah, exactly."

He started to raise his hand to run it through his hair.

"Hey. I said you need to stop that. You look a whole lot hotter with hair."

"Duly noted, Sophie." Then he finished what he'd started.

"Okay. I warned your ass. Bald isn't funny." Glancing at Alex, she couldn't suppress a fast grin. "You'll end up like Dough Boy over there."

"Funny, wench. Just stay focused for a change, will you?" said Alex, giving Sophie the evil eye.

"I got your focus," said Sophie, pointing to her backside.

Alex rolled his eyes. "I'll pass, thank you."

"Good thing you two aren't married," said Josh. "Manny?"

"I know the reasons for taking the body seem obvious, whether Argyle is dead or alive. On one hand, if he's truly dead, we can round up the rest of his followers or whatever the hell we want to call them, and this kind of junk will eventually be over. If he did fool us all and he's still out there—which I doubt, but say it's true—then the chase is still on, and that's what he lived . . . or *lives* . . . for."

"So doesn't that cover it?" asked Dean.

Sophie watched Manny carefully. He'd taught her much over the years, not the least was reading body language in a microsecond. That included the micro-expression concepts that Manny wanted her to bone up on. She was getting there.

His scowl had come and gone, and he had shifted his feet. Nervous or gathering his wits? She believed a bit of both.

"It would seem like that would be the only two viable options, Dean, but there's another possibility, no matter how remote."

Anguish and Sophie had played tag more than once since they'd met Argyle. It always got a little worse when she contemplated how Argyle's first true lackey, Eli Jenkins, had almost killed her on the cruise ship. Watching Manny, she felt that familiar torment spike higher than usual.

"You know when they say that imitation is the most sincere form of flattery?" asked Manny.

"Yeah, like some kind of hero worship that makes . . . oh shit, Manny. Are you saying this is some copycat sicko?" said Sophie.

He hesitated, and then slowly shook his head. "No, not like that so much, but in the ballpark. Back in 2008, a killer, Derek Brown, butchered two young women from the Whitechapel area of London, then disposed of their bodies, which were never found. He was caught before he could spiral out of complete control and emulate his hero, or essence of the hero, and his nauseating obsession completely."

"Jack the Ripper?" asked Josh.

"Yes. Brown said that he wanted to be known as a notorious serial killer and placed into that same category. He was totally consumed with the idea of recreating that same air of terror and intrigue, yet he was different. He'd been a sex offender for years, so his twist on the killings were his own."

"Like?" asked Sophie.

Manny performed his own version of pebble-kicking without looking up. "The obvious trait was hiding the bodies. Derek Brown's seven or so run-ins with the law in England had taught him, consciously or subconsciously, that he'd be better off if no one found the bodies. That way it would be harder to convict him. Jack was quite the opposite. He either didn't care if someone found the bodies of those women in 1888 or he wanted to display his 'work' for the world to see."

Raising his disconcerting gaze toward Sophie, she could see those complex, almost supernatural, wheels turning.

"The Ripper mocked Scotland Yard with letters and practically dared the authorities to catch him, which never happened, by the way. No matter who thinks they know for sure who Jack the Ripper was, he's never been identified. Brown wanted to remain low profile too. At least until he was ready, which, given his unpredictable psychology, may never have happened."

"Why?" asked Alex.

"Ego mostly, I suspect. The fact that they begin copying someone leads to comparisons of what they do and what their 'hero' did or does. They soon realize that the public isn't as enamored with their antics as the crimes of the copycatted killer. I think that's when they deviate and find what works for them and gives them their own trademark, as sick as that sounds."

"Okay, so what does *that* have to do with *this*?" asked Sophie.

"What if this copycat, so to speak, doesn't care about notoriety? What if he or she only wants to continue the game?"

"So one of Argyle's protégés cut from the pack and thinks he or she can continue where Argyle left off," stated Josh.

Manny shook his head. "No. A protégé would feel like they had to do what the Master required. He or she would be lost without direction. That's why they hooked up with Argyle in the first place. I'm talking about someone completely out of the fold. A person who studied everything relevant concerning Argyle. All of his theories, his actions, hell, even his personal habits. And of course, all of his enemies. This one person could be so deep into that psychology that they might believe they see and talk to Argyle or even think they *are* Argyle."

"So they don't have their own agenda, they just pick up where Argyle left off?" said Sophie.

"That's it, in a nutshell. It's very extreme but not unheard of. There are people in hospitals and prisons today that claim they are Jack the Ripper, Genghis Khan, Lizzy Borden, or whomever. Crazy or not, that belief makes them dangerous."

Josh moved opposite of the grave from Manny and Sophie, and she watched as he scanned Manny's face. She saw the glimpse of doubt, and a little something more.

"That would also mean, if your theory is right—which I'm struggling with—that this killer would not want to invite any of us to tea and crumpets," said Josh, looking at Manny with curiosity.

The quick smile Manny flashed seemed to catch Josh by surprise.

"You're a little worried about *my* psychology, yes?"

"Ahh shit. I hate working with a freaking mind reader. But yeah. I'm wondering if you are a bit obsessed by 'all things Argyle' and shouldn't step back some."

"That's a fair statement," said Manny. "Especially since Chloe's pregnant and Jen's getting ready for college. But you're off base, Josh."

Then Manny walked around the grave and stood a foot from his good friend.

More than once, Sophie had been on the receiving end of the look that Manny was now dealing out to Josh. Not pretty.

"I've got a lot to protect and even a workaholic's mind can work overtime. But you're out of your damn tree if you believe I *want* to be thinking the way I'm thinking. I need to see all of the possibilities, like it or not, and no matter how goofy-ass or improbable, that's what I get paid to deliver to you and the Bureau. And you don't get to tell me how to do that and just how deep I go. Are we clear?"

Sophie watched the commander of the BAU tilt his head as a tiny grin flashed and then disappeared.

"Clear enough. That still doesn't change my opinion that you should step back some. But I don't suppose that would happen even if I ordered it. But there is one more thing."

The two men glared at each other. Sophie wasn't sure what was coming next. She moved toward them.

Without turning away from Josh, Manny raised his hand in her direction. She stopped and waited.

"What would that be?" asked Manny.

Josh reached over and pinched Manny's cheek. "Do you realize how much your eyes sparkle when you get pissy?"

Dean laughed out loud almost immediately. Alex followed suit.

Sophie didn't. She simply released a pent-up breath, then smiled to cover her true thoughts.

Josh knew what he was doing by breaking the tension. That's why he led this group, but she also recognized truth, at least in part, when she saw it. She hated the feeling that Josh might be the slightest bit correct in his assessment, but he was. Then again, why wouldn't Manny be a little paranoid? Since they'd encountered Argyle, none of them had lost more or felt more pain than Manny. Not the least of those events was losing his first wife, Louise. Argyle hadn't been directly responsible, but if he hadn't been such a distraction, according to Manny, Louise would still be here.

Sophie had reminded him that he was just guessing and threw his famous words back at him: all things work for a reason. He'd nodded, said something about wrestling demons, and switched subjects. That's why they called Manny the Guardian of the Universe—he always put his emotions on the backburner and concentrated fully on a case, like he was doing now. But no one was free from the past. No one.

Sophie snapped back to the present when she heard "smartass."

This time, it wasn't directed at her. It was for Josh, from Manny with a smile.

"Hey, just had to remind you who was in charge, sort of," said Josh.

"Okay. Now that you two are done comparing weenies, what's next?" asked Sophie.

"Yeah, I guess we should get to that," said Manny. "And I didn't realize we were comparing weenies."

"I don't even know if that's in the Bureau's handbook," added Josh.

"Okay, now *you two* need to stay on track," said Sophie, feeling relief at their lighter tones.

"When Alex called to tell me about the missing body," said Manny, "I had him check to see who had been buried in this cemetery over the last week on the off chance that this was just some major screw-up by the city workers. There were four folks buried here during that time frame. We checked on the names and locations and found the plots, but that wasn't all we found."

"What does that mean?" asked Sophie, that sinking feeling returning to her gut.

"We found five fresh graves," said Manny.

CHAPTER-5

Rehearsing her smile one more time, the one Paige Madison had been practicing since she pulled up to the front of the old office building just off Fourth Street, she then got out of her car and brushed at her dark dress.

Scanning the old building, she frowned, and then let it go. Las Vegas had its glitz, an understatement to say the least, but it also had buildings like this one that reminded her of the other side of the tracks. But she wasn't ready to complain. Just getting a job interview in today's market was a lucky break.

Paige walked through the door and waited. The man behind the desk in the far left corner of the fairly bare, rundown room looked up, smiled, and then motioned for her to sit. She did.

His piercing eyes never left her as she sat down. She felt it. Yet he didn't speak. He watched her settle into the old leather chair, and then turned back to reading something hidden in a manila folder.

It must have only been a minute, yet it felt like a month, before he closed the file and turned his head, smiling one of those smiles that makes a person do a double take, especially a woman. Good-looking, in-shape potential bosses were a total bonus.

"Thank you for coming down on such short notice. Are you ready to see what we have to offer?"

Paige exhaled. "I'm a little nervous. This is my first interview in three months, so forgive me if I say something . . . well, stupid, okay? But yes, I'm excited to be here."

She flashed a sparkling, white smile. Her *best* white smile. She knew she wasn't breathtakingly beautiful, still she had enough to get a few roles in some Las Vegas shows. But even those limited show positions, which helped support her for the last five years, had dried up. At twenty-seven, it sucked to think she might be getting too old for some producers and directors.

Making money as a party girl was an option, like some of her friends had done. She'd even tried it one night. The dead presidents hadn't been worth the overall humiliation of going against everything she knew to be right. So here she was, applying for a job that had to do with medical research, whatever that entailed.

The tall, dark-haired man laughed. "Don't worry. We all have done that, or will most certainly in the future. I don't look for perfection. I want potential."

The tension flowed from her. His laugh was genuine and, in some odd way, comforting. It helped that he was a little older. This could be much more pleasant than she'd anticipated.

"That's good to know," Paige replied. "I have potential."

"I can see that you do. You're bright, and for this position, you're a blonde with fair skin. That is exactly what we need," he said.

"I guess that's a good segue into my first question," she said smiling. "What exactly does this job entail? I know the ad mentioned something about medical. What does that have to do with my features and hair?"

"I knew you had what we are looking for. I love it that you get to the point," he said as he stood.

She stood, too, following his lead. She'd not met someone with this kind of charisma in . . . well, forever. She found herself wanting to say "yes" to *anything* he asked.

"Rather than spend precious minutes trying to explain the complete process and complex procedures of what we're studying and why, let me show you. It's really quite fascinating."

He held out his hand, and for a reason she didn't fully understand, Paige took it.

"Is this normal protocol?" she asked as she followed him through the scarred, double metal doors.

The first thing she noticed was the sterile scent. If she hadn't known better, she would have sworn she was in a hospital or a doctor's office. To her left, there were three people dressed in green masks and surgical gowns working over a table but she couldn't see what they were doing. She stopped, releasing her guide's hand. She'd seen this before.

When her mother had fallen and broken her lower leg so badly that the compound fracture had actually forced the bone through the muscle and skin of her calf, Paige had ridden with her to the hospital. Before the ER nurse had kicked her out, she'd watched in a combination of fascination and anxiety as the operating room was prepared for immediate surgery.

Her heart sank as the scene before her brought back emotions she'd long buried. Her mom had died on that table. The doctors had screwed up the surgery—fatally.

After trying to cope with the loss of her mom and talking to a couple of shrinks, she decided to leave Ohio far behind. Just three weeks later, when she turned seventeen, she hit the road for Vegas.

Lyrics from an old tune sprang into her mind.

You can run, but you can't hide.

"Are you all right, Paige?"

Eyes wide, she turned to him. "What is this place?"

"It's a medical research center, as I mentioned." He grasped her hand again. "Don't be alarmed. They are following a new protocol that calls for—how shall I say it?—swift action in the event of an emergency."

"What does that mean? I don't even know what that research is. And I don't know your name either."

"Let me show you the rest of the facility, and I'll answer all of your questions. I'll start by giving you my name. I'm Doctor Fr–"

Paige raised her hand, turned, and started for the door. "On second thought, I'm not interested in any of this. It's creepy."

She was halted in her tracks. The man had a strength she'd not felt before. His hand was like a vise.

"Miss Madison. I'm afraid you'll have to stay. We need what you have."

"What? You can't make me stay. This is still freaking America." Paige began to struggle against her captor.

She intended for her tone to belie the fear that had escalated close to panic level. She'd been in a weird situation or two since moving to Sin City. Bullshit usually got her out of it.

Not this time.

With a yank, he had her close to him. Too close for a knee in the groin. Too tight to move.

"America it is. Land of the free, right?" he whispered.

The pinch on her arm caused her to yelp. The room immediately grew fuzzy. The next moment, her balance vanished as the tall man prevented her from hitting the cold cement floor.

"Thank you for staying, Paige."

She tried to speak, but her lips wouldn't move. Another moment later, the light left her world, and the black void threatened to swallow her.

Before she went out completely, she felt his breath on her ear.

"You've got the job."

CHAPTER-6

"Oh great, what the hell does that mean?" asked Sophie.

"I don't get your question," said Manny.

She flipped her black hair from her face then put her hands on her hips.

"I mean, who goes around digging graves for the hell of it? And don't give me that dumb-face thing, Williams. It doesn't fit you."

Manny exhaled. Sophie was progressing into a topnotch agent. With each case they worked, he saw her wheels turn faster than her typically sharp tongue. Yet sometimes her emotions, which played off the deep hurts of her past—as they did for most people—rose up and obliterated her logic. He wondered if her lack of beauty sleep was really the culprit or if she felt the same uneasiness about the situation at the graveyard.

He'd bet on the latter.

"Sophie. Take a deep breath and you tell me what it means. If it were you . . . why would you do it?" he said softly, his eyes scanning her face for the reaction he was hoping to see.

It didn't take long.

"Good God, Williams, I wouldn't do it. I'd rather have a great dinner or watch porn. But since you asked, you must mean other than the obvious intent to mess with us, or more likely, you."

"Yep, I do."

That's my girl.

She hesitated. Her expression of confusion appeared, and then disappeared.

"Well, I could do a few things with an extra grave in the mix. I could switch bodies, sort of like a shell game, and see if you could figure out who was where and why I did it. But that would take a lot of time, and no matter how good I was or how late I worked in this cemetery, somebody would be bound to see me switching bodies, I'd guess."

She shivered.

He didn't blame her. They'd seen a bizarre display of body parts in San Juan, thanks to Josh's adopted and insane brother, Caleb, yet the idea of defiling graves—as opposed to degrading bodies in a morgue—was way up the creep scale. *Although both could cause nightmares of untold qualities,* Manny believed.

"It wouldn't be as noticeable if you're just digging one grave. Normal course of business, right?" said Manny.

"Yeah. Not to mention the time it would take to do more than one, even with that backhoe Corner's determined to kill himself with."

"Hey, I ran that beast quite well," defended Josh.

"Keep telling yourself that, big dog," said Alex.

Manny ignored them and moved closer to Sophie.

"So what else?" he asked.

"Okay. When someone does something like this they could be looking for something," said Sophie.

"Maybe, or, given the personality of our quasi-Argyle theory, he might be . . . "

". . . giving something, right?" finished Sophie.

Manny's full-bodied profiler persona kicked in. He actually felt it. The way his brain worked disguised itself under the cover of a hate-love relationship. But he loved the way it worked in his mind today. At least most of it. It was like watching a movie in slow motion.

At the same time, he hated how the "gift" invaded his thinking process at the most private of moments. And there was no denying what his chosen profession had done to him personally, extracting a price that no one should have to pay.

Louise's face passed over his mind.

No one should have to pay.

"Manny?" nudged Sophie.

"I'm here, just collecting my thoughts," he answered.

Pity party later, Williams. Get your crap together.

"This kind of psychopath isn't like the CEO of a company or even the manager of a fast-food store. Those people want to wield their authority directly, and they get their rise from ordering people to do what they don't really like to do. They want to make sure people know who's in charge," said Manny.

"Which is a major power trip, but they don't really play games, as a whole," said Sophie, her eyes bright.

"You got it, Special Agent, so—"

"Are you saying this freak is screwing around and wants to tell us something? Really? 'Cause if that's true, I'm not going to be happy and I'm going to have to beat the shit out of someone."

"We'll get you a sparring partner or a punching bag . . . because that's *exactly* what I'm saying. What else could really be going on? We've just debunked the most likely scenario, at least in my mind, so whatever's left is probably the truth," said Manny. "I know. It's another way to say what we've seen a few times. But these people can't help themselves and remember what I said regarding the Ripper copycat. He has his own mark to make."

"So that's why Alex and I got the backhoe," said Josh. "So we could test Manny's theory."

"Wait. You've already dug up the fifth grave? And you didn't wait until Dean and I got here?" said Sophie.

Manny shook his head. "They've only dug to the point that a few more loads of dirt will get us to the coffin. You didn't have to be here for the surface digging." He grinned. "See? I'm sensitive to your sleep needs."

"Whatever, Manny. I told you before that bullshitters can't bullshit bullshitters."

Her mouth twitched into a quick smile, one of his favorite traits about his long-time partner. She was fully aboard, and he needed her to be.

"Why yes, you have. At any rate, I do want all eyes on this part of the process. We have to make sure we don't miss anything. You and Dean are as good as anyone with that."

Glancing at Dean, he realized how quiet he'd been throughout the conversation. "Dean? Are you breathing?"

The forensics expert was scowling. "Breathing, yes. Trying to get my mind around this situation is a bit more difficult. If someone had checked out of reality like you suggest and had the intellect to match your Good Doctor, whom I've not met, then I anticipate there will be minimal physical evidence to provide us a clue as to who the gravedigger might be."

"That's a fair assumption, but—"

"Let me finish, Manny. The fact that they had someone dig these graves would help with that possibility, but if I understand this psycho type, that person would most certainly want to be here to put the final touches on the game, or whatever this is." Dean stroked his beard, frowning harder than before.

Manny stayed silent.

"No matter how much information I could find on Argyle by Internet searches, I couldn't find details that would be specific to his Bureau files anywhere. The fact that this person is duplicating some of those very actions can only mean that he or she had access to our confidential files."

"That's a remote possibility. We've been hacked a time or two. I think it more likely that this killer's profile is similar to Argyle's, like we've been discussing."

"Copycat, almost?" asked Sophie. "So in the end, he'll still be a wannabe?"

"Something like that," answered Manny, feeling less confident than he sounded. What if Dean was right? Manny had dismissed the idea that Argyle had gotten further than Max Tucker in his endeavors to recruit converts at the Bureau. Argyle didn't have his claws in *that* deep, right?

"Okay, enough of this talk. Let's go see what this last hole in the ground has to show us," said Josh.

Without another word, he and Alex climbed into the backhoe and headed south. Manny jumped into the SUV with Dean and Sophie. Ten minutes later, he watched a silver casket rise ever so slowly from the black Michigan soil.

Josh swung the oblong box to his right and, just as he began to ease it down, the chain slipped and the rear of the casket hit the ground with a loud thud. He watched as Josh frantically worked the levers to avoid a complete crash.

Whatever he did, it worked, and Manny felt the group's collective sigh of relief as the front of the casket gently kissed the ground.

Alex jumped from the tractor's cab, Josh right behind, much happier than the first time he'd exited the machine.

"Not bad, huh? That could have been way worse."

"Yeah. I'll give you that. The last thing we needed was whatever is inside that box to be scattered all over the ground."

"You mean *whomever*," said Josh softly, changing his demeanor as quickly as the Michigan weather.

"How do you know that someone's in there?" asked Sophie, looking like she didn't want to know the answer.

Manny knew what she meant.

"Because it felt heavy. Too heavy for just a coffin," said Josh.

Manny moved toward the box.

"Only one way to find out for sure. Alex, grab that crowbar out of the tractor, and let's see what we have."

A minute later, Manny shoved the business end of the three-foot bar under the edge of the casket's cover near the midway point and lifted. The top slid easily and fell to the ground.

He stepped closer and peered inside.

CHAPTER-7

Chloe could do little more than stare at the message, an impossible feeling of disbelief forcing her to read the text again, and then another time. She reclutched the phone, sat it on the table, picked it up again, and ran her finger over the screen. She didn't recognize the area code but was fairly sure she hadn't seen it on her phone before. No, make that absolutely sure.

What the hell was going on? A prank? If so, the humor was totally lost on her. She suspected Manny would feel the same. Shaking her head, she quickly ruled it out. Anyone who had ever had an encounter with Argyle, or anyone like him, would never walk down this road and call it a joke.

It had been only two days since she told Manny about the new life growing in her womb. They'd shared the news with only a few of their friends and close family for a million reasons, with privacy at the top of the heap. God knew just how little of that precious commodity the two of them, and Jen, had enjoyed over the last seven months. They were doing what they could to steal back some of that alone time, as improbable as that sometimes seemed fostering a life sandwiched around the Bureau . . . and Manny being Manny.

Rubbing her baby bump, she exhaled. "Okay, Chloe girl, no reason to panic a 'tall," she whispered. "Just a hack job or something. Total coincidence. That's probably it."

Somehow, none of her optimistic explanations made real sense or made her feel better.

The next contemplation ricocheting across her mind forced her toward her Bureau training and how to analyze situations like this objectively. Yet that training was now dwarfed by a more urgent drive. Her maternal instinct was in full gear, trumping that training.

She tilted her head and focused on the inner battle. Perhaps that's how it should be. Manny had said so often. He'd say training was important but "feeling" was what kept the good guys ahead of the bad guys, and in most cases, alive. That's what this was. A feeling. Intuition. Whatever the hell you called it, she was beginning to see more of his point.

Profiling was based on the past experiences of a network of experts regarding the mind and body and how haywire, and predictable, they could be. But, in the end, each psychopath indulged in his fantasy just a little different than the rest. Manny saw those traits better than the other experts. That made his point of view the right one in Chloe's mind. Another slow grin made its way across her mouth. Not that she was biased or anything.

A loud knock at the door caused her to jump, startled by the interruption of her reflections, causing a trip-hammer in her chest. Instinctively, she reached for the Glock normally holstered at her right side, but it wasn't there. In fact, it hadn't been there for a week or more—since Josh told her she was no longer a member of the BAU and to take a couple of weeks off from the Bureau until he got organized.

She walked into the bedroom, pulled her weapon from the nightstand, and moved to the front door on full alert, just as the next round of knocking began, louder than the first time.

Taking a moment to muster the rest of her composure, and to gather a better grip on her Glock, Chloe pulled the hammer back, then swung the door open to confront the unexpected visitor.

CHAPTER-8

The stench drifting from the coffin was robust, almost overwhelming, but Manny had already gone beyond that and the rest of the rancid odor's effects. Sophie swore. Josh joined her. Alex immediately reached for his nose. Dean just moved closer. The rank smell crawled over Manny's skin, yet he barely gave it a second thought. The scene inside the metal enclosure was far more interesting . . . even in its repulsive, warped presentation.

The heavy man lying in the casket was hardly what Manny would have called funeral ready. Nor was the elderly woman lying nearly on top of him, angled away just enough to wedge into the oblong container, and to expose the gaping wound in the man's large stomach. The dead woman apparently hadn't been through any such ordeal because he saw nothing, initially, that looked like a cause of death. Her partner had been less fortunate. The striated bruising circling the wound to his stomach indicated, as far as Manny could tell, that the ragged hole had been inflicted antemortem. A chill ran over his scalp as he guessed at the pain the victim had experienced before death gave him relief.

He wished that the oddities regarding the two bodies had ended there. No such luck.

The two were clothed in similar multi-colored, striped tunics, reminding Manny of ancient robes he's seen in pictures of Jesus and the Apostles during Sunday school as a child.

Each robe was bound just below the chests of the victims with gold cords, designed to hold the tunic in place. The rope extended completely around them, as far as he could see. His stomach clinched as he realized that the cords were really just one twine and that the killer had fashioned it in a figure eight to keep the two victims close together. Inseparable.

Why would the killer do that?

Knowing almost without doubt that he'd find that answer before the day was over, Manny continued with his examination.

Starting at the woman's right shoulder, he traced down her arm and stared at the location of her hand. It was neatly resting on the man's crotch, fingers clenched in a postmortem fist intended to look as if she had a grip on his manhood.

"Sick bastard," Manny whispered.

He was struck with another idea and glanced in the direction of both victims' feet.

The man's feet were clad with leather sandals that were partially swallowed because of the swelling and rigor mortis. Manny could only see the right foot of the woman, and it was completely bare. If her other foot were without a shoe, then the killer could be drawing from an old tradition in many cultures. Woman without shoes were to be homemakers and submissive to the heads of the household, usually run by men. In Biblical times, that arrangement was the norm.

He frowned. The not-so-subtle implications were exactly that, making the reason for this distorted display hard to ignore, at least in his mind. She was to be submissive to her casket partner like the cultures of old demanded. But why?

The initial message was much less difficult to decipher than a typical Argyle riddle would entail. The potential copycat, if that were the case, was not nearly as clever or . . .

Sophie tiptoed close to his shoulder, then stepped back, her hand over her mouth.

"Shit," said Sophie. "Just when you think you've seen every sick thing under the sun, we get this."

Without moving his eyes from the vulgar yet curious content of the coffin, Manny spoke to Alex.

"Gloves?"

"Yeah, give me a minute. I'm getting them. This was worse than I imagined it would be."

"Maybe," said Manny, "but maybe not. This looks . . . different."

"How so, other than the obvious of finding two bodies in a grave that shouldn't be here?" asked Josh.

He looked at the group, shaking his head. "Did I just say that? Damn."

"You did and I'm not totally sure what's off. The whole biblical-time, Middle Eastern dress-code motif is obvious, but the question is, as always, why go there? And what did these two people have to do with this display? We need to dig deeper. There's more here."

Alex handed Manny a pair of synthetic gloves, then snapped on a pair of his own. "You can start the digging, Agent," said Alex.

"Some things never change. One thing you can count on is Dough Boy keeping rubber gloves close by," said Sophie, still holding her hand over her nose.

"Maybe. But how do you explain the fact that you have them hanging out of your jeans?" said Alex, handing a pair to Josh.

"Ahh, well, I got them from Mikus. He plans ahead," she said, grinning.

"So if he has them, he's planning ahead. If I have them, it's kinky?"

"That covers it," said Sophie with a wink.

"Don't wink at me. It scares me. What were you doing with those gloves, wench?"

"Figure it out, Dough Boy."

"Oh man. Really? And stop calling me Dough Boy."

"Enough. Later you two," said Manny.

Rolling her eyes, Sophie scowled. "You know, I was hoping you'd be less bossy and more fun once you got married and were getting laid," she said.

"I *am* less bossy. I just need you to concentrate, okay?"

"Great, now you're throwing guilt into the mix," she answered softly, only her voice was already different. More intense. More like the good cop she was.

She would forever be Sophie, but the woman could shift gears.

He waved the others closer to the coffin.

"Like I said when we started this little jaunt, it'll take all of us to figure out what's going on here. When we start moving these poor folks, we'll need to look for something that doesn't fit," said Manny.

"Seriously? Nothing fits here," said Sophie.

"Patterns, Sophie. Look for patterns and then breaks in them."

"Aye, aye, Captain."

She then wrapped her scarf around her face and stared into the casket.

Alex tapped Manny on the arm. "Don't you want me to bring another full CSU crew? There's going to be a lot of possible evidence to sift through. Maybe even the rest of the cemetery to canvas."

"No. Not yet. This was meant for us . . . hell, maybe even me, and I don't need anyone else messing with what that might mean. We're not screwing this up, got it?"

Manny heard the strain in his own voice. Apparently everyone else did as well because the silence was obvious.

Running his hand through his hair, he released a pent-up breath. "I'm sorry. We need to know just what's going on here, and I'm more than concerned that Argyle could be behind this."

Alex nodded. "We all are, Manny. And no problem. This time."

"Fair enough," said Manny, grinning.

"You said we need to look for something else. Like what?" asked Josh.

"I don't know for sure. Like I said, this repulsive display isn't difficult to understand. The problem is that it's also vague. This kind of clothing is obvious. That means seven or eight thousand years of history could be included in any meaning the killer intended. We're good but not that good. Although, I'd say, because of the sandals he's wearing and her bare feet, and the colors used, he's trying to make some reference to Christ's time on earth."

"You mean because of the whole humility thing that women had to swallow?" said Dean.

"Yeah, that's part of it. It might also have something to do with the whole feet-washing service that Jesus made famous at the Last Supper and our twisted unsub is trying to confuse us a bit more."

"Or, like you said earlier, if this is a copycat, he's not as good as the real deal," said Sophie.

"That ran across my mind, but what if that's what the killer wants us to think?"

"That's paranoid, even for you," said Sophie.

"Williams, you made my head hurt—again—but at least I follow you so far," said Josh.

"Good man, Josh. And it is, Sophie. So we might as well get to this and stop all of the conjecture, yes?" stated Manny.

Turning toward Dean, he nodded. "Dean, get your camera ready. I don't want us to miss anything."

"Got it. And I never do."

One last look at his unit and Manny knew, at least in part, what they were all thinking because he was thinking the same thing. How could anyone not?

Whatever they ended up finding, would they understand it? Did they really want to? Reaching into the casket, he grasped the old women's hand and gently dislodged it from the fat man's crotch. As he did, a piece of paper fell away from the woman's fingers, landing near the hole in the man's abdomen.

"What the hell?" said Sophie, bending closer.

Hearing Dean click the camera a few times, Manny waited and then reached over and picked up the small section of what looked like a remnant of a yellow legal pad. It was, however, neatly folded into a rectangle and gave Manny the impression that this psycho was tremendously detail-oriented and meticulous.

Not good.

His heart rate rose as he reached for the paper and began to unfold it carefully.

The breeze freshened and began to move the paper. He grasped it tighter.

Nodding at Sophie, she understood and placed her slim finger on one corner of the paper, holding it steady.

He reached for the last unopened corner and realized he hadn't taken a breath for a while. He exhaled and filled his lungs with sour air before continuing.

They'd seen notes before, beginning with the cruise ship. Killers like this one assumed that their brilliance was unmatched and they had to leave obvious messages so that their unworthy opponents would be able to continue the hunt. Despite opinions to the contrary, most psychopathic killers didn't want to be caught, yet couldn't resist taunting law enforcement if they became bored. But, for reasons he couldn't comprehend, this seemed different. The killer's pattern of revealing general then more specific clues, at the same crime scene, reeked of impatience. Something Argyle hadn't possessed, in Manny's eyes. Nevertheless, enough similar traits were displayed here to think the Good Doctor could be involved.

"Agent Williams? You're trancing again. You going to open the rest of this before I puke?" asked Sophie.

"Just thinking."

With that, Manny pulled open the last corner of the paper.

Written there in neat, block characters was:

NKJ-LK-24:4-5

Manny's brain went numb.

He wasn't totally sure what the letters and numbers meant. He did, however, recognize Doctor Fredrick Argyle's handwriting as it jumped off the paper.

CHAPTER-9

"Are you going to shoot me or invite me in for some of that vanilla latte stuff you've got me hooked on?"

Gavin Crosby, Lansing's police chief, stood behind the screened storm door, glancing at Chloe's hand, then at her face. His nervous grin explained to her that she'd been a little more dramatic yanking open the door than she'd intended.

She exhaled, then smiled at the man who she'd grown to care for over the last few months. Not only was he a great cop, but he had a love for Manny and all those in Manny's life. His love was similar to a father for his son, and it had spread to her like wildfire. He was tough, demanding, and strong enough to endure the emotional anguish of his wife nearly killing him with a shot to the chest—his Stella had lost touch with reality. Then he was forced to handle her subsequent murder. No easy feat, for anyone. Yet, he held that soft spot—which most men possess but hide almost jealously—and had shown it to her a time or two. If she could have picked a father, one not absent like her own had been, Gavin would fit the bill splendidly.

"Depends on what you've up your sleeve. A lass can't be too careful now, can she?"

His sixty-year-old eyes glimmered with amusement. "I promise, lady, my intentions are honorable. Now, if your mother was here, well, I would probably change my tune."

Chloe laughed and opened the door as Gavin rumbled in. Her mother, Haley Rose, and Gavin had been seeing each other over the last few weeks, and even though their relationship was short in time, there was no denying that special, undefinable spark between the two, and it had gone past its infancy.

"I'm sorry to disappoint you. I'm the only Irish woman in the place. Mum and Jen got an early start to Twelve Oaks Mall and promised not to return until her credit card is maxed or they get tired of trying on clothes."

"Yeah. I knew that. My bet is on the card-max thing. Manny's little girl can shop."

"She can. I'll get you some coffee. If you know mom is shopping and Manny is at the cemetery, that means you want to talk to me."

"Bright woman, you are," he said, showing off his best Irish accent. "I do have a proposition for you."

"I'm already married, but I'll listen."

Gavin laughed. "That's all a man could ask."

Brewing a fresh cup of latte for Gavin and pouring another mug of milk for herself, she sat the mugs on the table and settled across from him. Her phone, decorated with the message from the Netherworld and still firmly in her pocket, seemed to be burning a hole in her skin as she wondered whether to mention the message to Gavin or wait to talk to Manny. She didn't want Gavin to think she was overreacting, but then again, fresh perspective was a strong foundation for good law enforcement.

She started to speak, hesitated, then decided to wait, for now.

"Something on your mind, Chloe?" asked Gavin, his eyes narrowing.

"I was just about to ask what was on your mind, Chief. I'm dying to hear this proposition you have for a pregnant, apparently vacationing FBI special agent, who is currently sitting around on her arse. Which, by the way, I hear will get bigger over the next few months."

"Good points, all. Stella's got a little wider just before Mike was born," he said.

It didn't take a cop to hear the sadness touch and then leave his intonation. She felt his pain. She hadn't lost Manny, but it had been close, and that was as close as she wanted to get to traveling that road . . . ever.

"But it was good wide," continued Gavin. "I knew Mike was coming, so no problem for either of us. Besides, it looked kind of good on her. And, I gotta tell you, if that's the worst of your trials before Baby Williams gets here, you'll be way ahead of the game."

"Great wisdom. Still, I plan on wearing things that will make Manny look more to the top than the bottom," she said, grinning.

Gavin laughed out loud, then took another long draw from his cup.

"I'm not too good at beating around the bush, Chloe, so here it is; I want you to go to work for me here in Lansing as my new lead detective."

Raising her eyebrows, Chloe leaned back against the chair and stared at her friend and would-be boss, surprise etched firmly over her face. Leaving the Bureau hadn't crossed her mind, not once, until this minute. Yet she was already recognizing the merits of such a move.

Gavin raised his stout hand. "Before you say anything, let me tell you why this makes sense. And no, Manny has no idea I'm here talking about this."

She nodded.

"All right. Number one, you and Manny can't work together anymore, and in my eyes, that's good for both of you. Your relationship as husband and wife, and pregnant, would most certainly cloud one or both of your judgments at some place in time, and that could get someone killed. So, for a change, I agree with the Feds."

Shifting in his chair, he grew more animated. She was struck with the notion that he'd be a terrific car salesman.

"You'd get to work regular shifts, run the department, all ten of them, stay near home so you make all of those doctor's appointments that are coming, and a company car—sort of. We pay pretty well, and I'll start you out with a month's vacation and, when the time comes, as much maternity leave time as you need or want. Not to mention, I'm not getting any younger. I think my son Mike—who would have been here with me, by the way, but he's in a training seminar in Dallas— will be the next Lansing police chief in a year or two. He'll need your help."

He leaned back and waited, exercising *the first person who speaks loses* ploy. Yep. Car salesman for sure.

Stirring her coffee, she looked up at Gavin. "Sounds like you've put a lot of thought into it. But I love the Bureau, and that would be a difficult decision."

"I understand, but is that the life you want when the baby arrives?"

"You're just full of logical counterpoints this morning, aren't ya?"

"I do my homework," he answered.

"Gavin. I'm flattered and tempted. And, of course, I'd want to talk this over with Manny, but I have a question of my own."

"Fire away."

"What's in it for you and the LPD? I mean, we'll be fine if I stay with the Bureau."

"If you're implying this is some charity situation, and I'm trying to take care of all of you, you're wrong. I'd be a liar to say that wouldn't be a perk, but my reasons are almost entirely selfish. Did I say you'd be a great help to Mike? Look.

You're a topnotch profiler with great instincts, and you'd be the second best cop I'd ever had the privilege of working with."

"Second?" she chided. "Are you referring to that forty-year-old husband of mine?"

"Afraid so. If it makes you feel any better, though, you're a hell of a lot better looking than he is."

She laughed as she felt Gavin press in for the kill.

"Listen. You're perfect for this job. The City of Lansing would be lucky to have you, and I'll say it again: you're a helluva cop. As good as anybody. Your experience and training would be a Godsend. We need you."

"Any more whipped cream you wish to pile onto the shit?"

"Yep. I'll even throw in a better retirement package if you name the new kid Gavin."

"Now that might work."

Standing, Gavin went over to the coffee machine and made another cup of latte. Chloe listened to the sputtering and gasping of the machine as her mind evolved from cloudy to clear.

Manny's old boss was right on every level, and God knew she'd had her fill of cases that kept her up at night and her nightmares vividly alive.

Sitting back down, Gavin reached for her hand. "I know that's a lot to ponder, but you're a smart cookie and you and Manny will make the right call. But I can see you've at least bought into the concept."

"I just might have, at that."

"There's one more thing before I get my tired old ass out of your home. You started to say something when we sat down and then changed your mind; what was it?"

Chloe ran her tongue over her suddenly dry lips and sighed. "No fooling old cops. Let me show you."

She felt a bit of relief as she handed the phone to Gavin, the message still on display. The chief frowned, looked at Chloe, read it again, pulled at his gray mustache, read it a third time, then finally handed the phone back to her almost like it had grown too hot to handle.

"Did you call Manny and tell him?"

"No. I didn't want to seem like I was overreacting, and he's got his hands full this morning. I wondered, at first, if it could be some prank, or even a wild coincidence, but . . . "

"You're right. It's no prank or some shitty joke. The area code is from Nevada, probably from Vegas. Do you know anyone there?"

"I don't. Certainly no one that we would've told about the baby."

Taking out a pen and pad, Gavin looked at the number and wrote it down. "I'll give this to Buzzy in our tech department and see if she can find out anything. Meanwhile, I think you did the right thing by not calling Manny. It'll give us some time to see what we can find."

Her smile returned. "Okay. I like that approach. I hope she can find something, but it might be tough. This could be a pay-as-you-go, and if the sender is skilled enough, he or she could be bouncing this from all over the planet," said Chloe.

"I don't get all of that, so that's where you ladies come in."

Gavin headed for the door, opened it, and waved. "We'll get to the bottom of this and, meanwhile, start thinking about what color you want your new office to be," he said, smiling.

"Not to jump the gun, but that sounds great. And Gavin . . . thanks."

"My pleasure."

The chief took one more step and stopped. He reached into his pocket and pulled out his own phone. Chloe watched as he glanced at the number and then did a double take as his brow gathered into a deep V.

"Son of a bitch," he whispered.

CHAPTER-10

Detective Melanie Teachout glanced at her partner, Brent Lane, and slowly shook her head, causing her long, black hair to cover and uncover her face.

He shrugged his shoulders, raised his hands, then stepped to her side as they both returned their attention to the corpse that had been fished out of the garbage bin.

At least most of it.

Mel drew from her cigarette and puffed upward, releasing the swirling wisp into the early-morning Las Vegas breeze.

"You know that shit's going to kill you, right?" asked Brent.

"Yeah, well, thank you, Mom. You know the old saying: we're all going to die from something. Besides, I'm cutting down," she answered with a wink.

"Good to hear. And just an FYI, kissing people who smoke is like licking an ashtray."

She smiled at her short, good-looking partner with the dark-blue eyes, stopping at his wavy,

"Time of death?"

The CSI sighed. "Almost nine hours ago, if the liver reading wasn't affected by the heat."

"Any luck with the victim's ID?" Mel reached for her cigarette case in her pocket, keeping her eyes on the CSI.

"We're working on it. His first name appears to be Howard. There was no wallet, or cell phone, or credit card, or any other way to identify him further. We got his possible first name from a bracelet we found in his pocket. The inscription referred to the woman who gave it to him so we'll see where that leads. We're digging in with the usual procedures. We'll find out who this poor soul is, er, was."

Lighting another smoke, Mel exhaled and then slowly circled the body. She didn't scare easily, and God knew that homicide detectives had stomachs of iron, mostly. She also didn't get to where she was by letting her imagination run wildly unchecked.

Stopping on the right side of the body, she kneeled on one knee, reaching toward a small bloodstain on his dirty, white shirt just above his pelvic region.

Lifting the shirt slowly, she could only stare as the weakness in her knees kept her frozen in place.

After several moments, Mel Teachout rose and reached for her phone.

"Is it like the other two?" asked Brent softly. "Are there organs missing?"

"Yeah. Afraid so. Livers, intestines, now a kidney. This looks like it could have something to do with the human organ black-market business. That means someone far too organized is responsible for this shit. We could be over our heads. I'm thinking we call the FBI and—"

The target of her call answered. She felt herself swallow, hard. This was crazy-assed. She, and the LVPD, didn't make it a habit to call in help, but today she believed was an exception.

"Captain? We've got another one. I think this one seals it. Someone is harvesting the organs of the fine citizens of Las Vegas, and I think we need some help."

CHAPTER-11

It had been twenty minutes since the Ingham County Medical Examiner's office had transported the two corpses to the morgue at Lansing's largest medical facility. Still, Manny couldn't force the frown to totally vacate his brow. "Bizarre" had never been out of the realm his world encompassed, but this case had his mind racing while the facts tangoed with his imagination.

Two bodies positioned like these was an obvious setup, yet perhaps not as telling as the identity of the two victims could be. There was no form of ID on either of the bodies, so Sophie was working with Buzzy Dancer, the LPD resident tech expert, on that elusive task. With all of the technology available, including the LPD and the Bureau's facial recognition software programs, and IAFIS, the FBI's fingerprint database, it shouldn't take long to find out who they were, Manny hoped.

Using the thumb and index finger of his right hand, he rubbed his eyes, hoping to soothe some of the tension the last few hours had created. It helped a little.

Even better than locating the names of these two unfortunate souls would be what Alex and Dean were hoping to accomplish: identify the killer with some of their forensic magic.

The two CSIs had spent the last ninety minutes taking more pictures and extracting traces of anything that may and may not have originated with the bodies—fibers, dirt samples, hairs, spit, latent and observable prints, and maybe even a stray follicle or two that could be turned into a DNA lead.

Manny had decided he didn't care what piece of micro evidence would get the job done as long as one of them did. He just wanted a name. But it was more than that, wasn't it? He couldn't shake the feeling that his nemesis had somehow bamboozled law enforcement . . . again.

Since they'd returned from North Carolina, despite the incredible news that he was going to be a dad again, albeit well after Jen, the possibility of Argyle somehow still walking among the living had forced his gut into a perpetual knot. He kept telling himself all of the right things, but in the end, his gut did the talking.

The encrypted note taken from the male victim's hand wasn't helping. It, and the message it contained, were burning a hole in his pocket and didn't help his state of mind. The only positive thing he could think of was that people often try to emulate another's handwriting—maybe that's what this was. It'd be a couple of days before the Bureau's graphology experts could do the proper analysis, but that would go a long way toward settling his jumping belly.

How could it not?

For the hundredth time, he relived the moment he'd killed Argyle on that boat in Galway, without any doubtful compunction. Manny had shot the doctor as he'd reached for a weapon. He could still feel the small recoil and the roar from his Glock as he fired and Argyle's head disintegrated.

The feeling of freedom from the man's indescribable, perverted influence had been as liberating as anything Manny had experienced. One shot, one death, and one for the good guys. An action and a reaction. Dead was dead, and everyone at that rocky cove knew it had been Argyle who had been stuffed into that Irish body bag and shipped to the United States later that night.

It was that simple.

He shifted his feet. They didn't collect any of the doctor's DNA and run it through CODIS for a positive match because there had been no reason. They all knew who it was. Besides, that wasn't really a standard procedure in Bureau cases anyway.

"Maybe it should be," he mumbled.

If the wildly unimaginable were true and the doctor had managed to pull off a body-double stunt like the kind you read only in books and see in movies, then the questions of motive grew even more intense.

In the beginning, Argyle had been driven by revenge for the LPD's supposed role in ruining the doctor's professional career, but the reasons for his killings became more complex as time went on. His twisted motives had evolved into a game to outwit all of law enforcement, particularly Manny. That only gave more credence to the theories that true psychopaths of his magnitude develop a higher sense of narcissism and a deeper sense of self-importance. A God complex. Argyle had possessed all of that and more. It hadn't hurt the doctor's cause that he inherited a large family fortune. Crazy and rich had proven a deadly combination to over twenty people, maybe more. Only Argyle and God knew the true toll his bloodlust had tallied.

Raising his gaze, Manny slowly scanned the rest of the cemetery. He noticed how the late-morning sun forced the budding landscape to take on a fresh perspective as it inched farther into the sky. It was almost as if the blazing orb had an agenda to beautify what most would consider, at the very least, unpleasant.

Agenda?

That was the question pounding at Manny's sanity. What the hell was this truly about? Was there another step in Dr. Argyle's evolution or had he simply planned, in the event of his demise, a few parting surprises, orchestrated then executed by a few mindless lackeys?

There was sudden comfort in that logic. It made far more sense than the alternative.

He glanced inside again, shook his head, and closed the file.

"We know who these folks are, were, and it makes little sense to me so far," said Manny. "Her name is Abigail Roache, seventy-seven years old, and the man was her son, Matthew, forty-four. According to Sophie's info, they both lived at the same address. She was obviously retired, and Mister Roache was employed by, you guessed it, the City of Lansing, and—"

"Wait," said Alex, "let me finish your statement . . . he was a patient of Argyle too, right?"

Manny sighed. "He was. Four years ago he had a meltdown in the treasurer's office and had to get psychiatric approval to come back to work."

Opening the file again, he flipped the first page back, read some more, then closed it again. "Once he did, he apparently had no further incidents and went on his merry way as a happy employee."

"So, was he a disciple or just a cured patient?" asked Sophie.

"I'm not sure yet," said Manny, shrugging. "We need more info."

"That'll be coming in the next day or so. Buzzy is hard at work on gathering all that she can find on these two. We were able to get this much because he was an employee of the City. She's also going to pull all of the usual information on both. I'm banking on a weird sex thing for the kid. Maybe even one of those mom fixations, ya know?"

"What?" said Alex, rolling his eyes. "You mean like incest? Good God, woman, don't you ever give that a rest? Not everything is about sex, for crying out loud."

"It is if you ain't getting any. And since you got hand problems, I think that explains why you've been so damned cranky," said Sophie.

"I—"

"Stop. And she just might be right," said Manny.

"You mean why he's cranky?" asked Sophie.

"No, but you might be right there too."

"Some friends. Incest? You can't be serious," said Alex, his face showing his disgust.

"Remember how we found her hand on his crotch? That could have been a subtle way of sharing doctor/patient confidentiality. Maybe. At any rate, we've sent a CSI team over to the Roache's house along with Gavin's people to see what they can gather."

"Okay, my mind needs a bath," said Dean.

"Don't get too clean," said Sophie.

Dean smiled.

Manny turned to Alex. "Alex. What did you and Dean find?"

"Yeah, okay. I'm with Dean about my brain needing a scrub. Anyway, we didn't find a hell of a lot. The killer kept things pretty clean. We found a couple of prints and a few hairs that might not belong to these two, but then again, they might. We did get three weird fibers on the old woman that didn't look like they came from the material in the casket or any kind of clothing. They seemed to be more like carpet. Maybe from the trunk of a car or something similar."

"We also found some dirt and pebbles that didn't seem to match the soil composition of this area so we'll be waiting on the lab for the results of those tests," added Dean.

"What about the injury to Mister Roache?" asked Josh.

"I talked to the ME and she said that the position of the incision was strange. It was not quite in the center of Roache's gut, but more to the liver side. That made her a tad more curious, so she snaked a portable scope inside the cut and discovered that the liver, pancreas, and gallbladder were missing."

"Totally missing or misplaced? I mean, it's not like we haven't seen some of this weird shit over the last couple of years," asked Sophie.

"Missing. Not found anywhere in the casket or surrounding area," answered Alex.

"Why those three organs?" asked Josh.

Alex released a breath. "I don't know for sure. We'll have to see the ME's report on when, in relation to postmortem or antemortem possibilities, the organs were removed."

"There are usually only two reasons organs are removed, especially if the report comes back with antemortem removal," said Manny.

"Some form of ritual that the psychopath deems necessary to complete his mission . . . or transplants. Gallbladder transplants don't happen, but the other two organs can and are used every day to try to save people's lives."

Josh raised his eyebrows. "Are you talking black market?"

"I'm not talking anything. I'm simply listing the possibilities," said Manny.

"Well, the incision was done with a certain precision, so maybe that's an angle we should explore," said Dean.

Leaning forward, Josh raised his hand. "Let's get more info before we start thinking black-market organ harvesting, okay? This killer is Argyle-like, and we should concentrate on that. And besides, why would Argyle or any of his cronies go black market? They sure as hell don't need the money and that kind of criminal activity is usually controlled by gangs and organized crime. It's getting global attention, and the World Health Organization is becoming involved. I think it's too risky, even for the Good Doctor and his followers."

"Good points. But when did this cult, or its founder, ever care about risk?" said Manny. "We'll see what else the ME has to say. For now, I have to go with Josh on this. Psycho is psycho."

"What about that note and the writing, Williams? Is it Argyle's and what do you think it means?" asked Sophie.

Slowly pulling the evidence bag from his pocket, Manny spread it out on the hood of the truck, and then looked around the circle.

"It looks like his, but it could be faked. It happens. The folks in the lab can dig into it. The message is, well . . . Listen. When I was a kid, the only real book we took to church was the King James Bible. Over the last twenty-five years, the translations have grown to almost epic proportions and—"

"Wait. You think this is a bible verse?" asked Josh.

Manny nodded. "I know it is. It was taken from a new translation, the New King James. See here?"

The tight circle grew tighter.

"The NKJ stands for that. The LK stands for the Gospel of Luke. The twenty-four refers to the chapter and the five to the verse."

"So, what does it say?" asked Sophie.

"I looked it up and according to this passage, there were two men, white-robed angels, talking to three women. Mary, Jesus' mother, Mary Magdalene, and a woman named Salome. One of the angels asked the women an incredibly perceptive question."

"And?" said Josh, frowning.

"He asked the women why they were seeking the living among the dead."

CHAPTER-12

He laughed. Then again as he clicked the red button on his phone, placing it lightly on the desk.

The recipient on the other end of his communication must have believed him insane or joking. Either way, whatever the idiot thought, the purpose of his call was masked to cover the truth. His truth. After all, his way, his mantra, was the only one that held any significance.

The laughter had been genuine. But then again, over the last few years, had there been anything regarding his resurrection from the choking confines of societal expectations that was feigned? He could think of nothing that hadn't been of the sincerest motivation for him since his initial encounter with his true mentor.

What an encounter it had been. He recalled the chains falling away. At first, it was difficult to comprehend the way his mind had been utterly transformed and freed. He knew from hundreds of sessions what people really considered, what fantasies they so desperately desired to convert to reality, yet were unable to pull the proverbial trigger releasing that pure, unadulterated enlightenment.

"What a waste," he said softly.

The cell phone rested in his large hand. He could squeeze and feel it crack; he could squeeze harder and watch the phone virtually disintegrate as minuscule shards of black plastic and translucent glass slipped through his powerful fingers.

The phone, however, was needed as a lynchpin in the grand scheme of things to come. He'd laid the groundwork, for the most part, of what was to come next and, after all, that was important. Yet the unspoken, the perplexing, was far more defining.

Getting up from the desk located in the spacious backroom of the warehouse, he moved to the computer station and hit enter. The program that had been written especially for this project was vacillating on the screen as the power grid gave response to the rise and fall of the power surges running from one cell phone tower to another. The GPS for the phone he'd put on the desk had been fooled into believing it was coming from another area of Nevada and was being directed by remotely accessing phone sources in and around the U.S. Its function allowed the program to hijack a new location every fifteen seconds and mask the true origin of the signal.

He'd also had his programmer create a global connection that could hack into networks all over the world, disguising the source of his Internet connection, making it virtually impossible to trace his email and video-streaming communications. That would be important, beginning in less than two days, if his calculations were correct. And they always were.

Fortunately, he'd been able to test the project and found it completely serviceable for his complex needs—and all before the programmer had met with an unfortunate demise. He suspected that the programmer had no idea his life would end as it had, but then again, did anyone really suspect such a thing?

He wondered if anyone, other than the creatures of the desert, would ever stumble upon the programmer's body. He supposed some misguided camper or hiker may do just that, but it would be far too late to have any effect on his destiny.

Leaving a corpse to rot in an unmarked grave was not exactly his style but proved necessary to minimize the likelihood of detection until he was ready.

Two days.

That's all that was required. He'd waited long enough. Hidden in the sanctuary that was his own anticipation, he'd relented to a self-control that, at times, was difficult to succumb, but had done it anyway. The timing for this final play had never seemed quite right, but that had changed with the onset of one new development.

"Children will change your life, agents," he whispered.

*****

Staring at the phone, Gavin put it to his ear. "Who is this?"

No response.

Gavin licked his lips and then glanced at Chloe.

"Listen, asshole, this phone belongs to a law enforcement official, and I'll have your balls behind bars in a few hours if you don't identify yourself now."

More silence.

Waiting ten more agonizing seconds, Gavin spoke again. "Last chance, shithead."

"Soon, Commissioner, soon."

He barely heard the laugh as the phone went dead. The tone was unmistakable, the articulation one of a kind. He recognized the voice, yet . . . it was impossible.

The caller had been dead over a year.

"Are you all right, Gavin? You look like you saw, or heard, a ghost," Chloe moved toward him.

Regaining his composure, Gavin waved his hand toward Chloe, hoping to hide what he thought he'd heard.

"Yeah. Just some punk trying to get under my skin. Now. Let me get to the office, and I'll see about getting the ball rolling with your new job. I'll be back to talk to you and Manny."

"That works for me," said Chloe, watching him intently. "Are you sure you're okay?"

"I'm fine. See you when you can get that workaholic husband to come home."

Gavin slid into the front seat of his black sedan, his pulse still racing.

He glanced at the phone's screen and saw that, somehow, the number had changed. The area code was now a Detroit area number. *Impossible.* He knew what he had seen.

Pulling out of the driveway, he raced toward downtown Lansing.

Okay, maybe I'm seeing things, but I know what I heard. How could I ever forget?

Doctor Fredrick Argyle's voice was still ringing in his ears.

CHAPTER-13

Bending down to kiss Chloe, who was standing near the kitchen table, Manny felt the warmth of her breath and felt the touch of her soft skin as she fingered his hand.

For a moment, just for a fleeting tidbit of time, he forgot why the BAU and the LPD had decided to meet at his home to discuss the circumstances behind this whacky gathering.

She had always had an effect on him of some kind, but none as pronounced as when she touched him. Anyway, anywhere, and anytime.

The not-so-miniscule pulse of electricity was still there—and perhaps stronger than before because they'd grown closer. She had become his escape, his anchor on reality, and God knew after the last two weeks, topped off by the morning's developments, he needed both.

The image of the two of them relaxing on some exotic beach, umbrella drinks in hand, and Chloe sporting a hot-pink bikini covering less than it should have topped off his mini-fantasy.

"Hey. Where's your brain?" whispered Chloe.

"Oh, I'll tell you later. If you're a good girl," he whispered back.

Her knowing smile raised his internal thermostat a few more degrees.

"How do you know what I'm thinking?" he asked.

"Once a profiler . . . "

"True enough."

Motioning to her, they stepped into the family room out of earshot from Gavin and Josh.

"So, are you sure? Do you want to go this route?"

"I do. It's almost a no-brainer, Manny. Even before you and I were done talking on the phone, I knew it was the right call. I can't work with you in BAU, and unless I miss my guess, they'll want to reassign me to the terrorism unit."

"That's not something I want to see," he said.

She reached down and rubbed her calf. "Me either. Getting shot once was plenty, especially given my condition . . . " she said, patting her stomach.

He kissed her again, her warm mouth as pleasing as ever. He supposed someday he'd get used to how that felt, but today wasn't it.

"I'd never try to tell you what to do, but you becoming a Lansing cop makes me feel a whole lot better inside, especially taking over as a lead detective. And working with Gavin and Mike would be like working with family," he said, brushing her long hair from her face.

"Then it's totally settled," she said. "Now how about one more of those kisses. They curl my toes, don't ya know."

He obliged, but they were quickly interrupted.

"Are you two planning something?" asked Gavin, standing in the doorway. Josh was at his shoulder wearing a quizzical look.

"We are. Do you want to know what?" asked Manny.

"I'm not sure about Gavin, but I'm curious," said Josh, his expression staying the same.

Looking at his wife, Manny nodded. "Chloe?"

She exhaled then gave Josh a smile that could dazzle a corpse, taking his hand as she did. "Josh. I've loved working for the BAU, and you. I would have never met Manny without the opportunity you gave me, and I'm ever so grateful. But my life has changed, and for the better, so I'm officially resigning from the Bureau, effective immediately."

Tilting his head, Manny watched the tiny grin on Josh's face mushroom into a compelling smile.

Josh reached over and kissed her on the cheek, then stepped back.

"You're a talented profiler and a good woman, Chloe. I'll miss you and your skills. I can't blame you. I'd do the same, given your situation. Family is more important than anything else."

His look turned wistful and then darted back to the look Manny had grown used to seeing when his boss was working through something.

"I'm just getting that. Anyway, have you thought of what—wait! You're going to work for Gavin, aren't you?"

"She is," interrupted Gavin, looking at Manny and Chloe. "I've got her desk set up, and she can start whenever she wants . . . say, yesterday?"

Laughing again, Chloe nodded. "I was thinking Monday."

"Slacking already. Damn. Just like your old man," said Gavin, grinning.

"I had a great teacher, Gavin," said Manny.

"Maybe, but I had to protect you until you dried out behind the ears," Gavin said.

Josh headed back to the kitchen and the others followed.

"Should make an announcement?" asked Manny, reaching for his coffee.

Josh thought for a moment. "You might want to wait until after the meeting to decide. We've got a couple more issues to cover besides the reasons for this meeting. The timing may not be right."

"What does that mean?" asked Chloe, frowning.

"Just trust me on this, okay?" said Josh.

Manny didn't care for how that sounded. Plus, an air of edginess pervaded Josh's tone, and he didn't like that either. But he banked on his boss's judgment, at least for now.

"Are we going to like what's coming, Josh?" asked Manny, watching him intently.

Josh began to answer just as the front door burst open and Sophie, followed by Dean and Alex, marched into the living room.

As she reached the entrance to the large kitchen, Sampson jumped up from his spot near the pale-green sofa, wide tail wagging, and charged Sophie. Before she could react, he had a paw on both shoulders, his brown eyes almost level with hers.

"Sampson . . . " started Manny.

"Stop. I've got this," said Sophie. "I can handle tall, dark, and handsome."

"I wasn't going to tell him to get down," said Manny.

"You weren't?" said Sophie, never taking her eyes from the canine.

"No."

"What then?"

"I wanted to show you his new trick. He's a quick learner."

"What new trick? Oh shit."

Before she could move, Manny spoke. "Sampson, kiss."

Sophie's face was immediately saturated with the kind of jowl juice only big dogs could muster. Sophie could only stare, her countenance riddled with disbelief. His typically gabby ex-partner was speechless—a feat not easily accomplished.

Looking at his handiwork one last time, Sampson finished another lick the length of Sophie's face, plopped all fours onto the hardwood floor, and returned to his place by the couch.

The quiet was broken by Dean's chuckle. Then Alex's laugh. A moment later, the room was shaking with deep, wonderful laughter that even had Sophie grinning. Manny was glad for the break in tension—it would make for a better meeting.

Laughter was truly a mysterious tonic.

Chloe reached for a kitchen towel hanging near the dishwasher and rushed to Sophie.

Sophie accepted the cloth, wiping away the drool, the smile never leaving her face however, even after the laughter died to a dull roar.

"Good one, Manny. Excellent. I love your dog."

Manny's smile disappeared. Sophie's tone was one thing, but he quickly realized she hadn't stopped grinning, nor had she taken her eyes from him.

He began to back up, but was too slow. In the next instant, Sophie was on him, rubbing the cloth over his face with true enthusiasm.

She dropped down and stepped back, admiring her effort. "Looks good on you too, Williams."

Slowly sponging at the moisture on his face, Manny nodded. "Okay. That was fair. But I'm a little hurt that you didn't fully appreciate Sampson's affection."

"Oh, I did. Far more than the dose you got, Big Boy. Forget that I'll never get the smell of dog breath off me and my clothes. You're getting the bill if I have to buy a new blouse too."

"Oh, I'll pick up that tab," said Alex, brushing at the tears still on his cheeks. "That was absolutely worth it. I love that dog too."

"Great. Then it's settled. Sophie gets a new blouse. Sampson earns an 'A' for obedience, and we can get this meeting going because we've got a lot of information to cover. If you are all done screwing around," said Josh.

"Damn. You need to get home to the wife and soon," said Sophie.

"Yeah. Maybe. That sounds like a winner. But for now, let's get to work."

It was hard not to notice the stress in his boss's voice. It was the third time today that Manny had noticed the strain or, maybe, the uneasiness. It didn't take a profiler to see that Josh had other things on his mind.

Yet, Josh was right. They'd delayed the meeting, maybe subconsciously, long enough. They were here for only one reason: to solve a wicked case.

The job, particularly the details of this one, came flooding back to reality, like it or not. He couldn't lie. There would always be a part of him that liked it. Loved it, in fact.

The adrenaline began to pump through his body, especially as he considered the text Chloe had received. The hair on the back of his neck raised high as anger and fear hijacked his emotions. He would do whatever it took to protect his wife and baby—like any other man, he supposed. Yet, that inescapable excitement crawled around in his belly. As heart-wrenching, as stressful, as horrible as his divinely appointed vocation could be, the chase, the challenge of bringing a killer to justice, always sent him to a special place.

He wondered briefly if that made him little better than the men and women he'd brought down over the years. After all, he had to think like them to get to where he needed to be. Sometimes, it was far more than just *thinking* like them. He *became* them.

In the end, did it matter?

A bible verse flashed across his mind. The Apostle Paul had said that he became all things to all men so that a few might be saved. Manny understood that. He lived it. The Guardian of the Universe was who he was, period.

So be it.

"Manny? You want to start this meeting? You tranced out again, so that means you're ready," said Josh, a faint smile tugging at his mouth, causing Manny to think how much more appropriate that looked on his friend. He looked almost normal.

Manny nodded. Gavin, Alex, Dean, Josh, Sophie, and Chloe were now seated around the table, each with a file of information the CSU of Lansing had been able to put together on short notice. It was incomplete, but he had seen enough to make some assumptions.

Assumptions this circle of cops might think were crazier than he already did.

Manny let out a breath.

"What if I told you the calls, the text, and the cemetery circus are all created by one man?"

CHAPTER-14

"Damn, Manny. Really? I can't wait to hear this. I mean, how in hell are you getting that?" asked Sophie, moving to the edge of her chair.

Manny noticed the same look on everyone's face, except for Josh. He seemed far from surprised. In fact, Manny detected a slight nod from the BAU leader. As if he had expected Manny to connect the dots, as scattered as they were.

Manny frowned and moved on, ignoring his curiosity with his boss's body language, for the moment.

"Let's look at what we have. The what, the how, the where, and most importantly, the when. Like I said before, I don't much care about the why right now," said Manny.

The room grew quiet as his crew, and Gavin, gathered their internal ideas. Respectively, in their own ways, they were analyzing what he'd said. He was mildly surprised how much he'd come to recognize how each of them processed information and what each needed to do so.

He glanced at Josh. He was watching his phone and had not looked at the file. More odd behavior.

Two minutes later, Sophie looked up from her file. "What the hell, I'll go first."

"Have at it," said Manny.

"We got two dead people, mother and son, who just might have had a taboo secret or two. Empty graves as an apparent diversion and a note referring to a bible verse insinuating that someone dead might be alive. All from a cemetery that was run by the City of Lansing who had employees with ties to a therapist who happened to be the craziest bastard I've ever met, besides my first husband.

"Then we have a weird-ass text from someone somewhere in Nevada who had no way of knowing that Manny and Chloe were pregnant. That same number is used to call Gavin and he says it sounded like Argyle, according to what Manny told us on the phone. Right so far?"

"Good start," said Manny. "What else?"

"There's very little forensic material to draw from," said Dean.

"Which fits the intellect of an organized serial killer," added Alex.

"Let's not forget the missing organs," said Chloe.

"Let's not," said Josh softly.

"What does that mean?" asked Chloe.

"We just don't want to leave out anything," answered Josh, still staring at his phone.

This time, the rest of the agents and cops in the circle all switched their gazes to Josh. The tone of cool, collected, while admirable in meetings like this, didn't fit Special Agent Josh Corner. It never really had. He'd always been bright and the right man to lead the BAU, but he'd also almost constantly carried a sense of excitement and emotion with his responsibilities. His response, and, in Manny's eyes, his actions since they'd found the bodies in the cemetery, displayed a different attitude. It was if he was trying to detach himself from this party, and his folks.

Talking to Josh after the meeting was no longer an option. It had to be now. Right now.

Manny opened his mouth, but wasn't quick enough. Sophie had beaten him to the punch, and she wasn't happy.

She rose out of her chair and stood inches from Josh, never lifting her big, brown eyes from his face. She flipped her long hair over her shoulder, clasped her hands together in front of her, and leaned in. "Okay, Josh. Part of the thing that makes you really hot, besides your broad shoulders and those eyes, is your honesty. You know, how you talk to us and never keep us in the dark? If *I* can detect your complete asshole attitude this morning, you know Manny can. He's probably being polite by not mentioning it. He's a strange man that way. I'm not cramped by that shit. So, what the hell's going on with you? What aren't you telling us?"

One by one, Josh met the eyes of people in the circle. He then placed his hands on the table, staring at them, but not speaking.

The coffeemaker spurted and hissed, indicating that it had completed its task as the aroma of dark blend filtered throughout the room. Chloe got up and brought the pot of java back to the table, refilling empty cups. She then sat back down, grasped Manny's hand, and waited.

There had been situations in past meetings that made Manny uneasy, like when Josh's marriage had taken a walk on the rocky side. Or when Sophie admitted she was having an affair with a former Lansing DA's husband. But this setting was beyond making him feel "uneasy."

"You're both right. Manny saw it in my face earlier. You all know what it's like to hide something from him, so I didn't try. I knew the rest of you wouldn't be far behind, but for the first time in a long time, I was almost afraid to tell you all where this case was probably heading."

Josh swallowed and then cleared his throat. His voice faltered as he spoke. This time there was no masking his emotion. "The hard thing here is that I won't be with you. Furthermore, neither will Alex and Chloe."

CHAPTER-15

"This is unbelievable," said Brent Lane. "Four victims in less than five days. I ain't enjoying this one."

Detective Melanie Teachout nodded as she rebuttoned the top button on her green, silk blouse. "Even as cops we don't see everything in this twisted world; we only read about some of the shit that goes on. And this . . . this human organ dealing isn't the type of case I supposed we'd ever get."

She moved toward their bedroom window, taking in the view of the famous Las Vegas strip. The skyline really was beautiful. The buildings were as unique as they were diverse and offered tantalizing entertainment of all types. Her city was a place where memories of a lifetime were often made. Yet, underneath that beauty and freedom subsisted another world that most people only thought they knew. Not that other cities escaped the plagues that inhabited hers; it simply seemed more magnified here.

Reaching for her cigarettes, she pulled one from the pack and held it between her lips without lighting it.

She guessed it was because people came here to let loose from the ball and chain that was their everyday, boring, stressful lives, and to dive head first into the happenings that made the saying "what happens in Vegas stays in Vegas" more of a truth than just a slogan. Part of her thought that was okay. People need to live a little. The problem began when the line between reality and fantasy became blurred.

She felt Brent's arms wrap around her waist. Good God, she loved how he felt. She not only loved him, but it simply *felt* dead-on to be with him. He was right in keeping their relationship a secret for as long as possible. She didn't want a new partner, ever.

"We'd better get back to the office. We'll have some preliminary reports on the guy we found behind the Egyptian and the girl discovered downtown. What was her name?"

"Paige Madison," she said absently.

"Yeah. You were always better with the names."

"That's okay, you've got other skills. That's what makes us a great team."

"It does. Pretty weird to find that cell phone on her with a text and a call to Michigan."

"It was. The fact that one went to an FBI agent and another to a Lansing cop sealed the deal when I asked the captain for a little help on this one.

Pretty obvious the killer wanted us to find the phone," said Melanie.

"So we're going to get the FBI, huh?" asked Brent.

"That's what the captain said. She served in the Army with the supervisor of the BAU and called him, some guy named Corner. I guess he said they'd be coming out anyway for another case, so what the hell, right?"

"The more the merrier, at least on this one," answered Brent.

Melanie grabbed her weapon from the dresser. "Maybe. You're right about one thing, though, we've gotta go. At least we got a quick lunch. We may not get another for a while."

Brent smiled. "Is that what that was?"

"Nothing better than lunch delight," she said, kissing him again.

Picking up his gun and badge from the nightstand, he motioned for her to follow him. "The captain will be sending out an APB on us soon."

"Okay. I'm coming."

"I love it when you say that," he grinned.

"That's two of us," she answered.

He opened the door and motioned for her to go first.

"Always a gentleman."

"I try."

Three minutes later, they were headed north on Las Vegas Boulevard. Watching the dazzling strip go by, Melanie was struck with an idea. She turned to Brent.

"You know, I keep running over that part where we found the phone—with the call and text—and for the life of me, I don't get the connection. I mean why?" she asked.

"I'm sure we'll be clued in, but my first impression is someone has a beef with the Feds. That's not unusual, but the fact they dangled an invitation like that makes me a little nervous."

"Why?"

"Who on this planet wants the FBI to come looking for them?" he asked.

"Good question. I was wondering the same thing."

"Some peckerhead, I guess," said Brent quietly.

Melanie glanced at her husband and partner. She felt her blood grow a little colder as another answer danced into her head.

"Or a very bright killer with a vendetta," she whispered.

CHAPTER-16

Josh sipped his coffee.

"Keep talking," said Sophie.

The hesitation in her voice reflected the apprehension that Manny was sure they were all feeling. It wasn't difficult to see that Josh was wrestling with a demon or two. Manny just wasn't sure which one would speak first.

"I got a call from HQ a few hours ago that lasted longer than I wanted."

Josh hesitated for a long moment—no one interrupted the strained silence—and then continued. "Listen. I'm tired. I'm tired of shoveling shit against the administrative tide. Some days, it just doesn't seem worth it. Then I remember why we do what do, bureaucracy aside, and I take another breath. Let's face it, no one told me this would be a garden party. So let's get to this."

Standing, he pointed at Manny. "Tell them where this is headed, because you already have it figured out . . . at least mostly, right?"

Manny nodded and felt all eyes shift his way. He felt some weight lift from Josh's shoulders. Manny understood the burden.

"Part of the records we asked for and got was the credit card activity from the mother and son in the casket. You can see them on the third page in the file. Apparently the Roche's had just returned from a trip to Las Vegas. They had stayed at the Egyptian for five days, and they came home last week. There were over thirty transactions on Matthew's card. Not all that unusual when taking a trip to Sin City, except one charge was in a national department store for a pay-as-you-go phone."

"A little weird," said Alex.

"It was. Given they both have contract plans and updated smart phones. It was also odd because this throw-away phone still required the buyer to ID himself before activation. The days of walking into a store, buying a phone, ripping it out of its package, and making a call are dead, if they ever really existed. You have to log on to those temporary phone business sites, give them some info, fake or not, before you can activate the new phone."

"Still odd. But not entirely out of the question, especially if you're trying to hide something, from . . . say . . . your mother," said Sophie, shrugging.

"True. That was my first inclination. The CSU was able to get that company's records for phones purchased on that day—see page four—and activated within a couple of hours of the purchase. We didn't find anything with Roche's name, but she did find one listed to—"

"An F. Argyle. Shit," finished Alex, flipping his file closed.

"We shouldn't be surprised with that, especially given his range of influence. And that doesn't mean he's alive. It could be entirely possible, like I said before, that we're being led down the primrose path," said Manny.

"Let me guess," said Gavin, looking at his phone then glancing at the page open in front of him. "It's the same number that texted Chloe and called me."

"It is," said Manny, nodding. "Those facts mean that Mister Roche either had his credit card stolen and didn't realize it, or that he had a friend in Vegas. It also sets a motive to get rid of the Roche's, given his counseling sessions with Argyle four years ago. With Roche dead, he can't talk about his trip. Not that killers like this one need a motive, but at least it adds a little method to the madness."

"Why the mother?" asked Gavin.

"Maybe she heard or saw something." Manny sighed. "Or she was just important to the whole casket setup. Either way, she was innocent, I believe."

"Okay. I still don't know how the killer knew about Chloe's pregnancy," said Dean, rubbing his beard.

The chill came and went as Manny let the full ramifications of Dean's statement hit home. He stayed calm.

"I'm not sure. There could be some link between the text I sent to let you all know about the baby and access to the phone company's database. Those records get hacked often enough."

There was another way, as Dean had insinuated earlier. Manny chucked it out of his head, for now. He trusted everyone in this room with his life, but if he'd learned anything the last two years, trust was a fragile commodity and people weren't always as they seemed.

"So someone could have busted into any one of our accounts and seen that message? Or worse, they're monitoring one or all of us?" asked Dean.

"It's possible. That's why we'll have new phones and numbers before the day's over. Buzzy has also located a program that will block any outside source's direct access to our phone records, and it will track anyone who tries to gain unauthorized access to the new phones," said Manny.

"Damn, Williams. Two years ago you couldn't even *say* the word 'text,'" said Sophie, grinning.

"Yeah, well, I still don't care for this techie junk, but I have to play or be left behind."

"Okay, where does that leave all of this?" asked Alex.

"I think that's where Josh comes in, because that's as far as I can go. I will add that I think we're headed to Vegas, but not just for this case, right, Josh?"

"Right. The other side of this coin is that the phone that Roche bought was found in the possession of a young lady, Paige Madison, ninety minutes ago," answered Josh.

"Vegas? We're going to Vegas? Oh man, do I ever have outfits to wear out there," said Sophie, climbing out of her chair. "I've not been there in years. This is going to be—"

Sophie halted when she saw the look on Manny's face. She cleared her throat, brushed at an invisible piece of lint, then sat back down, folding her hands on the table.

She said, "Ah, what I meant is . . . what does this Paige have to say for herself?"

"Great question, Sophie," said Josh. "Nothing. She's not talking. She was the fourth murder victim in the last five days in Las Vegas. Each of them was discovered with one or more organs missing."

"Damn. So the connection is obvious. Whoever killed mom-and-son here has something going on in Vegas and wants the BAU to come running," said Sophie quietly. "The question is still why?"

The feeling deep in Manny's gut whispered the answer.

It was him.

The killer wanted Special Agent Manfred Robert Williams. And it didn't take a genius to figure it out.

The idea of being a cop, a special agent in his case, was to squelch fear by protecting the public. Putting the bad guys away and helping folks to sleep better at night. The irony wasn't lost on him. The public was safer with him and the BAU on the job, but he felt none of that safety in his own life. The constant concern of what, or who, was just around the corner for him and his family was growing old. It hung around his neck like some damned anchor, trying to pull him far into the deep and keep him there.

He felt his anger blossom. Two years of this shit was enough. He'd lost friends, witnessed horrible deaths, and felt unsafe, even in his own home. Never mind going crazy every time Jen left the house.

Argyle had invaded his home, touched his deceased wife, Louise, and had led him and his people on chases all over the world. He thought this crap would end when he killed the man, only to be stabbed later by one of his lackeys and almost checking out himself.

No more.

"It's me, and we all know it. And I'm ready. We end this once and for all," he said.

Glancing at Chloe, he saw his wife's strength. Her own anger was hard to miss, and her green eyes were steely, solid, and determined. He remembered just how much he'd never really wanted to get on the south side of that temper. This was one of those times.

Good girl.

"You're right. I'd be a liar, don't ya know, if I said I wasn't scared, but ya got to get this over and done with, man. I'll be going with ya, too," she said, her Irish lilt always more evident when she was emotional.

He kissed her and shook his head. "You got the next generation of Williams's growing inside, and whoever this is, knows it. That's not going to happen, okay?"

She stared at him, and then sighed, slowly nodding. "You're right—again. Besides, I'd be puking for days after the flight."

"There's another reason you won't be going. We'll talk about that in a minute," said Josh.

He turned to Manny. "You, Dean, and Sophie leave this afternoon."

"Hey, you forgot me," said Alex.

"Actually, I didn't. You're the second thing we have to discuss. You're going back to Quantico with me," said Josh.

Alex's look bordered on incredulous. "What? Like hell. I'm not letting these three have all of the fun. I'm going to Vegas."

Josh put his hand on Alex's shoulder. "There's a new developmental prosthesis that the military's been working on. The Bureau wants you to be the first to be fitted and run through beta testing."

Alex's jaw dropped, and then he regained his composure. "Sounds great, but it'll wait."

"Actually it won't. Alex. This thing looks like a real hand. It's almost science fiction with its potential. It could break barriers with what this could do not only for you, but for all those people who could possibly gain back something they'd believed they lost forever. In your case, a hand."

Watching the wheels turn, Manny saw Alex's expression change to acknowledgment, then back to reflect his fierce loyalty. It was what had cost him the hand in the first place.

"As great as that sounds, I'm not leaving my friends. They'll need me," said Alex with less conviction.

"They'll have help from the Vegas office. Besides, this is an order, Alex. The only way you don't go to HQ with me is if you don't work for the FBI, got it?"

Alex's stare moved from Josh to Manny, then back to Josh.

His eyes were flashing, but he kept his cool. "You're an asshole, Corner, but I get it," said Alex, pushing Josh's hand off his shoulder.

"Sometimes. But I know what I'm doing. I fought hard to get you this opportunity and you're taking it."

Josh put his hand back on Alex's shoulder. "Listen. I know how you feel. You think I want to go back to headquarters, let them go it alone in Vegas? I don't have a choice either."

Manny watched this scene play out and understood that Josh's mood was in part because he wouldn't be with his team.

"I have to spend three or four days in testing and questioning regarding my future. It seems they won't take no for an answer. I'm not given the choice for what's next . . . well, I have a choice, but since I have a family and a mortgage, I'm sort of screwed."

"Is this about the assistant director's opening?" asked Manny.

"I can't discuss what's going on. Like I said, you'll have to trust me."

"So is that why you've been so pissy?" asked Sophie.

Josh sighed. "Part of it."

He turned to Chloe. "I'm going to miss you."

Tilting her head, she gave him a half smile. "You are, aren't ya?"

"Okay. Shitty agenda item number three. The Bureau decided to eliminate Chloe's position and was going to send her back to the terrorism unit. I told the AD this wasn't acceptable. He told me he didn't care what I thought. I said she would quit. He said the Bureau would miss her, but so be it."

"Damn, dude, you struck completely out today," said Sophie.

"I was sure I was on the bubble here, so now I'm not feeling too underappreciated," said Chloe, smiling.

"What bullshit," said Alex.

"I agree, but Gavin fixed all that by offering to hire Chloe with the LPD. She's going to be an LPD employee now."

Chloe stood again, her impish grin reappearing. "What do ya all think?"

"I think you'll make a great LPD detective," said Alex.

Turning back to Gavin and Josh, who were now standing together, she raised her hand.

"Okay. It's totally official. I quit and I accept."

Walking over to her chair, Josh wrapped his arms around Chloe. "Like I said, I'll miss the hell out of working with you; you're one of the best. And I didn't have to fire you."

"So you were going to fire me?" she asked, holding him at arm's length.

"Yeah, I would have to when you said 'no' to going back to the terrorism unit, which you would have."

"You're such a smart man," she said, smiling.

Over the next thirty minutes, Manny watched and talked with the others as they congratulated Chloe and Alex for what was coming next for each of them. Yet, he couldn't escape the next pointed, unspoken segment of his journey and the unavoidable question that accompanied it.

Who awaited him in Las Vegas?

CHAPTER-17

The constant sounds echoing throughout any casino in Las Vegas were as varied as the time of day in which those sounds emanated. The sensory overload that was the very essence of Las Vegas was prominent on the outside of the colorful modern day castles and pyramids, but was no match for the inside of those monstrous dwellings.

From the soft bells and whistles to the loud jackpot ringing to let everyone know someone had just won a few dollars, the ambience escalated when the occasional obnoxious scream sprang forth to announce that some unsuspecting, would-be sucker had hit the right tumble of a slot machine's symbols, giving the winner a grand or two. The winners must believe they'd just forced the house into a serious cash deficiency and had to make some destiny-appointed amendment. That had to be true because why else would the fools turn around and give it all back?

He uncrossed his legs and turned his barstool slowly back toward the casino floor of the Egyptian. It was particularly busy for an early afternoon, which made his plan for the rest of the day a little simpler to put in motion. Not that it mattered much—he never really had a problem getting what he wanted. Today would be no exception.

Standing, he scanned the enormous room, taking in the motif designed to take the visitors back in time. He had to admit, he held a certain fascination for the ancient culture of the Pharaohs. The designers of the resort had done their homework. He did wonder, however, if the architects those three thousand years ago had carried his same appreciation for how business was conducted. He doubted it. One would have to see the world through his eyes to value the power of a Pharaoh.

He understood power.

"Are you leaving so soon?" asked the young barmaid in her best tip-me-well voice.

Standing, he picked up his whisky and tonic and smiled. "Leaving has such permanent connotations, don't you think?"

He could almost see her melt.

"You're right. It's just that I think a man like yourself shouldn't be without companionship, you know?" she answered, eyes wide.

"I couldn't agree more. Do you have any ideas on how I might remedy that situation?"

"I'm off tomorrow, if that works for you," she offered.

Looking down at her, he threw a fifty on the bar then tipped his white Fedora. "That is an intriguing possibility. Perhaps I'll return to escort you away from this madness."

"I'll be waiting."

A moment later, he was making his way amid the tangle of lights, smoke, and people, looking for what he needed to complete the day's quest. He was in no hurry; he guessed the Feds were still six to eight hours out, giving him plenty of time to put the finishing touch on the week's early activities. And what a week it had been.

Still, the best was yet to come.

Strolling leisurely, he moved past the high-stakes poker tables, circled the blackjack tables and the cashier's cage. He glanced up at one of the security cameras bulging from the low-slung ceiling just above the high-roller lounge, doffed his hat, and then mouthed a greeting. A special greeting intended for one audience. Only that person would understand it. His adversary had proved more than capable over the years, and he sensed that it was time for the journey to end for one of them. It wouldn't be him.

Bowing, he hesitated to make sure his target would get a good look, then replaced his hat and moved to the adjacent expanse of the casino's slot machine section. There were smaller gambling establishments in Las Vegas, but he doubted any was larger than the Egyptian's. That was why he was here, was it not? *Grand* and *larger than life* had always appealed to him .

Stepping around the corner, he stopped, tilting his head ever so slightly. His patience had proven fruitful. Sitting at a video poker machine was the reason he had spent hours here. She wasn't the most beautiful woman on the planet, but certainly a nice-looking forty-something who would fit quite nicely for the activities he had planned. He smiled. After all, he was here for her mind, as well as the rest of her.

Sitting next to the woman, he inserted a one-hundred-dollar bill into the machine. She glanced away from her slot to see who had invaded her space and did a classic retake, scanning him faster than an airport security machine.

"Hi. Holy smokes, you're a tall one. Good looking too, if I might be bold. I'm surprised your woman let you out of her sight," she said, smiling warmly.

"Hello, my dear. Why, I believe you're correct on my height and thank you for the compliment. But I'm currently out of a relationship. I'm sure you'll agree life simply gets in the way of that from time to time."

He watched as she drained her complimentary margarita and turned her chair toward him, brushing her knees against his thigh. "Well, I've lost too much money and had a few drinks, so this could get interesting for both of us."

"Indeed, it could."

Tapping the *deal* button, two queens, two kings, and an ace beeped across the screen. He held the two queens.

"You're going to lose all of that money," she warned. "My girlfriend just left and fed that damned thief two hundred big ones before she decided to go to the pool."

"I see. I thank you for your concern, but all things change, yes?"

"I suppose. But I'm not seeing it."

Tipping his hat, he smiled. "If I win this hand, I'll cash out, and escort you to your room for, shall we say, a late lunch, and then I suggest we partake in whatever else consenting adults do in this town."

Reaching up, she kissed him, her low-cut blouse allowing her fleshy breasts to touch his shoulder.

"Best offer I've had all day."

"I'm surprised by that," he said.

"Don't be. We cougars don't get as many opportunities as people think. We ain't hard bodies anymore."

"Too bad for the men who ignore you. You have many fine attributes."

She put her hand on his thigh and squeezed. "Okay. Now I'm getting pumped. Hit that button, and come on, queens."

Never looking at the screen, only at her face, he pushed the red *deal* button and almost instantaneously heard the machine chime that he'd won.

She tilted her neck and swore softly. "Unbelievable, you just hit four ladies."

"How fortunate, for both of us."

"Oh, you have no idea. This is going to be a day you'll never forget," she said, standing and taking his hand.

After claiming his winnings, he led his date toward the elevator that serviced the southwest tower of the resort.

As they rode up to the twenty-fourth floor, she stuck out her hand, smiling. "I'm at least a little old-fashioned and think we should know each other's names before we begin play time. I'm Grace Burleson."

"How charming and refreshing. I concur with your concept of etiquette. It's so very nice to meet you, Grace. You may call me Fredrick."

CHAPTER-18

Sophie released her seatbelt buckle, slowly stood, and steadied herself. She swore she would stop flying one of these days. Flying might go hand in hand with her job, but she didn't have to like it. Hate was a better word.

Walking ever so cautiously toward the front of the cabin, where the small refrigerator held bottled water and juice, she prayed for a smooth trip. Water would help with the slight case of nausea, she hoped.

Without warning, the Gulf Stream V skipped through an air pocket, and Sophie lunged to the right, screaming in pure panic as she hurtled into the air. Her eyes widened, her heartbeat soared as she grasped the air for an imaginary handle, desperately trying to recapture her balance. A second later, she landed unceremoniously into Manny's lap.

It took a moment to realize she hadn't been sucked out of the cabin through a hole the size of a pin and that she would probably live. Now all she had to do was to convince her stomach of the same truth.

She looked up at Manny.

"For crying out loud. This is total crap. All I wanted was a bottle of water and a tiny nap before we talk about your game plan, that's all. Damn, is that too much to ask?"

Manny laughed. His blue eyes were bright and alive. Even in the crazy set of events of the last twenty-fours, he was at ease. Strong, even confidant. Sophie couldn't negate the idea that the man seemed to be more and more at peace with what was coming next, even if she wasn't.

"What are you smiling at?" she asked.

"Nothing. I'm just glad I was here to help."

"Well, aren't you just a saint? And don't get any ideas. Chloe's hot and her boobs are even bigger with that pregnant thing, but if you ever had the best, you'd never go back to the rest."

Nodding, Manny's grin grew. "I'll remember that. Let me help you up."

By then, Dean was out of his chair, extending his hand.

"Me too. I wouldn't want you to be the cause of any domestic disputes. Besides, I'm a little jealous you're in his lap and not mine," he said.

"It's good to be the queen. But I don't need help getting up."

With that, she hoisted herself to her feet, flicked at a wrinkle on her sweater, and stepped toward the ice box.

"I guess not. Grab a water for me too, please, and since your nap's been interrupted, let's talk about Vegas," said Manny.

There it was again. That quiet confidence. She knew he'd been worried concerning his family since the BAU had returned from North Carolina. Who wouldn't have been? But none of that concern was evident now, at least on the outside. Still, there had to be *some* doubt.

On one hand, you believe the psychopath you put in the ground a year before was no longer a twisted, fearful threat. On the other, in just a few short days, that perception had been blown sky-high and, maybe, just maybe, all that seemed certain was cast into doubt—the bastard could actually be alive. Yet, Manny seemed to embrace the situation. It was as if he knew this was it. The final confrontation between him and whomever, or whatever, represented Argyle.

It was his version of the O.K. Corral.

Grabbing three waters, she stepped back to Manny, handing a bottle to him and Dean.

"Here you are, but you have to promise me something."

"Sure. What?"

Manny's large, hairy hand took the water ever so gently from her, his eyes not leaving hers. She returned his gaze and searched . . . the way he'd taught her. He'd always said that eyes were not only windows to the soul, but windows to the very heart of a person's intent. The very torment or blessing that engaged one's soul, the inner mind.

She felt her heart skip a beat because the candor in his gaze was blatant. The man was hiding nothing. That wasn't always so with Manny

Williams. Sometimes he hid his suspicions to protect the BAU and his family from unnecessary worry. Not now. Not this moment. No bullshit. No pretense. Simply straightforward Manny. For reasons she couldn't identify, it was almost scary to see that in a special agent.

Furthermore, he knew exactly what she'd been mulling around in her brain. His expression said so. That was even more disconcerting.

She bent to within a few inches of his face. Still, his gaze fixed on hers. She said, "I'm probably stating the obvious here, but you'll tell Dean and me everything, I mean everything, you're thinking. Since it's just the three of us, it'll help to get the skinny from your point of view. Not to mention, even though your theories are way out there, you've been known to be right, once in a while."

"Fair enough, Sophie. Fair enough. But you already know much that's on my mind, don't you?"

"Maybe, but I'm from Missouri and need to be shown."

"What? I thought you were from California," said Dean, grinning.

"So you've been paying attention?" asked Sophie.

Dean adjusted his yellow paisley driver's cap as his grin faded.

"Yes. I have. I'm not in tune to the two of you as you are to each other, but I see enough to know there's more going on than I understand sometimes. So you'll both have to go slow and tell me what the hell's going on."

Moving next to Dean, Sophie sat down, put her cold water in the holder, buckled her belt, and took Dean's hand.

"Are you ready to get into this man's mind?" she asked.

"Ready," said Dean, not sounding at all like he was.

"Ready is good," answered Manny.

He turned to her, that look of calm still etched on his face.

"And Sophie, you make me sound like something offbeat and perhaps a bit crazy," he said softly.

"Yeah, well, I'm sure you're crazy, on some level, like the rest of us, because of what we do, but you can dive a little deeper into that water than the rest of us. Offbeat is a given. So let's get to this."

She prayed she sounded more willing than she really was to hear what was coming next. She shook it off. No matter what they had been through, this was Manny. The Guardian of the Universe. Not to mention the person she wanted to be when she grew up, if that ever happened.

"Your wish is my command," he answered. "Let's open the blue Bureau folder and go over some of the notes I've put together over the last two days."

"We both did that already," said Sophie, looking at Dean, who nodded. "I get the connection between the two cases. I get all of that detail crap on the fact sheets. It doesn't take a genius to see the paper trail and that it was done intentionally. I want to know what you're thinking."

"Patience, Grasshopper. Let's look at the forensic report from Dean and Alex, okay?"

She nodded, crossing her legs as she fought her exasperation. The forensic report wasn't what she wanted to discuss. She went along anyway.

"We didn't find much, but there were two things that stood out. There was a degraded fingerprint on the note that we were able to identify through AFIS. It's 97.3% probable that it belongs to Argyle."

"No surprise there, given how organized this killer seems to be," said Sophie.

"True. The thing involving this print was that it had residuals of distilled water and glycol, which are used together to moisten the fingertips of someone who's been dead over a few months. There is even some reported success with this process on mummies in *Forensic Monthly*," said Dean.

Sophie gazed at Dean, shaking her head slowly. "*Forensic Monthly*? What is that? Porn for guys like you and Alex?"

Dean waggled his eyebrows, his eyes sparkling. "Oh, I've learned a thing or two from some of the articles. And the pictures . . . well, the pictures."

Rolling her eyes, she twisted back to Manny. "So it appears that someone may have taken the print from Argyle's corpse?"

"Or someone knew we'd dig deep and do that kind of analysis and set us up to think so," said Manny.

She frowned. "Damn. Really? That's stretching it."

"Maybe. But since we haven't been able to locate Argyle's body, we can't know for sure what we're seeing. That makes any possibility fair game," said Manny.

Clearing his throat, Dean went on. "The other situation Alex and I found interesting has to do with three hairs we found in the casket with mom and son. They were all from the same head of hair."

"Not belonging to one of the victims, right?" asked Sophie.

"Good guess. We couldn't match them with anyone, not even the city worker who dug up Argyle's casket. Which we were sort of expecting because they seemed to be placed on the son's lapel in a sort of row. Look at the picture."

Sophie did and saw the faint outline of three semi-blond hairs forming a loose "N."

"Maybe, if you've had a couple of beers. It's a guess, I think," she said doubtfully.

"Could be, but nevertheless neither of us could recall a random display like that before, so we went on the assumption that they were placed there for us to find. We did a little more testing and concluded the hairs came from a wig. Since they were short, we're taking a leap and saying it was probably worn by a man."

"Taking a few more leaps, aren't we?" asked Sophie.

"I don't think so. If I remember the first case file, Argyle was good with makeup and disguises, right? Besides, like Manny always says, run with your gut once in a while . . . so we did," answered Dean in a voice as serious as Sophie had ever heard from him. She listened just a little closer.

"Say you're right; what does that mean?" asked Manny.

"I think it means two things. Wigs like that one are often used to disguise someone's appearance, so this person didn't want to be recognized, obviously."

"Makes sense, of course. What's the second thing?" asked Sophie.

"Disguises can also be used to make a person look like someone else. If you look a little closer, the hair color is remarkably the same as Argyle's, at least according to the file photos," said Dean softly.

Leaning back in her seat, Sophie went over the information Dean and Manny had shared. She reviewed going back to the cemetery, then to Manny's house. She thought about the facts, but also dove into the other possibilities that the evidence and discussions hadn't revealed yet, the possibilities that stretched her imagination the way Manny wanted to see from her as she grew as a profiler.

There was a particular line of thinking that kept repeating itself. And since aliens and Big Foot were out of the question, she had to go with her own theory of deduction. *If you've eliminated all other possibilities, no matter what's left is most likely the truth.* Right now, that possibility made her skin crawl.

"Talk to us, Sophie."

"Damn it, Manny. I'm just not ready to go where I think this is going. Or has gone."

"Why not? I hate the saying, but 'it is what it is,' yes?"

"Yeah, whatever."

Taking a deep breath, she exhaled, and then reached out a hand to Manny and the other to Dean.

"I asked that you be totally honest with me a while ago, so I can't be a hypocrite, but I ain't as ready for this junk as you are. Never have been."

"What junk?" asked Dean, confusion and maybe a little apprehension in his expression.

Sophie sighed and pulled her hands back to her lap, then threw them up in the air. "Okay, fine. Here goes. When we first ran into that piece-of-shit Argyle, he'd used a few disguises, like you mentioned, and misled us to think that he was really someone else, a psycho named Robert Peppercorn, who had an alter-ego that went by the name of Eli Jenkins."

"Okay, got it so far," said Dean.

Manny nodded for her to continue.

"The thing for him was the game. He played us and loved it. He was such an arrogant prick that he left a message and clues for us to get to Jenkins, but not to him. We had no idea that Argyle had been the one behind Jenkins and his murders until *after* he'd escaped from the ship." "If he hadn't been so narcissistic, we may never have known that there was another killer," said Manny.

"Okay. So do you think that's happening again? But that really wouldn't make sense based on the evidence. I mean . . . everything points to Argyle being alive. If the evidence logic stands up, then Argyle is *trying* to get us to think that there's someone else involved," said Dean, frowning.

"Good logic, Dean," said Manny.

"But that's wrong, isn't it?" asked Sophie.

Twirling his finger in the classic "keep going" motion, Manny encouraged her to finish her line of thinking.

"All right, don't get pushy."

She sipped her water and gathered her ideas, then did what Manny asked, although he had no doubt already figured it out. "This guy is trying to get us to think its Argyle by sending us all of the right signals. Like with the phone, the cemetery, and even with Max Tucker's murder in North Carolina. All Argyle-like actions. But we know Manny scrambled the Good Doctor's brains in Ireland, so that man is surely dead and can't be the one setting this thing up."

"Makes sense," said Dean, nodding.

"It does, especially when you factor in Argyle's ability to create mindless zombie followers. But Argyle would never, I mean never, allow a student to outdo the master. The idea of having all the evidence point to him would satisfy his ego. And in a way, it would be consistent with how he set up Peppercorn."

"Okay, I guess I follow, but slow down," said Dean.

"Argyle wouldn't use the same trick twice. He turned the focus from himself the first time. This time the focus is on him. He knows we'd get that, so he's stepped it up another level, hasn't he, Manny?"

"I think so. One thing I can't get out of my mind is what Argyle said the night he died."

"What?" asked Dean.

"He asked me if it would truly be over and then he told me 'one never knows.' Like the joke was on us. I dismissed it as ranting and, even after I was stabbed in Puerto Rico, I figured that's what he meant. That he'd set up my death before he was roasting in hell."

Sophie hesitated, and then shrugged. "He never really wanted us to think this was a con by one of his lackeys, right?"

Manny's nod made her stomach clinch.

Son of a bitch.

God in Heaven she hated asking the next question. "Because he didn't die in Ireland, did he?"

"No, Sophie, I don't think he did," said Manny.

CHAPTER-19

For the tenth time in the last two hours, Chloe pulled away from the newest Rick Murcer novel and glanced at the antique grandfather clock in the corner of the family room.

Manny and the others had been gone barely three hours, and she was already going stir crazy. The silence was as uncomfortable as her bra. She was surprised at just how much she'd grown to hate that thing. Added to that was the fact that Haley Rose and Jen weren't due back from their assault on the new mall until tonight. More time to think.

She'd spent time alone, most of her adult life in fact, and it had been a welcome relief from the hectic pace of life as a special agent for the FBI. But this was different on a whole other level.

She'd grown accustomed to the sounds of Manny's breathing and his quick wit, or just his presence, not to mention that of Jen and her friends, who had all brought a different dimension to her life. Once experienced, that kind of bustle was almost heaven, and there was no going back, was there? Even Sampson's occasional room-rumbling bark had become a welcome change of pace.

Chloe stood from the sofa, reached down and stroked Sampson's large head as he snored at her feet, then moved into the kitchen. The aroma of her latest concoction involving bacon, peanut butter, pickles, and oat bread, topped with avocado and tomatoes, still lingered. She was tempted to make another one, dismissed the temptation, patted her belly, and then gave in.

"Hey, I'm eating for two," she whispered.

Five minutes later, she was headed back to the sofa, milk in one hand and a stacked sandwich in the other, when her cell vibrated in her pocket. She stopped midstride, then slowly placed her meal on the table.

Someone had texted her.

Even though she was totally aware that the other phone—the one that had received the horrible text—was now in police custody, that knowledge did little to reduce her anxiety. Maybe this person, this Argyle Wannabe, had found out how to reach her.

Pulling the phone out of her pocket, she dismissed her paranoia, nearly. Argyle, or anyone like him, wouldn't repeat the text scheme. It had served its purpose and as arrogant as these types of perverts were, calculated caution was usually a trademark for most of them. They also could be impulsive and not so bright, but she didn't think that profile fit her texter.

Shaking away the premise that Argyle had risen from the grave, Chloe glanced down at her phone, put her finger on the slide button, prayed, and then took a look.

At first, she couldn't read it, then she laughed out loud. Maybe more in relief than anything else.

Hey Chloe. We're leaving the mall a little later. We'll be home in a few hours. Granny Franson, I know, don't call her that, wants to know if you want anything to eat. Like those huge cinnamon rolls or something. Let me know, otherwise, see you soon.

Oh! You should see the stuff we got!!! Jen

Her fingers flew across the tiny keyboard.

Jen. Great. Looking forward to seeing you two at home, and your treasure. Bring extra frosting for the cinnamon rolls. Chloe.

The response was almost immediate.

Will do. XOXOX.

Glancing at the phone one last time, she reflected on how nice it was to be included in Jen's life and just how well her mum and Jen were getting on.

Her mum.

The woman had gone through a hellish stretch. She'd fallen, at least partially, for one of the most savage psychopaths to grace the planet and lived to tell of it. Added to that were the suspicions and subsequent testing and observation Haley Rose had to endure to ensure she wasn't one of Argyle's cult following. Chloe had suspected her for a brief time; in the end, she knew her mum. Haley Rose Franson was a tough, independent woman. No one could take her down a road she didn't want to travel.

Pulling out the closest chair, Chloe sat down, drank her milk, and finished off the bacon delight in no time flat.

Besides, Manny was convinced that her mum was untouched by Argyle's persuasion, at least in that mindless-follower way, and he'd come to that conclusion much quicker than Chloe had.

He trusted Jen to Haley Rose and that said all Chloe really needed to know. She also realized her own doubts, as well as Sophie's, came from having bad experiences with love in the past. That can wreak havoc on a person's psyche. Good God, she understood that merry-go-round.

So why the lingering doubt about your mum, Chloe girl?

She shook it off. She simply had too much time on her hands, especially with everyone else doing their jobs except her. She'd told Gavin it would be four or five days at least.

Maybe that was too long.

She reached for the phone and called Gavin.

"Chloe. What can I help you with?"

He seemed in a hurry and sounded far more like a police commissioner than a friend.

"I've got a few hours before Jen and mum get home and thought I'd come in and sign paperwork and get a look at my new digs, if that's okay with you."

The slight hesitation sent her into agent mode. She liked how that felt.

"Ahh, well, I'm glad you called. I was going to call you, but I didn't want to put any pressure on you to start before you were ready."

Gavin went quiet, then she heard the exhale. "Oh, what the hell, your professional life belongs to the LPD and me, right?"

"Why were you going to call? And yes, yes it does."

There was no hint of hesitation this time. "I need you to take a case."

"What kind of case?" she asked, her blood moving faster.

"The murder kind."

CHAPTER-20

The black Ford SUV pulled up to the wide, glass triple doors of the Las Vegas International Airport. Manny watched as the tall blonde wearing blue jeans and a green blouse and her burly, bald companion, dressed in kakis and a plaid shirt, exited the vehicle. They flashed their credentials to the security guards and then stepped into the private-flight section of the terminal.

Reaching for his bag, Manny turned to motion for Dean and Sophie that the FBI's personal escort service had arrived, only to discover that they had left his side for the slot machines some thirty feet away.

He shook his head. He'd been so wrapped up with watching for the local agents to arrive, and the facts of the case, that he hadn't noticed them leave.

Argyle's possible existence seemed artificial. Made up. Like some way-out plot in a made-for-TV series where the bad, evil villain escapes death and capture only to return to torture, and eventually kill, the protagonist. The good guy. Him.

He ran his hand through his hair.

The antagonist was alive and held but one purpose: to take out the good guys. Period. Except this wasn't a book or a movie; this was real life and that meant real problems. The thing is, he'd known it for a while. Argyle's final words had echoed in his mind a million times since Galway. Maybe two million. Each time the conclusion showed itself in a most despicable way, right into his heart of hearts.

Enough talking, Williams. Enough whining. Enough denial. Let's get on with it.

"You bastard! I'm going to kick the hell out of your shiny case."

The angry yell caused him to reach for his Glock, and then he stopped as he recognized the voice.

Sophie had just shook hands with her first Las Vegas one-armed bandit.

"Come on, Sophie, I think our ride's here," said Dean, pulling at her arm.

"Come on, my butt. This cheating slut just stole twenty bucks from me. I'm taking it out in whoop-ass trade," she answered, straining to reach the machine.

"Please try again. Please try again," said the electronic yet seductive voice of the slot.

His partner's face grew even redder. "What? Oh, you heifer. That's it. You're mine." She continued to try to break free from Dean, who, to his credit, was keeping a straight face. Manny guessed that if Dean wanted to stay out of the local urgent care facility, he'd do well to keep that demeanor.

The truth, however, was that his partner wasn't upset at the money lost in the machine. Hardly.

In three strides, Manny stood beside her, then he was in her ear, whispering. "Not now, girl. You can take revenge later, but we've got bigger problems, yes?"

She stopped struggling, then began to point at the machine, stopped, opened her mouth to speak, stopped, then stood still, slowly removing Dean's hand from her arm, her composure on the way back.

Manny motioned for Dean to back up as he stayed close to Sophie, speaking softly.

"Listen. I know why you're pissed. I'm not feeling any better. We have to keep clear heads. If he's alive, we have to get beyond that and do what we do, okay?"

She nodded, reaching her mouth to his ear. "I'm mad, but I'm scared too. I hate being afraid. Been there, done that. Argyle gave me sleepless nights, and no one does that to me. Now he's back from the damned River Styx, and I'm trying to figure out, exactly, how that happened."

"I understand that. I've had to check my underwear a couple of times myself. But if we don't keep it together, we're dead meat."

Her smile was electric. "Oh, Lord in Heaven, I've got to get that image of you crapping your pants out of my mind."

When Manny returned her smile, she kissed him on the cheek. "Thanks, Manny. I love you, you know? And for the record, I will kick that mechanical bitch's ass before we leave this town, if I'm alive to do it."

"I'll help."

By then, the local female agent was only a few feet away from them. She hesitated, took another step, and then stopped completely, her smile widening ever so slowly as she looked from Manny and Sophie to Dean.

She'd scanned the CSI thoroughly, her eyes lingering at his bearded face—perhaps a little longer than she intended, Manny noticed.

She abruptly thrust out her hand. "I'm Agent Kimberly Wilkins. This is Agent Ryan Frost."

Shaking their hands, Manny smiled. "I'm Manny Williams and this is Sophie Lee. I'd introduce Dean Mikus, but you obviously have met before."

"Great to meet you, Agent Williams and you too, Agent Lee. I've heard a lot about you, and it's good to have the BAU aboard for this case. And you're right. Dean and I go back to LA."

She glanced at Dean. "How have you been?"

Dean reached past her and shook Agent Frost's hand, then stepped back. "I'm doing just fine, Kim. Much better than the last time I saw you. I didn't know you'd been transferred to Vegas. And I didn't know you and Josh were in the military together."

"Yep. We were MPs on the same base. And I transferred almost a year ago. Talk about surprises. I had no idea you were with the BAU, or the FBI, for that matter. I guess I should read the staff roster information a tad closer."

He nodded. "It was time to leave LA. For a lot of reasons."

Her smiled faded ever so slightly. "I understand how staying could have been tough."

"Tough? Like how?" asked Sophie, her eyes narrowing as she stepped closer to Agent Wilkins.

"Ahh, well, that's a bit personal, and you're not here to discuss that," Agent Wilkins said. "We should go. We have a meeting with four folks from the LVPD. They're anxious for the BAU to do what you do and get them a profile. We get some doozy cases out here, but nothing like this one. Frost?"

She then spun on her heel and headed for the SUV.

"Okay. We'll load you up and get you checked into the Egyptian, then head for the office and get this investigation started," said Agent Frost.

He motioned for them to follow. Manny, Sophie, and Dean picked up their bags. Sophie and Dean were walking in front of him, talking low.

"What the hell is that about, Mikus?"

"Old history, Sophie. We can talk later, okay?"

"Ya think? I'm not blond, like your 'friend' up there. It didn't look like old history to my Asian ass."

"It is. Let's drop this until later. Besides, who compares to you?"

"Oh. Good answer, but you still got some 'splainin' to do, Lucy. She doesn't even have slanted eyes like mine."

Then Sophie strode ahead of Dean, stepped out into the Nevada heat where an FBI vehicle waited and threw her bag in the back before she climbed into the rear seat.

As they reached the SUV, Dean glanced at Manny and shrugged.

"She'll be fine, you just need to talk to her," said Manny softly.

He shook his head. "Yeah. You're right. Besides, we've got more pressing matters than my old love life, right?"

Manny nodded, and then watched as Dean joined Sophie in the back seat.

"More pressing matters indeed," he whispered, the perspiration already forming above his lip as he slammed the rear door of the SUV and climbed into the air-conditioned truck.

CHAPTER-21

"Are you ready for this, stud?"

Alex Downs reached over the armrest of the first-class seat and put his hand on his wife's leg, then smiled. Barb had always been there for him, and today was no exception. An old-fashioned girl in a new-world package. She was simply incredible.

His gaze met hers. He, once again, was hit with what most people had to be thinking when he introduced her as his wife. Hell, he still thought the same thing.

How did he ever catch the eye of a woman like her?

Her face was like that of an actress. She had long, platinum-blonde hair and the body of a goddess. Throw in an impressive IQ, and there was the perfect woman, at least in his eyes. And the best part, the very best part, was her love for him—story-book like. Barb only had eyes for him, and he never once doubted that, even before they were married.

"Stud, huh?"

Smiling, she kissed him. "Yep. My stud."

"You always make me feel better than I should, so I'll try to temper my answer. I—"

"Wait. Before you respond to that, I'm still trying to deal with that stud comment," said Josh Corner, sitting in the next seat over.

His grin was wide, and Alex couldn't resist smiling back.

"Hey. Sophie's on the way to Vegas—without us, I might add—so I thought I'd at least get to enjoy a flight without her smartass remarks."

"Yeah. I'm her replacement. But I'll be kinder, maybe."

"You better be. I took a few lessons from Sophie and might be able to thump you," said Barb, leaning past Alex.

"Got it. Who says I'm a slow learner?" answered Josh, grinning wider.

"We're cops. We're ALL slow learners, I'd say," said Alex.

Josh's expression grew more thoughtful, then he looked at Alex. "How *are* you doing, Alex?"

"I'm a wreck. Not so much because of the surgery and the testing, I guess. I mean, I'm feeling a ton of emotions with those possibilities too. It's just that I'm thinking of those three in Vegas and that case and what it could mean. It's been some time since we weren't all together, and it makes me nervous."

Josh exhaled. "I hear that. But they'll do what they do and be home before you know it."

"I'm sure you're right," answered Alex, realizing that Josh didn't feel as confident as he sounded.

"I am. Let's talk about your agenda."

"Okay," said Alex.

"We'll be landing, then going straight to Walter Reed. They want to get you prepped for early morning surgery. It'll take around six hours, and you should be back in the real world in eight."

"I get that. I'm still trying to understand the procedure. I mean I get the phantom limb phenomenon and how that works, but this concept of targeted muscle re-innervation is a bit intimidating. They're going to redirect electrical impulses through some electrodes to a healthy group of muscles that end up in the new hand?"

"I hear you, but according to the folks in the Defense Advanced Research Projects Agency, DARPA for short, you'll be able to move your hand by just thinking it. Not only that, you'll be able to actually feel sensations."

"Wow. It sounds like science fiction, for real. This is a prime example of what money and a few bright minds can accomplish," said Barb.

Alex heard the small hitch in her voice and was bumped with a subtle reality. This wasn't only for him, it was for her. Not for any selfish reasons on her part, but because she loved him and wanted him to have the best possible life. As much as he cared for Manny and Sophie and Dean, Barb was his first love and ultimate responsibility.

Damn. He could be short-sighted and self-centered.

Dumbass.

He took Barb's hand in his right one, his real one.

"We'll get to see it first hand," he said with a grin.

She winced and Josh groaned.

"Real cute," said Barb.

She kissed him again and unbuckled her seat belt. "I have to powder my nose so you two will have a few minutes to talk about whatever my presence is keeping you two from discussing."

With that, she walked to the restroom, leaving Alex wondering how she could be so perceptive along with everything else she had going for her.

"Smart woman," said Josh.

"She is."

The moment of awkward silence came and then left as soon as Josh spoke.

"This process doesn't involve severing nerves and, if everything goes right, minimal cutting of your muscle tissue. Just adding electrodes and letting them pick up on—"

"The pulses that are already there, I know. I did my research too. What that means is I should be ready to start the testing in a couple of days and then get my fat ass out to Vegas, right?"

Josh looked to the floor and then glanced back to Alex. "In a perfect world, maybe. But I'm not sure what the testing will mean. I won't be there the whole time because I've got a couple of crosses to bear myself, so we'll have to play it by ear."

Alex nodded, but there was something in Josh's voice he didn't like. He looked toward the restroom and saw the "occupancy" sign was still lit.

"Look, you been acting a little weird and you explained why at Manny's house, but there's something else, right?"

Josh folded his hands together. "Yes. There is."

Then he leaned closer and lowered his voice.

"Haven't you wondered how that text message where Manny announced that Chloe was pregnant got all of the way out to Las Vegas?"

"I thought it was strange, but that stuff can be hacked into, like Manny said, so that seemed feasible," answered Alex.

"It sounded right, but the system that Manny's phone, and the whole BAU, operates on is as secure as anything in the world. My people tell me it wasn't hacked."

Shifting in his seat, it was Alex's turn to tilt closer. "You know what you're saying?"

Clasping his hands together, Josh nodded.

"I do. We're still checking out the nine people who received Manny's text, but it appears someone on that list, somehow, was in contact with the man in Vegas."

CHAPTER-22

Placing the last of the gauze around her cold hand, he backed away from her and took a picture with her cell phone. The scene was exact and the setting perfect. Each of the four alabaster Canopic jars, representing the four Sons of Horus, were placed at the precise position Egyptian history dictated. The fifth jar, a creation of his very own, did not fit with the fascinating tradition of the old world, but was nevertheless the pinnacle of his creation.

"Grace, you were perfect. May you rest knowing that," he said, then tilted his head back, laughing out loud.

Reaching out, he took her cloth-covered hand in his.

"I'm afraid you don't know much now, unless, of course you'd subscribed to some form of ancient religion that prescribes to any afterlife perception. I wish you the best of luck with that premise. He laughed again, a little louder. "I was the last and only god you'll ever meet."

Releasing her hand, he moved to the opposite side of the king bed. As he did, he noticed that the hot Vegas sun was beginning to set over the mountains. Its rays danced and reflected off the spring vegetation and, of course, off the millions of windows making up the city's casinos and resorts.

For the first time in over a year, he nursed a sense of excitement. Not just with the prospect of ending the game—because it *would* end here, no doubting that—but also because of the steps he'd so painstakingly put into place to *get* to the end game. It was, as always, contingent on Special Agent Williams putting two and two together, no matter how clandestine the message. The agent's ability was no match for his own; still, he needed to make sure there were no mistakes. And there hadn't been any.

Without hesitation, Manfred Williams had figured out that Doctor Fredrick Argyle was not in the grave. Not the whole truth. Not by a longshot. And just as likely, the pathetic BAU had arrived believing they were going to squash the Good Doctor. Finally. Once and for all.

Except . . . that's what they believed the last time, was it not?

"Soon enough, my friends, soon enough," he whispered.

Continuing around the bed, he stopped, snapped another picture, then put the phone in his pocket. He reached a long arm over to the fifth jar, removed it from atop the dead woman's midsection, glanced inside, inhaled the scent one final time, then placed the finely crafted cover over the contents. He carefully placed the jar back on her

"Pretty amazing place, huh?" said Agent Wilkins, her voice expressing some of that almost-unbridled excitement.

"Yeah, if money and morals were no object," said Sophie, still staring out the side window.

"Oh, this glittering princess is far more than that. Most of the locals will attest to that. The shows can be the best in the world. There are a couple places designed just for families, and the cost of living is better than most think. And, although, it can become extremely hot for a few months, there's no danger of snow, or hurricanes, or even earthquakes."

"Damn, you sound like a tourist guide," said Sophie, a tinge of cool in her words.

"Maybe, but I'll retire here," she said, smiling a little too quickly. She'd caught the expression in Sophie's voice and chose to ignore it. Manny supposed that was a plus for her and this investigation.

"I guess we can discuss the pros and cons of Las Vegas at some point, but let's discuss the local take on the cases that we're here to help with," said Manny.

"That sounds good, Agent Williams."

"Manny is fine."

Kim Wilkins smiled, a real one this time, and it made her face come alive, allowing her beauty to shine. Some women are pretty, some are cute, and some had a beauty that showed through in a more subtle way. Her smile had released that subtle beauty, and it wasn't hard to see how Dean might have become enamored with her.

Not to mention, her expression told him a few things about her personality. She was genuine and very bright. He could sense she was not afraid to articulate what she was thinking, which told him she had no issues with confidence, toughness, or riding into the intense side of life.

He didn't think details were her strength, but given the way Frost was driving and his quiet demeanor, Manny guessed she knew that and subsequently hired folks to work around her that made up for her deficiencies, real or perceived. That action alone molded her staff into more of a team. Not many people in authority recognized their weaknesses, let alone acted on mitigating them.

Yet she still had plenty of poise to lead. All good traits, in his estimation, which made her a great call to run the Vegas operation for the Bureau.

"Okay, Manny it is. And did I just get profiled from turning my head and speaking to you?"

Dean answered before Manny could. "Oh, you and your agent Frost both. He's a profile addict but trying to quit."

"That's not really true, but sometimes it just happens," said Manny, flashing a grin.

"I bet it comes in handy too," said Agent Wilkins.

"Sometimes. Sometimes it's a bit of a curse."

"Well, I'd like to hear what you think, about both of us . . . maybe . . . but let's get to your first question."

The vehicle turned east on Tropicana as they swung away from the strip. He stared as they rolled past the MGM. It looked like a modern-day emerald castle.

Shaking his head, he turned back to Agent Wilkins. "Talk to us. We've seen the reports and have a few ideas of our own, but paperwork can't tell us what you all are seeing."

She nodded. "It looks like the classic organ-stealing scenario. The kind they show you at Quantico when you go through agent training one-o-one. Bodies dumped in a secluded area after an organ or organs are removed. The incisions on the bodies are made with a professional precision that some drug-crazed layperson couldn't have possibly done. Yada, yada, yada."

Manny raised his eyebrows. Sophie giggled under her breath, and Dean leaned closer. She'd gotten all of their attentions.

"So I take it you're not buying it?" asked Manny.

"No, I'm not. Two detectives began the investigation from the LVPD, who will be part of the meeting, and their captain contacted us because they believe this is an organ-trading operation connected with some highly organized gang or even the mob, but—"

"There are too many things that don't add up?" finished Manny.

It was her turn to look surprised. She cocked her head to the left. "Yeah, that's what I think."

"You mean the randomness of the victims. The timing of each murder that seems far too close together for killings related to this type of criminal activity," said Manny.

"Both of those. Plus, most times people aren't killed for their kidneys. It's a bit cliché, but folks are actually found in bathtubs filled with ice. They're in rough shape, but usually alive."

"And you're struggling with the way the bodies have been mutilated. Like its overkill?" added Sophie.

"No denying that. Someone has anger issues," said Agent Wilkins.

"Or wants us to think they do," said Dean.

Kim Wilkins unbuckled her seatbelt and then turned completely around, her knees firmly planted in her seat, as she looked at Dean, then Sophie, then settled on Manny's face with her dark eyes. The woman was shifting into a far more intense mode than anything he'd seen prior. He liked her mindset.

"What aren't you telling me?" she asked.

"The last victim, Paige Madison, had a cell phone on her that wasn't hers. You knew about that, right?" asked Manny.

Her facial expression changed, and she glanced toward Frost.

Her look told Manny she hadn't caught that part—there was that no-attention-to-detail quirk.

"It was in the report, Kim," Frost said matter-of-factly.

"I'm sorry. I didn't read the full report on the last victim. This isn't the only thing we have going, and I just figured it was pretty much a copycat of the others. My mistake, but tell me about the phone."

Manny brought her up-to-date on the text and subsequent call to Gavin Crosby as well and how that related to the reason the BAU was in Vegas. Minus any mention of the Argyle resurrection theory. He believed it best to not reveal that line of thinking. For now, she only needed to know that there was a true psychopathic serial killer hunting in her town. He sensed that might be enough for the moment.

Her face twisted into one of those "oh shit" looks as she sat back on her haunches.

"So you're right. This isn't concerning organ trafficking, as far as we can see. This is about something far more. We're here to prevent the locals from digging in too deep, give them a profile, get their help, then take over the investigation under jurisdictional guidelines for cases like these," said Manny.

Leaning forward again, she looked at Manny and the others and shrugged. "Okay. That'll teach me to make sure I read everything in those reports. I apologize for not doing that," she said. "What's next after the meeting?"

He was also right regarding her honesty and resilience. Her mistakes were water under the bridge for her, and now it was time to move to what was next.

Agent Frost turned north on Maryland, expertly speeding past a green Lexus in the left lane. The man was good behind the wheel. Not Sophie good, but good. Manny saw from the corner of his eye that Sophie had noticed too.

"We'll want to get checked in. The fact that there were two bodies found in the area by the Egyptian means the killer could be operating close to there. It's as good a place as any. Besides, the report from the cell phone company says the call came from within a quarter mile of the tower on that end of town," said Manny.

"That's what I was thinking," said Agent Wilkins.

"Well, one out of two. I feel so much better," said Sophie, smiling.

"Was that sarcasm, Agent Lee, or petty jealousy I detected in your voice?" answered Agent Wilkins, smiling back at Sophie.

Manny started to speak, to break up the conversation before it got rolling, but decided to let it run its course. Better to face the demon now, than let it raise its ugly head later.

"Neither. Just pointing out that if you screw up in the right situation, we'll all be dead, and then I'd have to kick your ass in the afterlife," said Sophie.

"Well, agent, why wait? I mean, I can have Frost stop the truck and you can see if your sparrow ass has overloaded your elephant mouth," answered Wilkins, never losing her smile.

Sophie tilted her head, glanced at Manny, then Dean, then reached into her bag, pulling out one of her pink throwing stars. "Ever had one of these stuck up your ass, agent?"

"Not since LA."

The tight silence was unexpected as the vehicle slowed for a red light. Sophie had been caught off guard by her retort, and she struggled to respond . . . without snorting and laughing. She couldn't pull it off.

Agent Wilkins followed with a full cackle of her own, causing Manny to join them. But not Dean; instead, he creased his thick eyebrows into a straight line.

"Okay, Wilkins. You got me. That was funny."

"We're even. I was wondering what that star thing was going to feel like," Agent Wilkins answered, a glint in her eye.

The tension-release only lasted a moment. The next instant, the driver's side window exploded and Agent Frost slumped over the wheel, the left side of his face splattered on the dash.

CHAPTER-24

"I'm sorry to take advantage of your goodwill, Chloe, but like I said, my son Mike is in Dallas at a training seminar, and I can't give my other team of detectives one more case. Hell, they live here as it is," said Gavin.

"No, you're not sorry," she said.

"Okay, you're right. I'm glad you came in, to rescue an old man." She sat in the burgundy leather chair across from Gavin, studying his face as he sipped the vanilla latte she'd brought him. Her new boss, at almost sixty, still had a passion for his job. The fact that his wife had shot him at point-blank range and then was killed a few days later hadn't sapped his spirit long term. Never mind losing his new daughter-in-law on the cruise ship just after her and Mike's wedding.

He, and his son Mike, had come out of those heart-wrenching situations far better than most. She wasn't so sure she would have. Father and son had each other, and it no doubt kept them sane.

She admired Gavin Crosby for that, and it was simply one more thing that contributed to her growing affection for him. He'd supported her from the beginning, even when some folks whispered that she and Manny shouldn't have gotten together so soon after Louise's death. Manny's brother-in-law for one. Being a profiler herself, she knew there was probably some draw to Gavin as a father image, since she'd never really had much of that. Chloe shifted in her chair. Little girls needed their dads, maybe more than little boys did, and if they didn't receive that attention at a young age, they sought it when they were older.

Ending the internal psych session, she finished with one more notion.

Sometimes she overanalyzed. Life threw everyone a curveball from time to time. She'd learned to deal with hers, mostly. That aside, Gavin was a good man. Manny had been right on that one.

"What are you staring at, detective?" he asked, frowning.

"I was just wondering how long that grumpy-ass look will stay on your face before you smile. And how can I be a detective? We haven't filled out paperwork. I've not done a psych evaluation, and where's my badge and gun?"

"This look stays until I hopefully see your mom tonight. As far as the other details and they are still details, I've invoked the Gavin Crosby quick-hire option."

His frown disappeared and a quick smile flashed, but just for a moment.

With that, he reached into his drawer and pulled out a gold shield and a holster fitted with a Glock 22, identical to the one she'd handed over to Josh Corner with her letter of resignation and FBI ID. Gavin slid them across the desk to her.

"You can sign the employment paperwork sitting on your desk and get it over to personnel later. Any more questions?"

"Why, yes, I do have more questions, don't ya know?"

"Shoot."

"Where *is* my desk? For one. And tell me about this case. You simply said on the phone it had to do with murder."

She liked how that sounded coming from her mouth. It felt good to actually be back in the saddle, as they say. Baby or not, she had been looking forward to returning to work more than she'd guessed. Stir crazy was still stir crazy, FBI or not.

Gavin's demeanor reverted back to the man-in-charge persona he wore well, accompanied with a brief, but obvious, glimpse of sadness.

"Your office is around the corner from my office to the left next to Mike's."

Pulling out a file from his top drawer, he hesitated, then reached over and handed it to her.

She looked down at the file. She didn't recognize the name, but the stamp that said UNSOLVED in bold, red letters stood out like a flashing neon sign. The folder and the papers inside held a musty, old scent that told her they'd been compiled over time, maybe a long time.

Opening up the folder, the first thing that stood out was a picture of a young man in his early twenties. The yellowing borders of the snapshot couldn't hide his bright-blue eyes. They held a certain glimmer that told her he liked to have fun. He had long, auburn hair, and his complexion showed traces of acne. A good-looking kid with a full life in front of him. She glanced at the date on the top of the file: 1996.

She then turned the page and felt her jaw drop. Beginning on the left side of the folder and continuing to the other side were a series of six smaller pictures featuring the young man.

These images from hell contained no hope of life, however. He'd been murdered in a manner that was far from humane. The savagery and mutilation were almost beyond comprehension. Someone had stabbed him dozens of times in the neck and chest to the point that his head was almost decapitated. For good measure, the killer had driven a pair of matching screwdrivers into each eye.

Closing her eyes, she gathered her composure and then scanned the horrific portraits again.

His body had been found in a sparsely wooded area, lying on thick grass, but near what looked like a narrow sidewalk. In the fourth picture, she could see the edge of a large, silvery swing set. Her profiler instincts kicked in. The killer had uncontained rage issues and had made it personal just by the number of stab wounds. She suspected that the victim trusted the killer and maybe they'd agreed to meet in this park setting or had run into each other there.

The killer had been strong. Several of the ribs were broken by the stab strokes. To nearly remove someone's head like that took a fair amount of strength.

Usually when a killer does something to another person's eyes, it means the killer has a sense of guilt and doesn't want the person to see them. She didn't think this was true here. This was a final statement and may have been done to punish the victim further. Maybe even for something they'd seen. She'd have to read over the reports, but she prayed the eyes were stabbed postmortem. If not, this young man suffered greatly before his end came.

Slowly, she closed the file and looked at Gavin. He seemed to have grown older in the last two minutes.

"Who was he?" she asked softly.

"His name was Alan Gordon. He was found like that after the first football game of the season. He'd come home from college to go to the game with his best friend, and after they'd parted ways for the night . . . well, this is how his friend saw Alan the next time they met."

"His story checked out?"

Gavin stood and looked out his wide office window toward the white dome that served as Michigan's capitol building.

Her eyes locked onto Manny's as the thin smile came and went. "He was here just two weeks. Two weeks, Manny. Hadn't even been assigned an official case yet."

He watched as she pulled her jacket from the floor and covered his face. She then swung her door open. It creaked and opened grudgingly, but she squeezed through.

Dean and Sophie climbed out the other side as Manny opened his door to escape. He hesitated, as the blood spatter laced across the windshield demanded his attention. An old quote came back to him that had been spoken by some long-dead philosopher.

For the dead, there are no more toils.

He wasn't sure why, but there was a certain comfort in that. Eternal rest sounded far better than eternal work.

"Rest well, agent," he whispered then exited the vehicle.

CHAPTER-26

"Maid service. Any one in there?"

Mary Lou Feighner knocked on the door again, this time louder.

No response. She sighed. Why couldn't folks just put the sign on the door?

Listening intently, like she'd been doing for the last eighteen years, she heard no movement or alcohol-impaired voice objecting to her inquires.

Slowly, she pulled the key ring from around her neck, causing her to wince. Lately, the arthritis in her neck gave her far fewer breaks from the pain that haunted her. Aleve helped. And prescription drugs really did the trick, when her stingy doctor would give them to her. Drugs offered her the only true relief she'd felt in years.

But what was she to do? She was a few months from retirement and as good as the Egyptian had treated her over the years, it was time to enjoy the years she had left. And maybe not alone, she hoped.

Hell, who knew? Maybe she'd find the man of her dreams. God knew she'd found a few that made up her nightmares. The universe is about balance, right?

"But then again, men are so much work," she said, sighing.

Moving closer to the lock, she slid the card into the key slot, and pushed the door open a foot.

"Housekeeping."

Again, no one responded with a *"what the hell are you doing in here"* so she propped the door open with the edge of her lumbering cart, snapped on new rubber gloves, and went inside.

The bathroom light was on, so she took a quick side trip and counted the towels and did an inventory of the hand soap shaped like a sphinx, shampoo bottles, lotion containers, and plastic cups. She frowned. Usually she had to replace *something*. Folks that visited Vegas weren't known for their neatness so much as they were known for letting their inhibitions slide south. That included making use of everything at their disposal.

The woman in this room hadn't touched a thing in twenty-four hours. Mary Lou shrugged. The clean bathroom meant less work for her, so whatever. As she moved out of the bathroom, she caught a glimpse of herself in the mirror. She stared an extra few seconds. Slowly shaking her head, she looked away. She still looked good but not the way the younger folks think of good. At sixty-two, there was no hiding the wrinkles and sagging, and not just under the eyes.

She laughed. It was all relative . . . relative to being above ground.

How did this old age thing creep up like this? And did it matter? She was still here and that meant something.

Moving into the neck of the hall that opened up to the sleeping section of the room, she glanced to her left, looked again, and yelped as she grabbed at her chest in surprise. Then she swore.

She'd seen some very bizarre things in this Las Vegas hotel, never mind on the strip, but this was at the very top of the list.

Someone had bought the fake mummy that was for sale in the gift shop and stowed it on her guest's bed. Probably just to scare the sin out of this poor woman. People were just plain crazy and had way too much money on their hands.

Looking at it again, she moved slowly toward the bed. This was a good one. It looked almost real. Taking baby steps, she inched closer and was hit with the odor. And it wasn't roses. To boot, she'd never seen those odd shaped jars with the tiny insignias before. Her unease grew.

Moving cautiously closer, the smell grew stronger, like someone had used perfume to mask a more pungent aroma.

Then she saw it.

The small burgundy blood spot that had blossomed into the size of a carnation, located at the top of the mummy's head.

Great God in heaven.

She backed away, her heart and mind racing. Grabbing her company cell phone with shaking hands, she was finally able to hit the speed-dial button for security as she continued backing toward the door.

She waited for security to answer, her eyes never leaving the bed.

She screamed as something touched her from behind. Whirling like she was thirty years younger and fifty pounds lighter, she came face to face with her supply cart.

"Shit," she breathed.

"What?"

Security dispatch had answered.

"This is Mary Lou on the tenth floor. You'd better get your ass up here to ten twenty-six. We got a dead mummy."

There was a brief silence. "You been drinking at lunch again?"

She yelled into the phone. "This ain't no damn joke. There's a dead woman, I think, wrapped up like a mummy on her bed."

"Calm down. How do you know it's real?"

"Cause I've never seen a mummy bleed before."

"Okay. Okay. We'll be there in a minute."

Hanging up, Mary Lou pulled her cart away from the door and leaned against the wall, tears in her eyes.

She wasn't just crying for the lady on the bed, but for herself as well. Some experiences in life change how one perceives reality.

Room ten twenty-six had done that to her.

CHAPTER-27

Standing a few feet away from Sophie and Dean, Manny watched the traffic meander slowly by in the only open northbound lane on Maryland. There was still some early-evening light, but Vegas was quickly approaching its time to shine.

The LVPD blues were doing their best to keep the congestion to a minimum, and it was helping at least some, and they had dispatched two teams from their CSU to help go over the crime scene. There were fifteen to twenty cops trying not to trip over each other. Manny sighed. The last thing he needed was more people milling in the vicinity where the shot had taken out Agent Frost and detoured them from their planned meeting at the FBI's office.

Running his hand through his hair, he wondered about making plans in this business. It was like trying to shovel sand against the waves; why bother? Fate had other plans, it seemed.

"What do you think?" asked Sophie.

Her voice was calm, professional. That usually meant she was nervous but focused. He wasn't sure he wanted her that way, but she was dealing, like they all were, with how close they'd come to checking out in grand fashion. It was interesting how people dealt with stress so differently. He believed it was part of what made everyone unique.

"Well, since we don't have any real witnesses yet, I'll have to go on what we know."

Dean stepped closer, shutting off his cell.

"We don't know that much, Boss," he said shaking his head "I did get a few things from the CSU working the SUV and Frost's body. The angle of the bullet that struck him was about forty-eight degrees, accounting for a little variance when it hit the window. But not a lot, since it was probably a forty-five caliber bullet that took him out," he said, gesturing with his hands.

"So that means the angle was window high, so he was probably shot from another car," said Manny. "Could it have been a random shooting?"

"That's easier to swallow than to think that he was targeted," said Sophie.

She leaned closer to Manny and Dean. "It's a hell of a lot easier to believe that it was random than believe that we were followed and set up at this particular intersection," she said quietly.

"It's not a matter of what we want to believe; it's a matter of what really happened. I don't want to think that way either, but look what we've run into in the past with Argyle and his cult. We can't be too cautious. We have to consider every angle, and we have to stick to the facts, yes?"

She nodded, but he could tell she wasn't feeling better just the same.

Hell, neither was he.

"What else, Dean?"

"The LVPD and every available FBI agent are canvassing the area, like you asked, as well as asking the local TV and radio stations to do a public service message and ask anyone who might have seen anything to contact the police."

"And?" asked Manny.

"Nothing yet, but it was only forty-five minutes ago."

Manny again scanned the area. They'd pulled up to the corner, stopped, waited, and then boom. Frost was dead. None of them had noticed anything unusual, but then again, they were talking and the SUV's windows were tinted in the back. That would have reduced their line of sight. Agent Wilkins was facing the back, so she wouldn't have seen anything suspicious.

He shook his head. He should have suspected there could be some kind of welcome party like this, but this was far out, even for a deranged psychopath.

He walked over to the intersection, Sophie and Dean following at a distance, and did a slow three-sixty. There were some low-riding, pale stucco buildings in the direction of the shot, a CVS drugstore, and a tire repair business on the opposite corner, but nothing that would really conceal a shooter who could have lined up with the angle Dean had mentioned.

Moving two feet to his right, he stood where the window had been blown out. Tiny bits of glass grated between his shoes and the road, the sound causing the scene to be even more eerie. Could this have really been a planned hit? It would have been easier if the killer were in a car and maybe even followed them from the airport. He supposed it was even possible for someone to get ahead of them, turn around, work their way south, and take the shot driving in the opposite lane. It would have taken great skill and perfect timing, but it was possible. It would explain the angle and why, so far, there hadn't been any witnesses.

He reflected on their time in North Carolina, when the truck they were riding in had been hit by a stray bullet meant for a deer. So a stray bullet was a possibility. This area wasn't the best in the city, and there were signs of gang activity. Yet that situation just didn't feel true.

The last option irritated his brain, but all things had to be considered. Did the shooter know exactly where they would be, made themselves inconspicuous standing on or near the corner, pulled the trigger, and then walked away?

Damn it. That would mean Argyle would have another contact or damn mole inside the Bureau or the LVPD to know what was going on and when.

But if that were true, why only one shot? One death? Why not get it over with? He supposed he knew the answer to that. Killing the rest of them like that would be too impersonal. This killer liked things up close. Killing all of them with one shot simply wasn't Argyle's style. If he were really involved, the game would continue. The killing of Agent Frost heightened the tension, and maybe the stakes, for the psychopath in charge. Manny was sure that Frost's family and friends wouldn't care much for that reasoning. He knew he didn't.

Yet somehow . . .

He felt the hand on his shoulder. His stomach did the tango as he turned to the source. Agent Wilkins stood three feet away. Her eyes were dry, her face hard, determined. She'd put her emotions on the backburner for now and was fully in the moment.

Good. They were going to need her.

"What are you thinking, Manny?" she asked.

Dean and Sophie had moved closer.

"Well, that's the second time I've heard that question in the last five minutes, and I'm not sure I'm any closer to knowing exactly what to say."

"I'd like to hear it anyway. We're not coming up with jack shit here and the CSU is ready to pack it in. No shell casings. No smoking gun. No footprints. No witness. No nothing," said Agent Wilkins.

"She ain't alone," said Sophie. "And I know those wheels are turning, Williams."

He nodded and went over the three likelihoods with the others, leaving out any mention of Argyle for the moment.

When he finished, there were a few moments of silence. He reflected on what he'd just said and how none of the ideas were out of the realm of possibility. Yet none of them seemed exactly right either. And the *why* of the attack was tugging stronger at his mind than before.

What was the point?

"I can't think of anything else you haven't mentioned," said Agent Wilkins. "It has to be one of those situations."

She tilted her head, scanning Manny's face with those hard eyes. "But who would want to kill Frost and why go to such means?"

Manny rubbed his eyes with thumb and forefinger. Smart woman.

"I'm not sure. I want to see the reports on the vehicle and any other forensic information before we go there. Dean will help analyze what the CSU finds, and we'll see what it tells us."

She stepped closer. "You have an idea, don't you? This isn't a time to be holding shit back, Manny. I've got a dead agent here. You're here not just for the organ-snatching crimes or because you got a text and call that made no sense. You know who's behind this."

Just then, another FBI SUV pulled up. The driver got out and looked at Manny, Dean, and Sophie. "Your bags are in the back," she said.

She started to hand the keys to Manny, but Agent Wilkins snatched them from his hand.

"I know you're tired and need some rest, but I need some answers," she said, almost pleading.

Sophie hesitated, then reached over and plucked the keys from Agent Wilkins' hand and headed around the SUV, Dean in tow. Manny watched as they climbed in, shutting the doors at the same time. He turned back to Agent Wilkins.

"I've got a theory, and I think I'm right. Evidence doesn't lie, however. But sometimes it can take you down a different path, and I'm trying to sort that out. Yes. I think your man was killed for a particular reason. And I may know who's behind it. But I've been wrong before, and it could have been totally random. I have to have those reports, and I need to talk to the two detectives working the organ cases before I can share anything as insane as what could be going on. Does that make sense?"

Her resigned look told him it did. And that the day had taken far more out of her than she'd realized.

"We meet at seven a.m. tomorrow morning at the Egyptian. I'll get a conference room there. I'll have LVPD CSU supervisors, detectives, and two of my agents trained in this shit as well. You'll get your reports and a little time to go over them, but not much sleep, I'm afraid. Like the rest of us." she said, determination returning to her voice.

"We didn't come to Vegas to sleep," he said.

Reaching for her hand, he squeezed, offering a reassuring smile before he got into the back of the vehicle.

"Do you know where you're going?" he asked Sophie.

"Yep."

She stepped on the gas, and they roared south on Maryland. As they reached Tropicana Boulevard in silence, he focused on the towering Sphinx almost a mile away. It was well lit in true Vegas style. He thought of his question to Sophie, posed it to himself?

Do you know where you're going, Williams?

CHAPTER-28

Staring at the analog clock resting on the wall above the HDTV, Alex Downs marveled at how slow time could actually move. Especially in a hospital and particularly the day before your world may revert to one you believed was gone forever.

Shifting in the bed, he glanced at the blue leather chair that Barb had been sitting in just a few minutes before. He could still smell her perfume. Or better yet, the scent that was her.

Funny. He was also hit with how much he wanted her to come back and hold his one good hand. To hear her say, in that confident voice, that he was a stud and this was like falling into bed with her. God knew how easy that had been from the very night they were married.

They were one. Even Manny's bible said something about that. It was hard to argue the point that true love seemed eternal. Maybe that's what his good friend and profiler extraordinaire was trying to show them. All of them.

Turning over, he closed his eyes. It was almost midnight, and surgery would be an early riser. Still, his mind drifted.

Love.

Though Barb was at the top of the heap in terms of having his heart, he'd grown to love Manny and the gang too. In fact, his love for Manny and Chloe had put him in this situation. Not that he regretted stepping in front of Chloe and taking the sword that had been intended for her in San Juan. He wasn't lying when he said he'd do it again. In a heartbeat.

Chloe made Manny happy and the man had dealt with enough of the other shit, the heart-breaking kind, to last most people for a lifetime and beyond. He wasn't sure if his friend could have taken another blow like that. Hell, Chloe wasn't even Alex's lady, and he didn't think he could have taken it either. He and Manny would have resided in padded cells next to each other for the rest of their lives, maybe.

"Hey. You sleeping?"

Alex looked over his shoulder, then sat up. Josh Corner leaned on the door, looking exhausted, but sporting that infectious smile that endeared him to his staff—and hid his tougher, sometimes tortured side.

"Nah. Sleep doesn't seem to be on my agenda just yet."

"I heard that. I tucked the boys in, kissed my wife good night, and proceeded to toss and turn for an hour. So here I am."

"I thought you were going to be in testing and interviewing until Jesus comes back?"

Josh shook his head. "No. Just until I couldn't stand another question from a man or woman in a black suit. Damn. You'd think they'd get a sense of fashion around there."

Alex laughed. "No plaids, huh?"

"None."

"You're not done, right?"

"Right. It'll pick up bright and early, and that's why I'm here. I just wanted to wish you good luck and let you know that I'll be over to see you as soon as I can."

"Thanks. But these surgeons are good, and I'm hoping luck has nothing to do with it."

Alex saw the expression change on his boss's face.

"I know this wasn't exactly the best week for this. For either of us to be away from the BAU, but bureaucratic wheels turn like no other. I couldn't get us out of this."

"I know. We should be there, but they've got help, and they're great at what they do."

Alex unconsciously reached for a hand that wasn't there. "Did you hear from them?" he asked.

Josh nodded. "I just got off the phone with Manny. They've had a couple of issues, but are at the hotel and have a meeting scheduled early tomorrow."

"What kind of issues?" asked Alex.

"Nothing they can't handle. Just more shit in the storm."

Shaking his head slowly, Alex turned back to Josh.

"Manny is as sane as anyone I know, and no one has to tell either of us about that almost-creepy profiler deal that rules his life. But Argyle alive? Really? Do you think—"

Josh waved his hand. "It doesn't matter what we think, at least right now. We've seen Manny make a few swings at the weird and hit most of them. I trust him to get to the bottom of all of this strange shit. And it is way on the wild side. I'm just hoping Argyle wasn't that good. I like him better dead."

"You're probably right. But are you sure?"

Josh hesitated, looked out the window at the city lights, then back to Alex.

"I want to be. Does that count?"

"I hope so."

"I'll see you tomorrow, Alex." Josh shook his head and, without saying another word, walked out the door.

A minute later, the shift nurse came through the door, stopped, and stared at Alex.

His heartbeat stepped up, and his eyes grew wide "What are you doing here?"

"Whatever I want, Downs. Whatever I want," she said, rushing the bed.

CHAPTER-29

Sophie burst through the revolving door. Dean smiled. Watching her drop her bag, raise her arms, and tell Manny that she already felt like Vegas was hers, made him laugh out loud. It must have caught Manny's funny bone as well, because for one of the few times since they'd left Lansing, Manny laughed out loud. A good sign.

His complex friend and resident genius when it came to reading people could take too much upon himself. A trait that haunted most workaholics, no doubt; yet he'd wager a few bucks that none of them had Manny's heart, which probably amplified his stress level times two.

"Just what part of Vegas is yours?" asked Dean.

"Damn, you're slow, boy. The colorful lights, the sounds of slots and screaming winners, the vanilla incense smell of this place. Hell, even the sight of working girls just trying to make a buck adds to the whole shebang."

"What about all those germs? There could be millions living on the chips, the slot buttons. Hell, never mind the restrooms and bars," said Dean, that old, uncomfortable feeling returning.

"Are you kidding me?"

Sophie then turned and kissed him full on the lips. Her mouth, like always, was a place somewhere between the third and fourth heaven. He felt warmer.

"How many germs did I just give you swapping spit? I don't hear you bitching about that, right?" she said, hands on hips.

He grinned. "Okay. Point taken. You'll just have to keep reminding me."

"In your dreams. Changing out of that yellow paisley shirt and hat might help."

"Whatever. Clothes make the man. I'm that man."

"Whatever."

She turned toward Manny. "And don't give me any crap. I know what time it is, and I know when we meet in the morning, and while I do care what you think, you ain't my mama, cool?"

Manny laughed again. "You seem to know a lot. And you're right, there are no mamas here. But I need you working on all cylinders. Plus, you need to watch who and what's going on around you. We have a dead agent and a psycho running to and fro who is looking for us."

"You're an amazing buzzkill, Williams. I can take care of myself and Dean too. We're good to go. Besides, maybe I, we, should be turning this place upside down, you know?"

Dean started to ask why, then realized the goddess he'd fallen head over heels for in San Juan those months ago was right. He didn't care for the ramifications, like getting little or no sleep and having his head on a swivel, but they just might find something or *someone* of interest. Then again, something or someone could find *them*.

"She has a point, boss. I'd be willing to help with this task, as unpleasant as it might be," he said, tongue firmly in cheek.

Manny's eyes twinkled despite being obviously tired and melancholy. "You're such a trooper, Dean."

Sophie elbowed him. "Unpleasant? I should kick—oh wait. I get it . . . yeah, he's right, Manny."

Raising his hands, Manny shrugged. "Okay. Here's the deal. Let's check in, get to our rooms, make a little bit of a plan, and then we'll rotate every two hours. That way we'll get some sleep as well as getting a feel for this place. Since three of the bodies were found near here, that makes perfect—"

Dean looked away from Sophie and followed Manny's eyes toward the concierge desk, then over to security.

Three uniformed officers, followed by three more from the resort's yellow-clad security team, hurried through the low door-gate, moving directly toward them. Movement from the left caught his eyes, and he watched as a man and a woman, who looked like cops, also zeroed in on the three of them. Feeling like he was banking a sharp curve on the roller coaster in New York, New York, Dean's stomach clenched and dropped to his toes. He guessed their plans for the evening were about to be scrambled.

The two plain-clothed cops got to them fast. The black-haired, attractive woman spoke first.

"Agent Williams? I'm Detective Teachout, and this is my partner Detective Lane."

Dean recognized the names as two of LVPD that were to meet with them in the morning.

Manny did too. Dean's guts twisted more as Williams released his infamous "oh shit" look.

Following suit, Sophie crossed her arms and shifted her weight in expectation.

"I am. This is Agent Lee and Agent Mikus."

Looking at Teachout, her partner, then the three blues and three security officers, he noticed Manny's slight nod as he skipped over any greeting. Full cop-mode came quicker for Manny than him, but adrenaline is a wonderful drug. Dean forgot about being mentally and physically exhausted, and was suddenly ready for what was next.

"I'd ask you what has happened, but I suppose I know. Where's the body?" asked Manny.

Teachout raised her eyebrows. "And I'd ask how you knew that, but your reputation precedes you, and I guess you've got to know something's wrong."

"Educated guess, I suppose," Manny answered.

"At any rate, this homicide is bizarre. Even beyond the others."

Manny gave her a quick, humorless grin. "I'd expect nothing less."

"Not like this. Never like this," she said, her voice struggling to stay calm.

"If you say so. Lead the way," said Manny.

Indulging in one more long look, Teachout shrugged and motioned for them to follow her.

Falling in line behind Sophie, Dean joined the law-enforcement entourage as they reached the security elevators and climbed in.

He found himself hoping for the best and dreading the worst. Sophie must have been thinking the same thing. She slipped her hand into his and squeezed.

She was trying to strengthen him, but it didn't work. He liked being touched by her, no question, yet her action only confirmed that another level of hell was coming their way.

As the elevator stopped and opened on the tenth floor, he wondered briefly how many levels there could be in this crazy bastard's world.

They walked into the room, and any sense of normal expectations was quickly, and finally, ushered from his mind.

Teachout was right.

CHAPTER-31

Standing near the corpse, Manny felt his heart break a little more. LVPD had just removed the victim's two vacation friends from the room. They'd burst through the blues and began screaming her name. The emotion was startling.

Grace.

He was reminded again that these victims were people with lives, friends, and family. They spoke, they danced, they cried, and enjoyed their lives, for the most part.

The unabashed horror on the faces of those women was obvious as they mourned their beloved friend. He understood both the horror and the love.

Manny gazed at the gauze-wrapped body. There were still times when he felt Louise in his arms, blood flowing from the scarlet wound in her chest, as her soul left this world. Who could ever forget something like this?

Healing would never be complete, he suspected, but Chloe Franson had walked into his life and helped turn his heart and mind in different directions. Not everyone had that kind of help. He prayed these two women would have each other to lean on until the sleepless nights and convicting nightmares evolved into something more tolerable, more sane, if that were possible for them.

"What's going on in there?" asked Sophie, pointing at Manny's head, her voice shaking ever so slightly.

His partner was tough minded, but he knew she was questioning how many more incidents like this could she handle before reason was replaced with unreason. Calm with anger. Determination with hate. Self-control with revenge.

Hell, maybe she was spot on. In fact, she probably was, but they were called to a higher standard. He hoped they could maintain that, at least for now. All bets would be off when they met this killer. And they *would* meet him.

"Trying to gather my wits, like the rest of you," he answered, exhaling slowly.

"Yeah? Well good luck with that. This isn't just creepy and warped, but this display is for us, isn't it?"

"Too early to say, but yeah, it could be. We need to process the room and look at everything closely before we make that jump," said Manny.

"What the hell does that mean . . . that this was for you?" asked Detective Teachout.

"That could be a long story. One we will share in the early meeting tomorrow. But for now, we

Then again, that's what someone like Argyle wanted. More smoke, more mirrors, more confusion.

"Agent?" she asked again.

There *were* a few things the LVPD could do for them. "Okay. I'd like the cell phone records of each victim pulled and cross-referenced to see if there are any numbers in common. I also want to see credit card records and, if you can get it done, GPS records for the phones, and for the victims' cars. Some of the vics may have had an OnStar service that can tell us if the vehicles had a common destination."

Teachout shook her head. "It sounds like busy work, Agent, but we can do that."

"It's not. I also need you to talk to the friends of each of these victims, but start with this woman's friends. We also need to look at all of the security video for this place, including the elevators, say for the last fifteen hours. Since your ME said the time of death was approximately four hours ago, we need to check to see if there's anything that shows her and the unsub meeting."

Teachout raised her arms in surrender. "Okay. You've done this before. I get it. We'll get to work."

The two detectives moved toward the door. As they hit the hallway, they motioned for the blues and the hotel security detail to follow them. A moment later, Teachout poked her head back inside the gold-trimmed door.

"Agents?"

"What is it?" asked Manny.

"What if we find another body?"

Manny shook his head. "You won't. At least not yet. He's not ready for another one."

"How can you be so sure?"

"Because we don't know what kind of message this scene was intended to show. He'll want to give us time to figure this one out. And laugh if we don't."

"So?"

"That makes the joke on us, Detective."

CHAPTER-32

Looking at his hands, he realized just how well he knew himself. His mind worked with his feet, his voice, his walk, his very biological infrastructure. Yet, it always boiled down to his hands. They were truly the extension of his mind's eye. Perhaps even the essence of his existence. He turned them over, smiled, and then laughed.

"Idle hands are the devil's playground, they say," he whispered. "So we shall stay busy."

Exiting the stall of the restroom, he browsed his image in passing, smiling again. He looked like he should, and wouldn't that be unnerving to all, especially Agent Williams.

Williams.

He felt the hate rise just at the concept of what that man had cost him dearly. Mostly, he was able to keep his emotions under wraps. Losing control gave little impudence toward the end game, but over the last three years, it was impossible for his hatred for Agent Williams not to expand.

And why shouldn't it? Hadn't he preached his whole life that getting in touch with one's true self was the key to finding who and what one was destined to be? By taking down those impossible expectations, one could begin to carve out that destiny, as the first prized pupil, Eli Jenkins, had so eloquently espoused. And make no mistake, he'd gotten in touch with his emotion regarding the Guardian of the Universe.

Walking through the door and entering the casino near the blackjack tables, he reeled in his loathing. The time was coming when he could release it all. And he would. But this wasn't the time, and he had much to do. He needed to savor the process and then move on when it was over. He would do that as well.

He moved to the back side of the gaming area, the smell of cigarettes and the boisterous banter of happy vacationers running interference for his next move. Next he sat at the high-stakes table, threw a thousand dollars in hundreds on the green velvet, and then sat where he could see directly to the main elevators' expansive foyer. The elevators were guarded by twin images of Anubis, who had the body of a man crowned with the head of a jackal. He wondered if the designer knew that Anubis was the god and guardian of the underworld who appeared on behalf of the deceased after their embalming was complete. He doubted it. To attribute so many gods to so many functions in any culture seemed asinine, but the irony here was hard to ignore. He played a large chip and immediately hit a blackjack. The other two men at the table congratulated him, and he nodded to them, but his eyes virtually never left the elevators.

He had no interest in the gods of some ancient civilization, but perhaps they were men like himself that the commoners, maybe even royalty, had perceived as something special. They wouldn't have been wrong in his case. His interest, however, was in the ones who carried badges and would be emerging from the elevator doors. He'd watched Williams and his idiots go up the elevator as the bitch of a detective intercepted them just when they began to move his way. Disappointing.

It would have been delicious to have them walk so close, mere feet, and never see him. No matter. That time was coming. He won a few more hands, lost a couple, and then played two large chips, beating the dealer on a hit that gave him a twenty-one. Before the dealer could pull another hand from the automatic shuffler, her replacement appeared from nowhere, and the pit boss, just for good measure, decided to replace all six decks at the same time.

Some things never change. He presumed the new dealer was the house "cooler." She was a pretty Asian woman probably in her forties with a quick, bright grin. Disarming and lethal.

Smiling to himself, he glanced at the elevators again. Seeing what he had been waiting for, he pushed his chips toward the dealer.

"Color me up, please."

"Are you leaving so soon?" the dealer asked, showing that smile.

"I am. But I may be back."

She nodded, called out her payout to the pit boss, then slid him his winnings—eight hundred more in chips than he started with. He flipped a twenty-five-dollar chip her way and left the table, just as the LVPD group reached the middle of the huge, colorful lobby.

"Thank you, sir. I hope to see you soon," said the dealer.

"One never knows," he said softly.

Then he rose and sauntered toward the group of cops who were heading for the golden front doors.

He felt so alive.

CHAPTER-33

"What kind of help can we give you, Dean?" asked Manny.

The room had been emptied and just he, Sophie, and Dean remained. There were two officers outside the room, but the door was closed and locked. The seclusion was something he thought the three of them needed. At least he did. The nuances of this horrific scene were going to be cryptic and, unless he missed his guess, more important than any of the murders to date. The killer had made a point to detail this scene. They had to determine why.

Dean placed his black crime-scene kit on the floor to the right of the victim and sighed. "You could get me a one-way ticket to some private Caribbean island and a year's salary in the bank for starters. But since that's not going to happen, you can start by moving away from this poor woman."

"I like the first idea way better," said Sophie, "But hey, we can move as far away as you want. We're not just pretty faces here. We can take a hint."

Dean offered a crooked, almost shy smile that transferred into a quiet confidence.

He was in total charge of gathering evidence in this room; he was probably a little uncomfortable with that prospect. Even though Dean and Alex had worked well together, and Dean was good at what he did, flying solo was different. Manny guessed Dean knew that.

"You don't have to tell me that, about the pretty faces, and no offense intended, but this room has already been invaded by way too many cops and hotel personnel. Even with gloves and the cute little booties everyone is wearing, this scene is probably tainted."

Manny nodded. "I think you're right on that. The good thing is that no one touched the body or the jars, and I believe that's where the rubber will hit the road on this one."

"Good point," said Dean, pulling at his beard.

The CSI reached into his case and pulled out a bundle of evidence bags, then separated five larger bags from the stack, arranging them across his case in a neat row.

"This is for the jars. I'm pretty sure when we check them out, you'll want to get these to the lab to verify their contents. Then I can process the rest of the room."

"Shit. You mean there are human parts or something in those?" asked Sophie.

Manny ran his hand through his hair. "These containers are called Canopic jars. They were used to hold human organs during the embalming process of Egyptian royalty," said Manny, moving closer to the body.

"Oh hell. Embalming? Organs? This just keeps getting better," said Sophie, shifting her weight.

"See the lids on the four jars around the torso? Each one is supposed to represent the keeper of a certain organ. I can't remember which is which—wait. Sophie, do a search on your phone for Canopic jars and what each one symbolizes."

Pulling her I-phone out of her jeans, Sophie slid her finger over the screen, and then looked up at Manny and Dean. "Why am I doing this? I mean, we're going to find out what's inside anyway—o*hhh.* The way the jars are laid out and the contents are going to tell us something important, right?"

"That's possible. Not to mention the names of each god represented on the jars could be crucial to what's next. If this is Argyle's work, and it could be, nothing is done without a purpose," said Manny.

"Yeah, what the hell else is new? Why can't we just get some pissed off woman who kills her husband because he was 'ho' hunting? It was simpler when we were Lansing cops."

"It was. But we're now the BAU and the FBI. We don't do 'ho' murders," he answered. Then he smiled.

Sophie's word sounded odd coming from his mouth. It must have sounded different to Sophie and Dean as well because she looked up from her phone, grinning, and Dean turned away from his case, snorting a quick chuckle.

"We'll get you into the twenty-first century yet, straight-laced boy," said Sophie.

"You can hope," said Manny.

Her phone played a short ditty Manny didn't recognize as she began scrolling and swiping with amazing speed. He still had a difficult time texting more than one line a minute.

"Okay. You're right. The four jars have names and protect different organs and are some mythical god's kids. His name is Horus or something. The human head jar, Imesty, protects the liver. The falcon head, some weird name— Qebekh-seenuef, I think that's how you say it— protects the guts. The monkey, or baboon, I guess—Hapy—takes care of the lungs. And last, but not least, this dog or jackal head, some dude named Duamutef."

She turned to Manny, shaking her head. "Man, these kids grew up with these names? They're hell to pronounce let alone live with. I bet they got their asses kicked at recess. Anyway, this one watches over the stomach."

She looked at Dean than back to Manny, shifting to a more serious look. "Good God. This sick bastard has all of those body parts in the jars?"

"I think so. The CSI reports of the first three killings have shown those organs missing from the victims."

The elephant in the room grew larger as Manny stared at the fifth jar sitting on the woman's chest. It was larger than the others by half. The top of the jar was a detailed carving of a lion/human hybrid. Its golden mane was full, framing a face with the piercing blue eyes of a man, which then morphed into the nose and maw of a lion, changing back to the strong, square jaw of a human. The ears were lower on the side of the head—one human, the other, lion-like. The carving then tapered down to the neck of the jar, which was approximately two inches wide, then the base of the jar ballooned out in a typical urn shape. He could see something silhouetted against the thick glass, but it was unrecognizable because of the dark amber color of the jar. He wasn't sure that he really wanted to know, yet his mind raced at the possibilities. But he had to be sure before he let the forensic crew get involved.

"What are we looking at?" asked Sophie quietly.

"If you mean what's in the jar, I don't know for sure, but I have an idea. I think the top is the key to the content," answered Manny.

"Why?" asked Dean, more evidence bags in his hand.

"The lion is a symbol for a ton of things, but mostly it's known for its fearlessness, its swagger. Its heart."

"You mean like the heart of a lion: bold and brave," said Sophie.

"Right."

"For crying out loud. There's a heart in that jar?" she said, her tone rising.

"I don't think so. For two reasons. If I remember right, the Egyptians believed the soul and a certain amount of intellect was seated in the heart. To remove it from the body would be akin to damning the person to the underworld, so they left it in the body. The cover combines the lion with a man so that reduces the significance of the courage factor, but increases the intellect, the cunning, the craftiness, even the arrogance."

"So?" asked Sophie.

Manny didn't answer. Instead he tilted his head toward the top on the jar, staring at the design closer. The workmanship was past flawless. It was difficult to get that kind of handiwork done in these days of automation and presses that stamped out and mass produced synthetic images. The person who did this was an artist, and an accomplished one at that.

He was suddenly compelled to touch the carving. The brilliance of the work called to him. Even through the gloves, he could tell the wood was real and dense, maybe Brazilian teak. Smooth, almost sensual to the touch, it even maintained a bit of its original scent.

Squinting, he moved as close as he dared. The carving was perfect in every way. It had also been well thought out by someone who believed themselves superior. Right down to the Argyle-like chin.

Manny reached out and grabbed Dean's arm. "Dean. I need you to remove the part of the wrap over her heart."

"I'm not at that–"

"Now."

Dean started to speak, shrugged, grabbed his scissors, and began at the left side of her chest. He made four passes, started the fifth and stopped, looking over to Manny, then Sophie. He carefully removed another carving with a large set of tweezers. It was a small, bluish-green scarab; and the material and workmanship seemed to be the same as the Canopic top.

"What the hell?" asked Sophie.

"According to the Egyptian myth, the scarab guarded the heart from telling all of its owner's past sins to the god of the west, ensuring a great afterlife. I wanted to see how far this game had gone."

"And?" said Dean, putting the scarab in a clear bag.

"Too far." At that second, he knew his first inclination was right and he felt his stomach churn. "Dean. The head. I'd like you to unwrap the top of her head."

Grabbing the scissors from the bed, Mikus did as he was told without a second look.

After the third cut, Dean stopped and stepped away. "Shit."

"It's gone, isn't it?" asked Manny.

Dean nodded. "It looks like he used a drill."

"Drill for what?" asked Sophie, not smiling.

"To remove her brain," said Manny.

CHAPTER-34

Life is, and will always be, about choices. Josh Corner knew that. He more than knew it; he lived it each day. He supposed everyone did to some extent, but his choices seemed to hold so much more weight than those of the average person—his choices affected so many lives. Leaning back in his blue leather chair, he snorted softly.

"It's always about you, isn't it, Corner?" he said under his breath.

Manny would probably remind him of the good things this life had dealt him. He'd even call him blessed. He'd remind Josh of the great salary he pulled down and the health benefits afforded a ranking FBI supervisor. He'd tell him to pull out the family photo of his two sons and beautiful wife and never underestimate the blessings of a healthy, strong family. Not to mention that Josh Corner was loved. That his boys worshipped the ground he walked on and even though his wife and he had gone through a few rough patches, they were the lovers that destiny had intended for each other. And better yet, they each knew it.

On cue, he reached into his suit-coat pocket and pulled out the picture of his family. The soft glow of his work computer's monitor shed light on the familiar image in his hand. The worn photo verified what he had just run over in his mind.

Manny would be right.

It was sometimes easy to not think about the struggle that life could be for folks who lived paycheck to paycheck, working diligently to keep the proverbial wolves away from their collective doors. Never mind those who had no paycheck at all.

But this pivotal decision was *his* and no one else's. He guessed that his self-consternation and narcissism would be okay today, given the potentially far-reaching impact of what he had to decide.

His stomach rumbled, and he ran a hand across his midsection. Thirty-five and courting ulcers and acid reflux wasn't what he'd had in mind at this point in his career. Then again, the last three years since the cruise ship, and the meeting with the Good Doctor, had changed his golden career path to an uneven rocky trail that seemed to wander into the wilderness, hadn't it?

Finding out that Argyle had been an integral part of a government-financed program for mind control and other potential travesties, leading to US Marshall operative Braxton Smythe's arrest, forced Josh to ask himself some more tough questions. For instance, why the director knew about Smythe's and Argyle's little project and never bothered to tell the BAU how that project had gone south? The director had stonewalled his line of questioning and changed the subject more than once. And, Josh, being the good soldier and the company man the Bureau believed he should be, hadn't pushed it . . . until now.

The director hadn't taken kindly to his research requests. He'd tried to be discreet. Except the information he'd finally gathered held a life of its own; and there was no question AD Dickman knew where Josh had delved.

So here he was, and he couldn't help feeling guilty. More like convicted. His team had been intentionally broken up under the pretense of higher priorities.

Divide and conquer.

Reaching over to the blue dish near his keyboard, he unwrapped a butterscotch candy and popped it into his mouth. He wasn't sure whether the taste or the smell was more to his liking. Both worked.

The surgery for Alex's hand was a gift, no doubt, but could have waited. Yet, the director had ordered it now, end of discussion. Then Josh had been brought in for intense situational testing and to undergo a new psychological profile under the guise of a grander scheme for his career path. At least that's how it felt.

Manny, Sophie, and Dean had been sent to do what the complete team was designed to accomplish. They'd have help, supposedly by the local office, but it still wouldn't be safe, especially if his research proved to be true. Manny's ability as a profiler was otherworldly at times. Yet, he doubted that Manny really suspected, at least not totally, what was transpiring in Las Vegas.

Hell, what exactly *was* transpiring in Las Vegas? He wasn't sure he had a clue either.

Manny and the others were special at what they did, but a team was a team. He and Alex should be there. But orders were orders, and if he wanted to play ball and get ahead, he'd do what the hell he was told. The AD had gone as far as voicing a subtle, veiled suggestion that he should toe the line, for one could never tell when tragedy may strike. Hell, the message wasn't that subtle.

His stomach rumbled again.

Orders.

He had his, even if obeying orders meant putting his staff at risk. Except these people weren't just his staff members. They weren't just his *people*, but his friends.

They'd had each other's back almost from the first time they'd met, before the three of them had joined the FBI. Add Dean into the mix, and they were the sum total of his family away from his family.

So this is what friends do, Corner?

Rubbing his face, he stood, then reached over and turned off the computer. He began to put the family picture back in his wallet, took one last look, ran his finger along each of the three faces that meant more to him than he'd imagined possible, then put the image away, in more ways than one.

As he hit the door and rode the elevator to the parking garage, he refocused on his job, Alex's operation, and his BAU out west.

Besides, his imagination was simply running on the wrong wheel. The FBI would never intentionally set up an operation to fail in order to put its agents at risk. That was absurd. He just had to trust the system and play his part. That's what good employees, and great husbands and dads, do.

Right?

*****

"You'd better go now. They've probably got monitors watching me," said Alex, trying to catch his breath.

Barb kissed him again. "Even in the closet? It'd be a heck of a monitoring system. And can you imagine how red their faces would be?"

Moving to the side, allowing for more room so they could get dressed, Alex laughed quietly. "True, but the real nurse will be checking in soon. How am I going to explain that my wife took a uniform from the locker room and dressed like a nurse to fulfill some sexual fantasy?" said Alex, putting his green gown back over his arms.

Barb giggled, pulling her bra over her shoulders, smiling. "Sounds to me like you just explained it. Just don't forget to tell them whose fantasy it is. And no worries. They're not due back in here for twenty minutes. I'll be long gone by then. As hot as I am, I can't stay all night. I need beauty sleep."

Her comment about being long gone struck him. She was a special woman, and for her to return to his room dressed like that proved it. He didn't want her to leave and go back to her hotel, but she was right. And she was correct on another item. She was indeed hot, but . . . well, there was hot and then there was *hot*. Beauty sleep? My ass.

He smiled. He sounded like Sophie.

Two minutes later, he was back in bed, and she was leaning over him again.

"Okay, I really have to go now, but I'll be back bright and early." She smiled. "You should sleep better."

"Yeah. You wore me out."

"Good."

For the second time in an hour, he felt her lips on his for a goodbye kiss, and he watched her leave. It wasn't any better this time.

Well, a little better. Making love with your wife in a hospital closet while she was half-dressed as a nurse was on a very limited number of bucket lists, he guessed. He'd never tell anyone that it wasn't on his, but Barb's.

Yep. Special woman.

Staring at the ceiling, Alex was still having a difficult time talking to the Sandman. He began to count the holes in the pale, white ceiling tile right above his head. Some were small, some were larger, and the pattern appeared to be totally random. But he knew enough about the science of acoustics and design to know that wasn't exactly true. Random sometimes looked intentional but the reverse was true.

He suddenly sat up and reached for his phone.

"Shit. I should have thought of this before . . ."

After hitting Dean's speed-dial button, he waited.

CHAPTER-35

Manny stood on at the side of the Scarab bar, hands in his pockets, and then leaned against one of the ornate pillars, which was supposed to resemble Cleopatra. Sophie hurried toward a bank of slots and then disappeared around the corner. That made him smile, at least a little. It had been an hour since the second CSU had arrived to help gather evidence, and Dean had seen fit to kick them out of the room.

Alex had nothing on Dean when it came to protecting his territory.

He was impressed with Dean's ability to direct and advise the new team in how he wanted the organs and jars processed and what else to look for. He wasn't only bright, but more of a natural leader than Manny had guessed. Dean had always been reserved, content to fulfill his role within the team, all the while wearing clothes that made him impossible to ignore. Manny would profile that later.

With Alex in the hospital, maybe Dean felt the need to step up. Whether it was the leader coming out, or he was pacing up because his friend was in a hospital bed on the other side of the country, there was certainly more to Dean Mikus than met the eye.

What was it Sophie had said? *You gotta watch out for the quiet ones.*

Dean had made it clear that Manny and Sophie should go do something else for a while, maybe two hours or so, and then booted them from the room.

That was okay with him. He'd been able to call Chloe for small talk and a goodnight wish. He'd liked that. Talking to her, just the two of them, had stopped his brain from running into that sometimes god-awful, full-bore investigator gear, and forced him to take a break from where that often carried him. Thinking about being a dad again, and focusing on the excitement in Chloe's voice when she spoke of the Baby Williams, was something he embraced—in fact, *absorbed.* Jen had been a life changer those seventeen years ago, and still was. Now there was a second installment of parenthood on the way. He wondered if he'd ever get used to the idea of children being complete miracles.

Dean's forced exile was good for another reason. It gave Sophie the opportunity to blow off a little steam in the casino. She was on overload, or almost, and the whole concept of what they'd discovered had brought the two of them down the elevator in silence. Yet he also knew she was processing the information. Just like he was.

Manny preferred the quiet to organize his thoughts and run through each possibility. He suspected that Sophie could get lost in the noise that was a Vegas casino almost as well as the sound of her own voice. Still, he'd noticed something else today. She wasn't typically prone to showcase her emotion much, but the body of the woman had shaken her more than normal. He guessed the shooting of agent Frost and now the mummy of an innocent woman murdered brutally weighed on her as much as any two deaths they'd encountered. With good reason. This was more personal.

Throw Argyle, tiredness, and jet lag into the mix and there was a perfect recipe for a break from reality. Manny knew exactly how she felt.

He squeezed the conference room key he'd gotten from the head of security, looked at his watch, pulled out his room key, and was unexpectedly struck with a conundrum. They had maybe six hours until the meeting, but he was running on fumes. Sleep sounded just this side of heaven, but after the past three hours, there was no guarantee that he'd get any sleep, or that the nightmares wouldn't decide to show up in a big way. And what about talking to Dean when he'd finished? That had to happen. They needed to be ready with all of the information they had available. But the prospect of sleep was quickly winning the battle.

"Maybe I need to do something else with my life," he said out loud.

"Nah, that's what I thought. It doesn't help."

He glanced at the young bartender who'd just spoken to him. He smiled.

"It doesn't?"

"No. Just a different set of rules. You look like you need a drink," she said, grinning.

"You know, I do. But it'll wait."

"Working?"

"Is it that obvious?"

"Yep. At least to me. Cops always have that look."

Turning to face her, he asked. "Which one is that?"

"You know. The haunted one. That *weight of the world on their shoulders* thing is hard to miss."

He raised his eyebrows and returned her grin. "I suppose you see all kinds in your profession."

She rolled her pretty brown eyes. "Yeah. You could say that. People are a hoot mostly, but every once in a while you see someone that's different. Like way-off-the-charts different. Not just physical, ya know? Just . . . well, that person has one of those presences that makes you do a triple take."

Moving closer, Manny found himself intrigued with her insight.

She had the gift, the one that allowed her to read people in a matter of seconds. Not the obvious expressions and what they showed of themselves on the outside, but what made them tick, the subtle nuances of body language and the hidden agendas in what they said. Whether it was as simple as an unsure glance or a vestige of anger showing through someone's eyes, this girl would catch it.

"I think I'll have that drink. Water on the rocks."

"Coming up," she said, her nerves in perfect order. She wasn't intimidated by who and what he was.

"You studied psych in college?" Manny threw the guess out there, certain he was close.

"I did. More than studied. I have a master's in abnormal psychology. I know, I know. But at least doing this job, I can control how much I want to see."

"Can you?"

"Usually. But like I said, every so often, I see someone special."

Taking the water, he took a drink, his exhaustion forgotten. "You said that. Define special."

"Why, officer! Am I being interrogated? No wait, profiled. And you're no officer. You're a something else. A profiler? FBI?"

The wave of excitement was hard to contain. This woman was right on. He understood that he might be an open book to some, but to make that guess put her in a different arena.

His excitement then vanished as quickly as it had appeared. What if she was a plant hired by Argyle? Or worse, what if she was one of his twisted followers?

No. the situation was too random. He thought about how luck plays into solving cases, and maybe this was one of those times. Stranger things happened.

The hand on his arm got his attention, but he didn't turn to look at Sophie.

"Okay. I just won fifty bucks from one of those crooked little metal bitches, so I thought I'd find you and get something to eat," said Sophie.

He felt her eyes on him. She moved over to a barstool and sat down, nodding toward the bartender.

"Who's your new friend?"

He pointed to her nametag. "Her name is Pricilla. Pricilla, meet Sophie, and I'm Manny. We were just discussing people and what makes them special."

Still no nervousness. If anything, she seemed more comfortable. Her behavior wasn't normal for someone who had two FBI agents a few feet from her.

"I'm right, aren't I?" said Pricilla.

"Right about what?" asked Sophie.

"She thinks I'm an FBI profiler."

"Oh really?"

Sophie's eyes narrowed. She was immediately suspicious. *Good girl.*

"Let's say you are right. What gave me away?"

Pricilla tilted her head closer. "It's how you ask a question. You search folks when you ask. Most people just ask. And I wanted you to talk to me. That's why I spoke to you. You're pretty easy on the eyes, and you were standing there alone, deep in thought. Sometimes that works out to a dinner and the next step."

"Pretty good. What else?"

Looking down, she then looked back up. "Also, the badge on your hip sort of helped."

Manny dropped his hand down, touched the cold steel, and shook his head. He'd needed it to get into the crime scene and had forgotten to put it away.

Sophie was already laughing, Manny had to join her. Pricilla only smiled wider.

"Okay, you got me there. But you are trained, aren't you?"

"I tried the police academy route, but it just wasn't me. Rules mess me up. Besides, like I said before, I get to run into folks here that aren't so ordinary, like you. But I never get that twice in a day, like today."

Manny stood. "Thanks for the water, Pricilla. We need to go—wait. What does that mean?"

He felt his heart begin to thump in his chest.

For the first time, he saw some give in Pricilla's face. His question had sparked something . . .

"Ahh. Well. There was this guy earlier today. He was different. Bright. Tall. Uninhibited. Good looking too, but he . . . hell, I don't know for sure. He just wasn't like most guys who try to pick me up. I turn ninety-nine percent of them down. He was so charming and engaging, I would have gone with him."

"Did he tell you his name?" asked Manny, knowing that he had. It was part of the game, no doubt.

She exhaled, her smile now gone. "Fredrick. His name was Fredrick."

CHAPTER-36

Reaching for the volume button, he cranked it and the hard sounds of 1970s rock-and-roll burst through the vehicle. Some habits were simply hard to break. Perhaps that's how it should be. He'd broken down everything he'd once held sacred and replaced it with something better. Although he doubted many believed the end result of his development was better.

Tsk. Tsk.

Doubters had their place, but not in his world, and after all, this world was his, almost in a vacuum. Nothing was out of the question, out of the realm of possibility. For that matter, *no one* was out of his sphere of influence, one way or the other.

For instance, take this little safari. Who in his right mind would follow a convoy of law enforcement vehicles back to headquarters and do what he was about to do?

Lions roar, sheep cower. It was that simple.

What makes a "right" mind? That was the crux of the problem with society. Most people just didn't get it.

If being a sheep, a conformist, someone who has bought into the moral and emotional bindings that are accepted by the masses, defines a "right" mind, then so be it. Those parameters were no longer restraints he levied against himself.

Doing what he desired, roaring loudly, seeking whatever he wanted, and in the end, accomplishing the ultimate goal he'd set for himself, was far more than a prerogative, but an eternal right, in his mind. Only the strong survive. He lived that statement over and over.

His thoughts circled back.

His goal.

He gripped the wheel more tightly. It was all coming together, here in the City of Cities. No more games, no more riddles, no more trite messages that only had previously lengthened the joy of the game for him. Agent Williams would figure out what was coming down the pike—except the part that would affect him and the BAU the most. But this time, he'd be too late. Far too late.

Pulling to the east side of the building, he saw that three of the four vehicles that had left the Egyptian before him had already arrived. The fourth, an LVPD cruiser, was missing, but it didn't matter. The most important units were parked in the proper location, and the occupants had entered their fortress.

Exhaling, he lowered the radio's volume, left the window half down, and exited his car.

Standing there, surveying the front of the building, he realized just how much he enjoyed the feel of the desert heat as it engulfed his face. It almost spoke to him. He couldn't help thinking that the warmth outside would be a precursor of the real heat to come, on the inside.

Walking away from the Jaguar, his stride said that he was moving like a man who belonged in the law enforcement domain, especially this one. In a way, he did. Every yin has a yang.

He strolled up the orange-brick steps and came face to face with a female agent on a smoke break. Glancing around, he could see that they were alone, for a moment at any rate. A moment would be all he required.

"Good evening. I'm Agent Schneider from the BAU. I need to get inside to speak with Agent Wilkins. I was supposed to arrive with Detective Teachout but was detained."

The short, ebony woman released her breath. Bluish smoke swirled and danced around her head, the smoke's odor tugging at his nostrils.

"I'll go get her. I can't let you in without—"

Moving quickly, he reached out, grabbed her head, and snapped her neck with a flick of his hands. Maintaining his grip around her neck with one hand, he then used his other hand to pull her ID and security pass from her lapel.

Once done with that, he lifted her from the ground, took two steps to his right, and tossed her body behind the row of blossoming evergreen hedges.

Thirty seconds later, he entered the door, looked at the room assignment chart, and was moving down the hallway toward the back offices. He passed the CSU lab entrance as he turned to the left, striding down the L-shaped corridor. He saw the sign he was looking for and continued toward the room. As his gait brought him closer, he could hear muffled assertions. The voices grew louder as he approached the door.

Someone wasn't happy.

My, my, my. Such tension.

Being around law enforcement as much as he had, he still marveled at the inability of organizations to work together. If they had, he may never have made it this far. Maybe.

Standing tight outside the office door, his smile grew as the conversation became clear.

"You need to fill us in, Agent. We've been in the middle of this thing from the beginning. I hate this cloak-and-dagger shit you Feds pull every time something weird rolls down the lane," said Detective Teachout, obviously upset.

"Stay calm, Mel," said Detective Lane.

Agent Wilkins sighed. "Mel, I lost a good agent tonight. And we're still trying to figure out how. So don't give me any of that attitude shit, okay? After that, I questioned Agent Williams and I got only part of the story on just why the BAU is out here. And you think you're frustrated? Give me a freaking break."

"I'm sorry about your loss, believe me, Kim," said Teachout, her voice softening. "But I need to know if this is some organ-harvesting ring or a smoke-and-mirrors cover up. Never mind trying to explain that twenty-first-century mummy found in the Egyptian. I know the BAU is good at what it does, but you have no idea on what the hell's going on here."

Now is as good a time as any.

Stepping into the room, he stopped three feet short of the two detectives standing next to the large oak desk, just to the right of Agent Wilkins.

"Perhaps, if you asked pleasantly, I can help with that last question," he said.

"Who in the hell are you and how did you get in here?" asked a startled Wilkins.

"Getting in was easy and me . . . well, Agent, I'm the reason you're under duress."

Before any of them could pull a weapon, he did what he always did—took control.

With a swipe of his arm, he backhanded Lane and heard him thump with sickening conviction against the wall, blood flowing from his nose. Reaching for Teachout with the other arm, he pulled her from her feet and, in one motion, slammed her face first into the tiled floor with a resounding smack. She lay motionless.

One more step and he had Agent Wilkins by the throat. She tried to pull her Glock from the desk, but as she rose into the air, it was just out of her reach.

He pulled her close, squeezing the air from her throat ever so slowly. The gurgling sound forced his adrenalin to storm the rest of his senses.

There is nothing like being in complete control. Nothing.

"Look closely, Agent. I could send you to your funeral and would love to do so, but I have a job for you," he whispered.

Her eyes were bulging, yet she didn't seem to be really seeing him. His training told him she was and that she would not forget this moment, ever.

He pulled her closer, licking her face ever so slowly. "Such a time we could have. Maybe when we meet again. For now, however, I want you to memorize every detail, each line, each subtlety of my face. To feel my hand around your throat until the fear almost drives you insane. To realize that you shook hands with death tonight and survived to speak of it. And speak of it you will. Agent Williams must know who you've seen. Clear?"

There was an almost indistinguishable nod as her eyes began to close. Pulling her back to the desk, he released his grip and bent toward her ear. "Tell him it's time. No more surprises. No more riddles. Just me and the wild west."

The next second, he struck her with a short jab to the chin and watched her eyes roll up in her head, fully unconscious.

He walked away from her desk, reached the door, looked both ways, and then strolled out of the room, whistling an old Rod Stewart tune as the sound of his steps echoed throughout the hall.

Tonight would truly be the night.

CHAPTER-37

Standing at the service elevator, Dean Mikus watched as the Clark County Medical Examiner rolled the body inside.

"You got everything, sir?" asked one of the young techs.

He couldn't have been more than twenty-five, if that. He still had remnants of acne dotting his cheeks. That, along with his slight build, made him seem even younger.

Youth is wasted on the young.

He was starting to get exactly what that meant.

Not that thirty-six was ancient, but nights like this affected him far less when he was younger. Dean wondered briefly what the south side of thirty felt like again, especially tonight. He was exhausted, hungry, and he didn't mind admitting, a little rattled. Younger nerves were exactly that.

"Yeah, I'm good. I need to meet with my folks, so I put her in your capable hands."

The young man nodded. "I'll take good care of her, sir. It's the least I can do."

One of the women fell against the wall and bounced back upright, saluting the others. Her actions set off a round of laughter from the group that proved his first impression of them. Drunk and having fun. Right now, that sounded just fine, especially if there was a juicy steak and a huge, buttered baked potato involved.

The elevator pinged again, and Dean stepped in. The ride was short, yet he could feel some of his tension fade. Safety in numbers wasn't just a saying and included the mental, not just the physical.

Reaching the main floor, he stepped out and began walking across the checkered floor, heading for the night manager's office to get a key card to where Sophie and Manny should be waiting for him, when his phone vibrated. Reaching into his pocket, he realized he hadn't heard or felt it ring or vibrate for a few hours. Maybe it was the room location. Maybe it was his head's location.

"Or maybe you're just not that cool to talk with," he said under his breath, smiling as he looked at the screen.

Alex had called an hour ago. He hit the voicemail button. A moment later, Alex's voice began to speak to him. He was surprised at how good his friend's voice sounded and he welcomed it.

"Hey, Beard Boy, call me. Yes, I'm fine. But I need to ask you something. I had an idea about how the bodies were laid out in the casket in Lansing."

There wasn't really a sense of urgency, but on the other hand, why would Alex call if it weren't important?

Dean hit the redial button just as his phone signaled it was shutting down. The red meter indicated that he had one percent power.

"Damn it."

He'd broken a golden rule and not charged his phone when he had the chance.

Sophie's new phrase of the week echoed in his brain.

Dumbass.

Stuffing the phone back in his jean's pocket, he hurried toward the desk. Just as he reached the red granite top, he heard Sophie call his name. Turning to the sound, he saw her. She was dressed in tight slacks and a red blouse, draped in a black vest, walking like she owned the place. No way to control the smile. She strolled to his side and stood close.

"Talk about a sight for sore eyes," he said.

"Don't forget it either," she said, kissing him on the cheek. She tilted her head. "You look like hell. But then you've been working, while Manny and I grabbed a couple of hours of shuteye. We thought it might be the only chance we get before the meeting."

"Good plan."

"Maybe. I couldn't sleep, and he probably couldn't either."

"You're right, I couldn't."

Turning over, away from the damned clock, she tried to close her eyes and go back to sleep, yet she knew it wasn't going to happen. Each time she closed her eyes, she saw young Alan Gordon's face, or what was left of it. The condition of his body was disturbing, no question. And if the well-placed screwdrivers were any indication of the killer's anger, and not some oculophilic expression, a fascination for eyes, then the killer would have probably had a few incidents prior to escalating to this kind of killing. He would have had problems with fighting in school, maybe even a record for petty vandalism or shoplifting.

That profile description could have fit a large number of young men, and make no mistake, this killer was a young man, in the city of Lansing, but narrowing it down to who had the opportunity, combined with a mini-profile, was always the cornerstone for investigations like this one. Despite his reluctance to embrace the science, Gavin, and his partner, had done a great job of that.

According to the interview files, they'd interviewed all of Alan's friends, including Mike Crosby, his teammates on the basketball and baseball teams, his close classmates, and even several teachers. All expressed shock at the crime because Alan was well liked. It was obvious that he had been popular, bright, and athletically gifted. There didn't seem to be a soul on the planet that wanted to harm him. His parents were so devastated that it took until three days after the funeral before they could talk to the police. They were cleared almost immediately; their mental state of mind and alibi had made that an easy call.

Gavin had made a short list of names that were mentioned as the interview process had hit second gear. He'd then cross-referenced those names with the potential profile. Then he checked each of them against the infamous *where were you Friday night* line of questioning. The six young men checked out, leaving no clear cut suspects and an almost complete guessing game for what should have been a fairly routine investigation.

Sliding to the edge of the bed, Chloe reached for her robe and headed for the kitchen. No reason to fight it now. Maybe she would get time for a nap today. The case wasn't the only thing on her mind, not by any stretch. It would be just past two in the morning, Vegas time, and unless she missed her guess, Manny wouldn't be sleeping. Far from it. He could function for a couple of days before he truly needed to recharge. Longer if he caught a couple hours of shuteye on the fly.

Her heart picked up the pace. Whoever, or whatever, the team ran into in Vegas was smart, clever, and extremely dangerous: the profile of a perfect psychopath.

For a moment, she almost regretted anything she ever learned or understood about the human mind, especially the sick ones. Even the new job required more of that than she'd hoped, at least so far.

At any rate, Argyle or not, there was no stopping the trepidation attacking her thoughts regarding what was truly happening in Vegas. As good as Manny was, no one was perfectly aware all of the time. But Sophie and Dean, and the rest of the local office would have his back, right? That was all she could hope for. That knowledge, and the occasional text or call, did wonders to keep her nerves from being completely jangled.

Reaching for the switch on the coffee machine, she changed her mind, opened the refrigerator, and poured milk into her waiting cup. Decaf coffee was probably okay for the baby, but she was not going to indulge anymore. It could wait. Besides, cookies dunk much better in milk.

Chloe went to the living room and sat down near the stack of files. One was marked "tips and leads." She'd opened that file for a short time last night, but was past the time when she'd be able to look at it without nodding off. Not the case this morning. The slight clack of toenails on the hardwood floor told her Sampson was on his way. The big dog made his way around the corner, licked her exposed ankle, and plopped down on the carpet with a grunt.

She couldn't stop her smile.

Early or not, he was on watch. Somehow, that made her feel better about where Manny was and what he was doing.

Opening the file again, she began sifting through various notes and comments from anonymous calls, or at least folks who believed they were anonymous—the LPD's caller ID caught most of them. Gavin had done a good job organizing the calls by ID number and name, then categorizing the tips by opinion versus what someone may actually have seen or heard. There seemed to be nothing of significance. Chloe shook her head. Most crimes back then were solved with a break: a witness saw or heard something. Or perhaps a person overheard a conversation. Forensics had put a dent into that practice, but there was still nothing more convicting than an eyewitness.

Only in this case, there was nothing remotely close to that. None of the tidbits of information, at first glance, contributed anything toward a viable clue or killer.

Chloe thought her first course of action might be to go over those tips and the list of suspects again, just to make sure nothing was missed.

"Good luck finding them," she whispered, understanding that people didn't stay in one spot so much these days.

Flipping the page, she saw that Gavin had listed other calls to the station by unidentified numbers, which back in the late nineties probably meant pay phones. There were nine calls from three different phones. The first seven calls had conveyed pretty much the same as the other dozens of tips: *I may have heard a scream. I was sure I saw a person run through the shrubs. I think the killer was a demon right from hell, look there.*

That was her favorite. Unfortunately, it came up every time a murder like this one was committed.

Almost ready to turn the page, she looked at the last two calls, then stopped. The first one said that the caller suspected someone who rode a motorcycle because she heard it race away from the park around that same time. There was a little red note beside it, saying that none of the prime suspects owned a motorcycle.

The second call was two days later. The caller stated she was angry that the police were such assholes for not checking out her lead. She *knew* that the killer rode a motorcycle and that if they didn't dig further, the murderer would get away with it. She said that God told her so.

There was another word written by Gavin or his partner: CRAZY.

When a caller says "God told me so," their tip usually becomes an automatic disregard. Chloe understood that.

She thumbed through the rest of the file and saw no evidence of a DMV report being pulled for the young men who may have fit the initial profile. She frowned. That should have been done. It could have led to something.

Flipping back to the page with the pay phone calls, she ran her finger over the one word comment, frowning. The fact that the tipster called twice weighed on her.

CRAZY.

Chloe wasn't so sure.

CHAPTER-39

"This freaking case, or I should say, these cases, are making me more goofy-ass than normal," said Sophie, her mouth half full with a large bite from her New York strip.

She was sitting next to Dean as they finished up the meals Manny had ordered from the Casino's finest restaurant.

Manny glanced down at his plate and was surprised at just how much chicken felluccini he'd actually eaten. When the waiter, accompanied by two security guards from the resort, had brought in the trays, the enticing aroma had immediately filled the conference room. The scent of steak and pasta had been out of this world. Another reason to like Vegas.

"That may be the idea, Sophie," answered Manny.

"Great. But I see what you're saying. You mean like diversions?"

"Yes. That's what I mean. This killer has got a few irons in the fire, including what Dean has given us on the mummy homicide.

Stuffing the last piece of baked potato in her mouth, Sophie raised her hand, finger in the air, telling Manny to wait until she'd finished. She had something to add, he hoped.

Dean pushed his plate away, leaned back, and exhaled.

"While she's finishing, I just have to say that this filet was one of the best I've had. It was distractingly good."

"No argument from me as far as this fettuccini either," said Manny.

Sophie swallowed her last bit. "That's what I was going to say. I just hope it wasn't our last meal, ya know? I want some of that hot brownie covered with homemade ice cream before we check out."

No one laughed. He was sure Sophie meant leave the resort to go home, but her somewhat Freudian comment drove home the nervous truth that they'd been, in all reality, summoned to Las Vegas by someone who knew they'd come. That suggested he was ready for them. If Manny were in the killer's shoes that would entail only one thing: that the BAU wouldn't be leaving Vegas, at least alive. None of them.

But they'd been in that situation before and things had worked out, right?

His stomach twisted some. Not exactly. Louise had been lost to him and Jen.

That hadn't worked out.

Damn it, Williams. Not now. Get your head straight or this won't end well.

"That dessert sounds great, but we've got just a few hours before we meet with LVPD and Agent Wilkins's group. We need to be ready to give them a profile that makes sense. And right now, we need to sort out a few things," said Manny.

"Deal. Okay. I'll go back to what we talked about with the diversion idea. One thing you always said is that a serial killer, even as he evolves, will hold on to a semblance of a pattern, right?"

Manny nodded. "That's right. They may have progressed to take trophies, for instance, or at least some type of keepsake. That trait is usually more prevalent as the killer progresses from one kill to the next. He might also deviate from his behavior, sexually or otherwise, if that type of gratification is the true goal, which, often it is," said Manny.

"So it's about what gets him off? I mean, they get comfortable with one way of doing things, they don't usually change, right? That is, until they aren't getting their jollies anymore," said Sophie.

"True. You also have to consider the physical features of the victims. The killer can be fixated on a certain body type or whatever, right?" asked Dean, leaning forward and putting both hands on the mahogany table.

"All of that's true. Yet, the killers, if they're bright enough, can throw intentional curves at an investigation to get us to take off in another direction. We saw that three different times since we became part of the BAU. Anna Ruiz and Caleb

Corner did a couple things to get us off the trail. But in the end, like we talked regarding that psycho in England who wanted to replicate Jack the Ripper, they will, they must, revert back to what is motivating them. They have no choice. It's what drives true psychopaths."

"So what's the motivation here, Manny? I mean, if Argyle is alive, let's say, his ultimate goal was to destroy everyone that he felt screwed up his career and caused him grief. Which is basically Gavin and you, Alex and me some, and Josh and Dean even less."

"That's true, but he's also devolved into something more. He enjoyed the killing, any death at his hands, and the mind screws he threw our way. Which, in a sense, was worse than killing each or any of us, in his mind. He took it a step further and wanted us to suffer. And in a way, he was right."

"But you don't think he wants that to continue?" asked Dean.

"I'm just not sure, yet."

Manny scanned the Egyptian's ancient motif etched into the wall designs of the conference room. Each row of hieroglyphics was evenly spaced and the mural of the bright-blue Nile running serpentine between detailed pyramids was extremely well crafted. He wondered if it had been easier to solve murders in that era. He was pretty sure the mode of justice had been simpler and taken at face value. Guilty or not guilty with no fancy-ass lawyer getting them off with a slap to the wrist.

He was assaulted with a sudden epiphany.

Maybe he'd been approaching these murders, and everything from the circumstances surrounding Argyle's missing corpse to the unfortunate mummy woman, with the wrong perspective. When one tries to read a book too close to one's eyes, it's impossible to see the words clearly.

"I think it's time to look at these murders as individual cases. We keep trying to tie them together; at least I do, without looking at each one as a single act and not leading to the next. That still could be true. I think the phone found on the last victim here in Vegas bears that out, so what are we missing by jumping to conclusions?" asked Manny, feeling a little excitement ripple through him.

Sophie nodded. Her expression suggested she hadn't yet arrived aboard his train of thinking, but at least was considering it.

Dean raised his eyebrows and leaned back away from the table, his mind obviously running at full bore.

"Listen. I said when we first started that we couldn't overlook some copycat situation. And I still believe that. What I didn't consider, because I was wrapped up in the thought of Argyle being truly alive, is what the evidence actually was saying."

"You mean like stepping back and seeing what we *have* versus what we *think* we know," said Sophie.

"Exactly. What do we really know about each of these murders, starting with Max Tucker's in North Carolina and Braxton Smythe's involvement, to this very moment?"

"Well, they're all dead and—Wait!" said Sophie, her eyes coming alive. "Tucker, then the guy who stabbed you, and then the couple in the casket were all, I don't know, like tying up loose ends, right?"

"That's right. While this killer took the opportunity to send us a message or two with the folks in the casket, and that was effective, he also got rid of someone who could put a finger on him. He had to know that just by the text and the phone call to Gavin, that would be enough to get us on the plane to Vegas," said Manny.

"So why the murders out here? Are you saying these Vegas murders are part of a setup to get us out here?" asked Dean.

"Let's back up to the evidence. Remember, while playing mind games is part of the MO for a killer like Argyle, these guys will eventually go back to the reason they're doing what they do," answered Manny.

"That's just it. We don't have that much data," said Dean. "We still need video reports from the casino and the intersection where Agent Frost was shot. Plus, I need to get the analysis reports from Lansing and the CSU in Detroit for the rest of the fibers and soil samples we found. Not to mention it'll be six to eight hours before I get jack shit from the Clark County's ME office and the forensic units here in Vegas."

"I get that," said Manny. "But maybe we have enough. Maybe the killer knows what it takes to process a crime scene so he made it easier for us."

"Are you talking, you know, the barmaid, Argyle's empty coffin, and the five whatever kind of jars you call those with putrid smelling organs inside?" said Sophie.

"Yeah. I am. What do all those three things tell us? Never mind potential hairs planted or not. Pay no attention to victim profiles or what they may have in common. Ignore the text message content to Chloe and the phone call to Gavin. Hell, ignore the murder of Agent Frost. Step up and see the overall, and much simpler, profile."

"All of that information and circumstance is just fluff?" asked Dean, not hiding the doubt in his voice.

Sophie's eyes were bright, yet puzzled. It wasn't making sense to her, just yet. He wasn't quite sure himself if he was right. Only that it *felt* true. That had been good enough a few times in the past.

Manny exhaled. "Remember that we discussed a million times that serial killers don't want to be caught, although some psychologists suggest that they do. That some have suppressed emotions somewhere and hate what they do, but are helpless to stop. Maybe we're—"

His phone rang, interrupting his next words. Agent Wilkins.

"Manny?" Her voice was soft, almost weak.

"Yes."

"You need to come to the office, now. We've had an incident."

"What kind of incident?" he asked, his stomach clenching tighter.

There was a brief silence. "Your killer visited us. People are dead, and he wanted to make sure I told you what I saw. Just get here."

The phone went dead.

Standing, he motioned for Sophie and Dean to follow him.

They hurried through the conference door. Sophie caught up to him.

"Who was that?"

"Agent Wilkins. She said our killer showed up at the Vegas office."

"Shit."

Bursting through the front doors, they hurried to the SUV and climbed in.

Sophie tore out of the lot, lights and siren blasting a path toward North Vegas. She hammered the accelerator.

Manny felt her glance as he conveyed to her and Dean what Wilkins had said.

She nodded. "This bastard is crazy."

"It seems so," said Manny.

Leaning over the seat, Dean touched his shoulder. "What were you going to say in the conference room?"

He started to run his hand through his hair. Instead, he slammed his fist down on the dash, leaving a leather crater the size of a tennis ball.

So easy to look too hard and miss something.

And that's just what happened, Manny was sure of it. "It fits perfectly, and I'm an asshole for not seeing it. What I was going to say in the conference room was maybe I'm wrong. Maybe this killer is different. Maybe he wants to be caught."

CHAPTER-40

Patiently, with the scrutiny of an eagle soaring in the blue, he scanned the stage he'd created in the back of the storage building. There could be nothing out of order. Nothing. Not one wire. Not one camera. Not one angle skewed. Any mistake, any miscalculation, could jeopardize everything, given the considerable talents of his target. He'd even had to consider the impact that the rest of the BAU, the LVPD, and the local FBI presence would have on what was next on his very particular agenda and adjust accordingly. He'd thought of everything, yet one couldn't be too cautious.

The Bureau had much at its disposal. More technology. More research facilities and sources. More access to proper training and procedural policies as they pertained to people like himself. More Manny Williams.

The Lansing-cop-turned-Special-Agent had been somewhat of a credible addition to the Feds, yet, in his entire splendor, he'd not figured out this end game. Nor would he. Not even Manny Williams would be able to fly in this plane. By the time he could see what was coming around the bend, he'd be far too late to stop it.

"The proverbial day-late-dollar-short scenario," he muttered as he strolled over to the object that would be the center of his cinematic production.

Placing his hand on the purple crushed velvet material running down the back, he ran his fingers ever so slowly and made the turn around the object. Each step had been wrought with a care and precision that would make the most anal retentive of men envious. His hand never left the sensual feel of the velvet as he reached the front of his creation, stepping over the perfectly placed cables. Moving back, he rested his other hand on the chair and then looked over the other three objects in the display. Each placed in perfect symmetrical relation to the others. *A stunning fabrication of deadly beauty.*

A sudden, unexpected rise of emotion invaded him. He was *proud* of what he'd created, and to where it would lead.

Despite what people assumed they knew about men like him, his emotion could run deep. Louise Williams had seen it. Haley Rose had seen it. Lexy Crosby had seen it. And he supposed, in some inexplicable way, Agent Williams had known it, if not seen it firsthand. If nothing else, the Special Agent had a talent for getting into the minds of others.

Rage. Hatred. Joy. Thrills. Were not these states of mind witnesses of his connection to the rest of humanity? His control over them displayed his superiority. As inferior as the rest were, no one could deny that connection, try as they might.

His previous training told him that unreasonable fear grew in people who saw just how close they were to becoming like him. Except they really had no concept of who or what he truly had become. Not really. How could they? Fear ruled them far more than any other emotion.

Many of the other supposed experts on the human mind, and its complex operation, only thought they understood. If he were a betting man, and he was, simply ask Grace Burleson. He'd bet that Agent Williams had wrestled more than once with the concept of just how closely related he was to men like himself. Neither he nor Agent Williams was unfamiliar with the acuity of thinking like a fox to catch a fox.

Walking over to the bank of three computers, he set the program he needed on ready. He'd only need to push the ESC button to set it in motion. Next, he inspected the three cameras, meticulously checking the angles of each, cleaning each lens and adjusting the tripods. The chairs and the object they surrounded must be in full sync to garner the desired results. They were.

Repeating the complete process from beginning to end one more time left him with confidence that all was ready for the final curtain.

In a few hours, at least by the day's end, it would be over. For all of them, and for him.

Think like a fox indeed, Agent Williams.

One final look, then he turned on his heels and moved through the metal doors, and into the meager front office. He picked up his last required prop from the desk and exited the building.

As he opened the door to his Jaguar, he watched the sun beginning to show itself over the eastern mountain range and he thought the timing to be more than appropriate. The scene inspired him to recall a quote he'd once heard regarding revenge.

Justice is revenge.

Today would be a new day, and justice finally would be his.

CHAPTER-41

Rubbing remnants of what little sleep he'd enjoyed from his eyes, Josh Corner sat up and reached for the phone that vibrated like an angry wasp on his bedroom nightstand. Glancing at the lit screen, the first thing he noticed was the time. Six-oh-six a.m. The second thing was who was calling. Apparently Assistant Director John Dickman didn't need any sleep. He'd heard that about some mythical monsters. No sleep gave the monsters more time to think up crazy, minding-grueling, questionable tasks for the people who worked for them.

He lingered on the AD's last name for a moment. Dickman. How appropriate.

"Corner here," answered Josh, surprised at how alert he sounded.

"Did I wake you, Josh? I guess it doesn't matter. I have a big day lined up for you and wanted to make sure you're ready."

The 'asshole' in the AD's voice was entirely too obvious. He could almost see the crooked, sadistic smile plastered on Dickman's face.

"I believe I am ready, sir. I need to get a shower and help get my boys ready for the day. Then I'll be wherever you'd like me to be."

The slight hesitation told him that his plans weren't on the same agenda as his boss's. Not even close.

"No time for that. You have to be at the training facility in twenty-three minutes. This will be intense and last well into the night. We've got to cover ground you've not been exposed to previously. What's coming next will tax you to your limits, Agent Corner."

It was Josh's turn to hesitate. He'd promised Alex that he'd be there when he came out of surgery and wait for him in the recovery room.

"Sir, with all due respect, I promised Agent Downs I'd be there when he woke from surgery. And . . ."

"You shouldn't promise things you can't deliver, Corner. What is happening here will shape your, and your family's, future. Downs will either be fine or he won't. Your presence will not affect that one way or another. Is that clear?"

"It is sir, but he's on my team, and God knows I feel like I've left Manny and the others sitting on some kind of ledge by not being there with them in Vegas."

"Do I sound like I give a flying-pig's ass what's going on out there? They get paid for doing their job, just like you, Agent."

Dickman's voice had increased its 'ass-hole' intensity. He was growing impatient, maybe even angry, with Josh.

He frowned. This wasn't quite like him, or at least the Assistant Director he'd known the last few years. Josh was no profiler, but Dickman sounded . . . well, almost anxious. The words of an old song popped into his mind.

Everyone's hiding something.

"I understand that, sir, but this is my team we're talking about," answered Josh, trying to keep his growing frustration in check.

"Agent Corner. You'll do what you're told, got it?"

The emotion was entirely gone from Dickman's voice. Cold hardly covered it.

Josh didn't care for it. Not one iota.

Without truly knowing why, Josh decided to let his emotion loose. For three weeks, he'd gone through this shit. Even before they'd left North Carolina, Dickman had been planting seeds that there were more important things in the life of a BAU supervisor than his team. The AD had tried to beat home the point that the Bureau was all that mattered, and everything, and everyone else, was there to serve the Bureau's purpose. Their individual needs, troubles, and joys were of no consequence. Josh had even gleaned from a couple more intense conversations that field agents were expendable, if need arose.

Any field agent.

The idea of Manny or Sophie or Dean or Alex, or even himself, being just an expendable body had two effects on Josh. Bullshit and bullshit.

"I now fully understand, Assistant Director. Where is it that you'd like me to be this morning?"

"Now you're making sense. I'd—"

"Actually, I don't care what you want. I won't be there. I've got somewhere else to be. Oh, and you can stick this new project up your ass. I'm no longer interested. I've got a team to take care of. *My* team to watch over."

He turned the phone off and waited. Only there was no call back. No telling ring or vibration that let him know Dickman wanted to talk. There was an air of unease about that, but the feeling of relief was far more inviting and prevalent.

The hand on his back alerted him that he'd woken his wife, Connie. She ran her long finger down his spine and stopped at the base of his tail bone.

"I guess you heard," he said softly. "I'm pretty sure I'll be asked to give my credentials and my gun back to Uncle Sam soon."

"That's okay, Josh. I'm proud of you. It was the right call," answered Connie.

"Yeah, I guess it was. Maybe your mom won't mind if we move in for a few years," he said, still not facing his wife.

"Could be. But at least we'll get you back. All of you. And besides, maybe the boys and I will get to finally see you more than a few minutes a day.

Maybe even meet this Manny Williams and his friends."

He turned toward her, kissed her, the scent of her never more alive than it was at that moment. "That would make me the happiest agent on the planet. And they're special folks and friends. But I've got one more thing to do before I get my total tit in the wringer."

"I figured that."

She kissed him again. "Just remember that and what's waiting for you when you get back."

"I never really did forget, you know."

"I *do* know."

With that, Josh got dressed, looked in on the boys, both sleeping with their covers on the floor and facing their Marvel superhero posters. The smile led to teary eyes.

A minute later he was outside. He jumped into the SUV, glanced at the clock, and sped toward his next-to-last destination as an FBI special agent.

CHAPTER-42

At Manny's gesture, Sophie slammed the SUV into reverse and backed away from the flashing red and blue lights pulsating from the three ambulances parked in an ominous row.

The EMS units were lined up directly in front of the gated doors of the brick, low-rise building that served as the FBI's Las Vegas regional office. It was hard to ignore the resemblance to a three-casket funeral.

The well-maintained building faced north, but hints of the rising sun from the east got Manny's attention, at least for the moment. They had endured another night with minimal sleep and the pileup of dead bodies—apparently an integral part of working with the BAU. He'd heard that the sun rose early in the west, except a few minutes before five a.m. was far sooner than he'd expected.

A lot like the phone call he'd received from Agent Wilkins. The killer had been bold, unpredictable, and arrogant. Argyle-like, to say the least. The Good Doctor had been almost this bold in Saint Thomas just before they'd captured him on the cruise ship. He had killed several people, including two local cops, and had beheaded one woman. He still got to experience that one in his mind's eye and in a nightmarish deep sleep every so often.

Now this son of a bitch had killed another young agent and—

"Manny, let's go. I think they need us in there," said Sophie, giving him the curious look she brandished when she was counting on him to make the next call.

"I know. I'm trying to get through the killer's motivation for this. But I suppose it'll come to us."

"It usually does, one way or the other," said Sophie. She opened the door and stood outside the SUV.

"I think we have an inside track," he said, getting out of the vehicle.

Dean followed behind Sophie and Manny as they walked in silence past the LVPD blues teaming up with several agents to secure an area that was past the need for it. Reaching the red brick steps, they climbed and started through the open door just as two EMS techs emerged from the shrubs, protecting the front of the building. They were carrying a young lady whose neck was tilted in an unnatural angle. Her dark and dead eyes were open, forever holding the last vision she'd beheld before leaving this world. He stopped. It was painfully obvious she'd been killed by strong hands. The bruising that was forming around her chin and neck verified what he'd suspected.

The killer, her killer, had tossed her away as if she were an old rag doll or an empty beer can that had served its purpose. Furthermore, she'd had no idea that this day would be her last.

These young people signed up for the sexy part of what the Bureau had to offer and it didn't dawn on them that they could be dead before they drew their first paycheck. He still remembered that feeling of invincibility when he pinned his badge on for the first time. He also recalled how fast that feeling had evaporated when, on his second day, he was the shooting target of a drug-induced bank robber. This agent probably never had that experience.

She never would.

Another day, another body. The fun never stops.

Manny turned away and moved through the doorway. He saw Agent Wilkins sitting on one of the sheet-covered gurneys on the right side of the hallway. Detective Teachout was resting on the other end, receiving attention but not really wanting it. A moment later, a second gurney appeared. It was carrying Detective Lane, but the man wasn't sitting up. The enormous, bloodstained bandage running from his eyebrows to chin told part of the story. The unbridled concern of EMS personnel told him a bit more. The expression of stark horror that suddenly appeared on Detective Melanie Teachout's face finished the trifecta.

Detective Teachout didn't move; she could only stare. Manny suspected she had to wait for the reality of the moment to strike.

It did.

"Brent? Brent?" she said softly. Her panic was way above the scale for a working partner. Not that partners couldn't care for each other deeply, he was keenly aware of that. She was trying to control it, failing miserably.

She spoke to him again.

Nothing.

In a flash, apparently her patience at the very end of its delicate rope, she was over him, her face near his, tears streaming. She gripped his bloodied shirt with both hands and shook him ever so slightly.

"Brent. I'm talking to you."

No response.

A member of the EMS team reached for her, trying to pry the LVPD detective from Lane. Teachout brushed one tech away, but the other one had gotten close to her. "Detective. We've got to get him to the emergency room now. Do you understand?"

Teachout stood up, wiped at the reoccurring gush of tears, and nodded ever so slightly. "I'm going with you."

The second EMS tech returned her nod. "Let's go then."

They positioned themselves to roll the gurney out the door, when a hand rose feebly into the air.

Manny watched as Teachout quickly grabbed his hand. "I'm here, Brent."

The delayed, unexpected response was stunning.

"Great. That's awesome. I think I need a drink, though. And could you get me a straw?" he answered. His voice was weak and distorted from the swelling in his face, but Brent Lane was coherent enough to talk and even joke.

Manny felt his emotion rise in tune with the rest of the room, especially with Detective Teachout's state of mind. It seemed the good guys had won, at least for now.

Then the EMS team was out the door, followed by Detective Teachout, her own bandage taped to the side of her head.

"Detective, wait," said Manny.

She stopped, swinging his way. "I have to go, Agent. He needs me."

"That's true, Mel, but right now we need you more. These people will take good care of him, and there's nothing you can do until they let you get into the same room. That's not true with us. You can help us get this guy."

"Manny, I can't just let him go without me."

She was adamant, but the look on her face told him she was already beginning to lose the fight to go with Detective Lane.

"I know how you feel. Only with all of us talking together, we can get our one version of what happened. Help us to put this freak away. All

I need is ten minutes of your time. Then you'll be free to get to the hospital."

The hesitancy in her step, and confusion on her face, told Manny she understood exactly what he was saying. Yet, separating the heart from the logical wasn't an easy formula for anyone to accept. Manny found himself hoping that would always be true. Conflict like hers told him that humanity still had a chance to be better, something bigger than taking care of number one.

"We've got him until you get there, Detective," said one of the EMS techs.

Taking a tentative step toward Manny and Agent Wilkins, she quickly did an about-face and kissed Detective Lane on his gauze-covered lips. Then she stepped back into the hallway.

"Let's talk," she said.

CHAPTER-43

Dodging the intermittent spikes of late-spring rain, Chloe reached the front stoop of G's Coffee House, pulled open the door, and settled into the early-morning line. Gavin had agreed to meet with her for a bagel and coffee so they could discuss the cold case.

Her new boss's schedule, he'd said, was going to be crazy for a day or two, but he'd relented when she told him she had a few questions regarding the procedural part of the investigation. His voice had stiffened. She pictured him bristling at the thought, like most good cops who had their investigative skills brought into focus. Still, Gavin had kept his composure, pretty much. He hadn't been able to completely rid the indignation from his voice. She understood.

She'd been grilled nonstop for hours over a decision she'd made while in the Terrorism Unit. She'd shot a suspect they'd been trying to capture alive. He would have been a great resource, but she would have had to let two agents die in the process. She'd done the right thing, but paid a certain professional price. The thing was she'd slept well knowing that those two people would be able to keep going home to their families.

Surprisingly, the flip side of her actions had haunted her for a few months. Would the Bureau have been able to save more lives if the suspect had been captured? Perhaps, though there was no definitive way to prove it. Besides, what was done was done. She still felt like she'd made the right choice, but. . . .

"Good morning, detective," said Gavin.

She'd been deep in her own world and hadn't seen his approach.

Turning toward the voice, she smiled. "Mornin' yourself."

"I've got a table in the back corner. We'll have some privacy. Follow me."

The stiffness hadn't completely left his voice and the wide grin that he used to greet her, on most occasions, was absent. It caused the one she greeted him with to disappear. This wasn't going to be a pleasant conversation, except she'd already guessed that, hadn't she?

They reached the back section of the shop, past the large stone fireplace, and settled into chairs at a two-person table. Her decaf latte was steaming (the aroma was still one of her favorite) as she sipped it during the first sliver of silence.

Gavin folded his rough hands and his eyes were fixed where they joined together. "Chloe. Do you know why I set you loose on this case?"

Reaching into her carry bag, she pulled out two folders and a yellow legal pad with neat notes chronicled in the order she deemed appropriate. She placed them on the table and then put her hand on his.

"I think so, Gavin. You probably were too close to it, and, in my estimation, it may have caused an error or two in judgment . . . or I'm just not seeing what you saw, if we're being perfectly blunt."

Sipping his coffee, Gavin was shaking his head ever so slightly. "You're right on both counts. I was too close to this one. Alan and four or five other young men were always at the house. He and Mike were good friends. But it wasn't just them. There were three other boys who hung out. I've gotta tell you, it was crazy, and no creature on the planet eats like a teenage boy. But Stella and I loved it. We knew where Mike was practically every moment.

It's not something you think about much when you say yes to becoming a cop, but there are some stupid-ass people out there that wouldn't mind making you and your family suffer for putting them away. We'd even get a threatening letter every so often but, mostly, we felt safe."

He drank again, and Chloe stayed silent. Gavin's take was going to be important, so she had to pay attention.

"The parents of the other lads were ecstatic that they were hanging around with a detective's son, and at his house to boot. I think it made them feel that their kids were safe."

Gavin's speech had quieted, grown more reflective. Chloe could see him struggling to keep his emotions at bay. Even grizzled old cops like Gavin fought to stay attached and detached at the same time. She knew from experience that such a balance was nearly impossible. Still, a cop had to try.

"I-I got the call that there had been a murder in the park at around ten p.m. Back then, murder was still a big thing in Lansing, so, looking back, I wasn't so sure that we truly had a homicide."

"My partner at that time, Jerry Hastings, was out of town fishing near the Mackinac Bridge for the weekend, so I was the first suit on the scene. I took one look and reality smacked me as hard as it possibly could. For the only time in my career, I found a place to puke my guts out. Not so much for the blood and twisted display of Alan's body, but because of who Alan had been to Stella, Mike, and me."

"You don't have to relive this thing, Gavin, not like this. I—"

He raised his hand, stopping her midsentence. "Actually, there aren't many days that go by that I don't relive that first few hours. It's like one of those damn, never ending, repeating DVDs, you know? I keep it to myself, though. I haven't even told Manny. He was just coming on the force and getting adjusted to his new life was enough on his plate. I'm sure he did what all of the other blues did—shook their heads and went on with their duties."

He turned his cup in his hands, fiddling with the rim. She waited. After a few moments, she began what she'd come to do: question Gavin on what was done in this investigation, and what wasn't.

"Ready, man?" she asked.

He nodded. "Fire away."

"Why no DNA processing? There were two questionable sources of blood that, based on the area of origin and subsequent spatter patterns, could have come from the killer. The second one, in particular. It was found nine feet from the body, and the wider pattern indicated that it dropped from around six to six-and-a-half feet."

Chloe shifted in her chair, handing Gavin the yellowing photo.

"I think there's a possibility that Alan may have defended himself and his attacker was bleeding. Maybe a bloody nose," she said.

"I agree, and that was in my report."

"It was, but you didn't push it or follow through. Why?"

"You know that a single spatter isn't enough to determine the correct point of origin, axis and angles and whatever other kind of physics shit you want to throw in there. Hell, the wind could have gusted just enough. Who in the hell knows for sure? You also know that exposure to the environment could affect the DNA results. Just being on that piece of cement for an hour could, and most likely did, render that potential piece of evidence worthless," answered Gavin, his voice back to more like she'd grown accustomed to hearing. She'd never believed gravelly and surly could sound as good as it did.

"I get that and that isn't the case so much these days. I'm sure Alex has lectured ya a time or two. And at the risk of pissing you off, I've got to press this. Why didn't you at least try, man?"

"Good God, you don't let shit die, do you? I'm not a praying man, but Manny's going to need help with you," he said.

Chloe grinned, but continued to press Gavin. "You could be right with that. But I think he knows what he got himself into, almost. Anyway, we can talk about your prayer life later, just answer the question."

"We didn't really have a forensics team as such. It'd be another year before the department hired Alex to get us up to speed. Also, there was the cost. LPD didn't have a ton of money budgeted for that stuff either so, all things being even, I didn't think it'd further the investigation."

"And?"

Leaning back in his chair, he tilted his head toward the ceiling, gathering his responses, and, in Chloe's estimation, trying to keep his infamous impatience in check.

"I-I. Shit, Chloe. I just didn't think it'd be a problem putting this killer away. I thought it was a clear-cut crime of passion and finding this guy would be a snap. Someone must have seen something or the killer's remorse would bring him into the station. Something."

"I can buy that, a little anyway. But why not go back and try to do something with the sample later?"

"Mostly for the reasons I stated before. But I guess the real reason was not being able to find the biological evidence bag that the sample was in. One of the evidence boxes for Alan's case is missing or misfiled, along with forty other files and boxes from other cold cases. It happened when we moved to the new facility a few years ago."

She nodded. That wouldn't be the first time something like that happened when a new storage building was needed. She'd even heard of techs throwing away old files simply to avoid having to move them.

"We may have to dig into that before we're done, depending on how you answer my next question."

"Have at it," he said.

"I will, don't ya know."

Opening the second folder with the transcripts of possible tips and leads, she pulled the first one from the top and placed it on the table, halfway between them.

"Let me guess. You want to know why we didn't follow up after that crazy woman called the second time about hearing a motorcycle drive away a few minutes after Alan was murdered." said Gavin.

"That's right. How did you know?" asked Chloe, frowning.

"Because that's what I would ask. Listen, Chloe. There were hundreds of bikes registered in the area. Hell, we even found eighty or so owned by women. It would have been like finding Bigfoot in the woods to even get a few possible suspects that way."

"She may have been ready for the loony bin, but—"

Gavin waived her off. "Having said that, we realized as the case grew older that it was worth at least some sort of effort to see where the lead took us. We went to work on it. We started by thinking like you're thinking: let's narrow it down by who might have fit our initial profile. Who knew for sure? Maybe we'd get a break. Then we added those several suspects who could have had opportunity and some unknown motive into the mix."

Chloe threw up her arms. "Where is *that* research? It's not in any of the files."

"It's with the lost box, which includes the samples of blood spatter and a couple of more files. Sorry to say."

"Great. Do you remember what you found?"

"Hell yes, girl. I'm getting old, not senile. Besides, I did most of the legwork on that angle."

"Well, speak up then, man."

"We found nothing that helped much. I had an age criteria, along with county residence, and anyone who'd been in even a little bit of trouble with the law. We narrowed it down, right away, to twenty-four possible suspects. We interviewed each one, with the exception of two: one woman with an amputated foot and a young man who had just moved here with his family and had been out of state during the murder. All had an alibi that worked for us."

"Okay. But I need to ask. Was there anyone's name on that list that made you blink?"

"Define *blink*."

"Don't play with me here, Gavin. Ya know damn well what I mean."

"Yeah, I suppose I do. But after I talked to him, there was no way it could have been him—even though he had a motorcycle and his parents couldn't tell me exactly where he'd been. His sister said she knew where he'd been because she saw him there."

"Where was where?"

"At the football game a few blocks away from the murder scene."

"Let me back up. Why did he make you blink?"

"Because he'd gotten into trouble in school for fighting and owned a motorcycle."

"Did anyone else see him at the game?"

"Three or four kids, besides his sister, said they remembered him there, but couldn't remember what time."

Closing the file, Chloe knew what she needed to do next.

"Don't give me that look. I talked to him two more times after that and got the same answers. The story was consistent from him and his sister."

"Gavin, I'm going to talk to him. Is he still around town?"

He shook his head. "He is. But it's a dead end, Chloe."

"You're probably right, but I need to start somewhere. And I'm sure your staff ain't gonna like it when we get to pulling each file box in those evidence rooms to find some fifteen-year-old cold-case file. So we need to do what we can before we go there."

Looking into the bottom of his paper cup, he got up, put it the trash bin, and sat back down.

"His name is Joseph Belle."

Chloe felt her mouth fall open. Joe Belle was a name she recognized. He was the younger brother of Louise Williams, Manny's deceased first wife.

CHAPTER-44

"We were talking about jurisdictional issues, and the next thing I knew, the unsub was in between Brent and me. He moved quickly, and I've not been swatted like that since we busted up a fight between Hulk Hogan and Andre the Giant years ago in the arena at Caesars," said Mel Teachout, doing her best to keep her trepidation under control.

Manny thought she was doing well, considering the circumstances. She was obviously shaken, but doing a hell of a job compartmentalizing that trauma so she could help the team get closer to her attacker. And Manny was determined to stick to his word and get her out of there as quickly as possible.

Although he doubted that it would be much longer before they met their tormentor face to face, Detective Teachout may be able to help them get the jump on this psychopath.

Argyle.

It still had a ring of unreality to think his name and entertain that he was still breathing.

"What kind of look did you get at him, Mel?" asked Manny.

"Wait. You got smacked by Hulk Hogan? Damn. Only in my dreams. What happened?" said Sophie.

"Sophie. Not—"

"I got this Williams," she said, raising her hand to cut him off.

He smiled inside. *Good girl.* Getting Mel to talk about something else, anything else, and then come back to his questions would relax her just a touch, and she'd do a better job remembering what she experienced.

Despite what she'd just been through, Mel gave Sophie a wry smile. "Ahh, well, yes, yes I did. It hurt like a bitch, but it was a good hurt, ya know? The man had muscles on his muscles and that tight little Speedo wrestling thing he was wearing was something else."

"Oh man. Was he . . . well, was he . . . like, big?"

"Oh yeah. Everywhere. I mean everywhere. He picked me up like some discarded doll, kissed my growing bruise, and said he was sorry. Don't tell anybody, but I didn't wash my cheek for a week."

"I'm *sooo* jealous. All I get is serial killers. I mean Manny and Dean are hot enough, but Hulk Hogan?"

Mel started to speak, stopped, and then gave Sophie a grateful nod.

"Our attacker was kind of tall, but a little stocky, maybe six-two, and like I said, strong as a bull. He might have been wearing a fake beard, or maybe a wig, because the beard and hair didn't seem to match color totally. You see that out here when old geezers are trying to impress some young hard-body, so I recognized it."

"What else?" asked Manny.

"He was sweating. I remember seeing perspiration on his forehead, right below the bill of his Fedora. Odd what you see in your mind's eyes when this kind of junk goes down. I didn't really get more than that, other than his arrogance. He had no fear and seemed to know exactly what he was doing and how to do it."

"You're sure that's it?" asked Manny.

He was interested in anything she had to say about their attacker, and she was doing a tremendous job of recalling the details. That being said, the feeling that something was off with this whole situation grew. Not that it was out of character for someone like Argyle to be egocentric in anything that he did. In fact, that trait was what usually got killers like him caught or killed.

His mind was racing to add up what she was saying with what he knew, or at the minimum, what he assumed he knew.

Searching her face, he waited for any sign or micro-expression that would tell a tale she didn't know she knew.

It didn't take long. The faint twitch around her eyes and the slight raising of her chin told him she had more to say. "Yeah, Manny, there was one more thing. His voice. It was deep, but it . . . hell, I don't know, sounded like he'd been eating glass or some damn thing. He either had a really bad cold, was disguising his voice, or had some kind of injury to his throat."

Manny's frown couldn't have been deeper. This shit storm was getting more cloudy and clandestine by the moment. Some of the attacker's moves made even less sense to him, given who they were dealing with.

"Thanks, Mel. Now, as promised, get your fanny to the hospital to see your husband."

She took three steps toward the heavy metal door, stopped, and turned back in Manny's direction.

"I never said we were married. How did you get that?"

Manny grinned. "Well, there are laws, even in Nevada, for kissing your brother, uncle, or cousin like that. Besides, that faint white area on your ring finger tells me you keep your wedding ring in your purse or at home when you're working. Detective Lane wasn't as cautious. He was wearing a gold band, yet his file said he was unmarried. Not that hard to guess really."

Mel Teachout nodded, then winced, the pain from being hit hard showing itself again.

"Damn, Manny. I feel sorry for your kids, if you have any. They probably can't get away with anything."

"Oh, she's still daddy's girl, and she might be better at reading me than I am her. She knows I love her, and the last time I looked, love is blind and fierce, Mel. Our loved one's get that. Brent loves you and would agree with you talking to us before going to him."

She began to tear up, steadied herself, and offered a grin of her own. "I suppose they do. I'll see you after I get an update on Brent."

With that, Detective Mel Teachout was through the door.

The pregnant silence had reared its head far more than Manny could remember in meetings like this, yet it seemed appropriate. There was a horde of new impressions, different facts, and just flat out inconsistent behavior from the killer that he wanted to take a moment to reconcile. He was sure his first impressions, after Mel was finished speaking, were true, but he wanted to hear what Wilkins had to say, and by the way she was staring at the white writing pad in front of her, her pen making little more than abstract patterns, Manny guessed it was part of her courage-gathering routine as she contemplated the next part of this meeting and what she had to say.

Just then, one of the forensic experts from the Vegas office strolled through the door carrying a stack of paper reports and three DVD discs resting on top of the reports.

The sleeve on one of the discs showed the FBI's seal, the other two had "LVPD" imprinted on the spine.

Manny felt his heart jump.

They'd gotten the video from the security cameras inside the FBI's office in record time.

And, unless he missed his guess, the other two were the security footage from the Egyptian and the city's traffic department focusing on the street corner where Agent Frost was killed.

It was time to get a first-rate look at the Good Doctor.

CHAPTER-45

Raising her hand to knock on the faded wooden door, Chloe dropped it to her side and turned to go down the concrete steps she'd only seconds before climbed. She rethought her actions, and faced the door again.

Whoever said that police work wasn't for the faint of heart had hit that button straight on. It was strange enough to knock on anyone's door and ask about a fifteen-year-old case. Let's throw in that the home belonged to Manny's ex brother-in-law. Oh, and just for the hell of it, let's make Manny's new wife the cop knocking on the door.

"I should sell this to Hollywood," she whispered. "Ya just can't make this stuff up, don't ya know."

Shrugging, she exhaled, and rapped on the door. The worst thing that could happen is he would shut the door in her face and she would have to get a warrant. Or maybe she would have to shoot him.

Somehow, the latter option seemed more plausible. She wasn't sure she wouldn't feel the same way.

After fifteen seconds, the door swung open, and an overweight, thirty-something woman with short, dark hair and matching tattoos on either side of her neck, reading JOE in script, stood in the doorway. Her smile disappeared in a New York minute when she recognized Chloe.

"What the hell are you doing here, Chloe?" asked Linda Belle, her voice as cold as a Michigan winter's day.

As bad as that was, Chloe thought it could have been worse.

"I'm here to talk with Joe, if he has a minute."

Linda sighed, a hint of sadness, or maybe anger, in her dark eyes.

"I don't think that's a good idea, Chloe."

"I understand. But I have to ask him some questions about Alan Gordon."

"Alan Gordon? The friend of his who was murdered?"

"Yes."

"Why does the FBI want to talk with him about that?" her voice became more guarded and she moved back a step.

"I'm not FBI any more. I work for the Lansing Police Department now. Gavin gave me this case to get my feet wet and to see if anything was missed."

Chloe remained patient. She knew how tricky this might be. The more comfortable Joe became with her, the better this might go. Linda could be a key to that.

Linda hesitated, shook her head, then answered. "That's good for you and maybe for Alan. The thing is that Joe is out of town. His job takes him on the road every once in a while. He'll be back in a few days."

The ice was still there, but melting.

"I see, where is he?"

"I'm not sure. He'll call tonight, but he's been out west for three days."

"What does he do?"

"I'll let him tell you that, if he wants to."

The ice was returning.

Don't push too hard, girl.

Handing Linda her card, she gave Joe's wife her best Irish smile.

"I'd appreciate it if you'd have Joe call. I realize that I'm not number one on his list of people he cares for, but I'd like to see what he remembers about that night."

Linda shifted her feet and bit her lip. Her nerves were getting the best of her and it made Chloe curious. Was it Manny's new wife standing on her stoop or something else?

"The cops already talked to him, I think three times, because he owned a motorcycle and whoever killed Alan might have ridden one away from the park. That's why you want to talk to him, right?"

"That's true. But there is a problem with a few of the cold case files being misplaced. Joe's interviews are part of those missing files. And yes, that's why I want to talk to him. Besides, he may remember something else."

"Maybe."

Linda's eyes were giving her away. Chloe played a hunch.

"Did you know Alan Gordon, Linda?"

At first, she did nothing, then she lowered her gaze, nodding her head ever so slightly.

"I did. Hell, who didn't? He was a funny guy, great looking, and smart as whip. Most of the girls thought he was hot, and he had great friends. If there was such a thing as a cool clique in high school, Alan was right in the middle of it."

"Like Joe?" asked Chloe.

"Yeah, Joe and Alan were tight. They were part of a group of five or six guys who hung out together. Mike Crosby was part of that group, and you probably heard that those guys used to hang out at the Crosby's all of the time."

"Gavin told me that. Kind of like a second home."

She nodded again. "I started dating Joe a few weeks before Alan was killed. Back then I was quite a few pounds lighter and was pretty hot myself. I'd dated around, but one day I looked at Joe and it was like I'd never seen him in that way before. I think we were truly in love in just a few days. It seemed like that anyway. I was even a little jealous when Joe would hang out with his boys and leave me out of the picture, but I got it. It was almost cool to see those guys watch each other's back, you know?"

"Tight mates then? All of them?"

"They were. The boys in that group were totally devastated when they found out about Alan."

Her voice cracked, then she recovered.

"Joe still has nightmares every once in a while. I guess it's one of those things that scars you for the rest of your life."

"I can see that. How about you, Linda? How did Alan's death affect you?"

Chloe suspected she knew that answer.

"Me? I-I . . ."

Her face grew soft, then hard. Real hard. "You know, I'll give your card to Joe."

Linda's action indicated she was either scared or knew something. Chloe gave it another shot, realizing she had nothing to lose.

"Can I ask you one more question?"

"That depends."

"On what?"

"If I can ask you one afterwards."

"I can do that."

"Okay, then fire away," said Linda.

Moving a step closer, she scanned Linda's face. "Did you know of anyone who would have wanted to hurt Alan?"

Linda looked at her feet and then shook her head. "No. Everyone liked him, like I said."

Her voice said one thing, her body language another. Or maybe she was still nervous talking to Manny's new wife. Either way, Chloe was going to ask that question again in the very near future.

She had to be sure nerves were the reason Linda had acted like she had.

"My turn."

"Ask away."

"Were you and Manny an item before Louise was killed?"

It was Chloe's turn to hesitate and capture some threatened composure. She hadn't expected that question. Yet, if she'd thought about it, the question was probably on more than one person's mind.

"No, Linda. Not a chance. He . . . well, he's Manny. He loved Louise and would never have been part of something like that. The Boy Scout thing is real for him."

Linda tilted her head. "But you were attracted to him, right?"

"I was. It was difficult, for me, not to be. But my mom raised me right. Still, the temptation was strong."

Letting out a breath, Chloe hoped her honesty would satisfy Linda on some level because she wanted to ask her another question. Not to mention, a little confession is always good for the soul.

"Thanks for telling the truth, and I think you are."

"You're welcome. I just have one more thing, okay?"

"Sure, I guess."

"You understand what I was going through, right, Linda? You loved Joe, but you were attracted to someone else in that group of cool boys, weren't you?"

Joe's wife took two steps back, her eyes growing wide. Chloe must have hit the jackpot because Linda's surprise was indisputable.

So was the sharp slam of the door.

*****

It was time, wasn't it?

Gavin Crosby looked at the small red circles Chloe had drawn as she'd gone over each page of the files that had been in her possession regarding Alan Gordon's murder. He ran his finger slowly over them. The woman had been precise. Each word, each statement, each picture, each line item she'd deemed important to reconsider had been right on, in his eyes. He'd been right to give her the file. That, in turn, had given him courage.

Funny word, courage. The dictionary gave it a one-word definition: bravery. He'd been far from that, hadn't he? He'd endured Lexy's death and Mike's reaction and almost-complete melt down. He could've been more supportive of his son, but he had his own grief to deal with.

Then Stella's murder had left him alone because of that damned Justice Club shit. He'd known something was up with her. Ignoring the signs seemed like a good idea at the time. He kept telling himself she'd come around. He should have gotten her some help. That would have been the brave thing to do.

Chicken shit.

Over the years, after Alan's murder, he'd done his best to make sure the boys, especially Joe, had gotten the attention they needed. Seeing their friend like that was a hell no one should have to visit, particularly high schoolers.

At first, he thought the kids had done well, maybe even better than expected. The kids in Alan's school had graduated and most moved on to college and then families. Wasn't that all anyone could ask for? A normal life?

Gavin closed the file, rubbed his face with both hands, then stared at his palms.

There had always been something wrong with Joe's interviews. They'd been basically the same answers, except they hadn't been. A word here, a darting eye there, a request for a pop or a glass of water when the intensity of the questions had increased. The truth was, and still remained, that there was something wrong with Joe Belle's answers to what had happened to Alan Gordon. Gavin should have dug harder, but he was sure he would've hated the answers.

Wasn't one death, one ruined life, enough?

Courage.

Bravery.

He'd not held those ideals close to his heart during that investigation. That would have cost him something and it hadn't been a price he was willing to pay.

"We all pay eventually," he whispered.

Gavin had watched Joe over the years, knowing firsthand what a killer with that kind of rage could develop into, given the right, or wrong, circumstances. Thank God, that hadn't happened. And Gavin had been grateful for that, for reasons most people couldn't imagine.

Until now, that is.

Hitting the intercom button, he told his secretary that he was leaving for the day. He then made another call, pulled out his credit card, paid the charges, and hung up.

Turning the piece of plastic over in his hand, he couldn't ignore the irony.

It was time to pay the other charges, and he prayed it wouldn't cost more than he could afford.

He knew it would be costly. There were always hidden costs, weren't there? The trick was to be able to face them or walk away.

This time, there would be no walking away.

nurse, the doctor, and Alex looked his way, almost in complete sync.

Josh caught his breath, trying to calm his thumping heart, then spoke.

"I need you two to leave."

He pulled his ID and stepped closer. "I have to speak to this man, and I want complete privacy."

The doctor blinked, then shrugged.

"Okay, but we have a tight schedule, so hurry up."

He left the room followed by the nurse, just as Barb, Alex's wife, strolled through the door, coffee in hand.

"Okay, Corner. What in hell are you doing? You think I'm not nervous enough so you got to pull this stunt? Wait. It's Sophie, isn't it? She put you up to this. Damn. I'm going to—"

"Relax. She did nothing of the sort, although that would be a hell of an idea on her part."

He moved closer as Alex sat up, Barb moving to Alex's other side.

Tilting his head toward Josh, Alex's expression changed. Trepidation didn't fit the pudgy CSI, yet Josh could understand. His sudden appearance was, at minimum, unexpected.

"Listen. I'm here for your help. I made a choice this morning that will probably affect my employment with the Bureau, which may come to fruition within a few hours. Meanwhile, I'm going to do what we, I, should have done all along."

The emotion in his voice surprised even Josh. Good. About damn time the "yes man" hit the bricks.

"What decision?" asked Alex.

"Good question," said Barb.

"Let's just say I'm not going to be getting any Christmas cards from AD Dickman. He wasn't happy when I told him to stick this process and promotion where . . . well, you know the rest."

Alex shook his head, then flipped the sheet from his chest, and put his legs over the side of the silver-railed bed, never moving his eyes from Josh's face.

"I'm not having surgery this morning, right?"

"Only if you want to. I'm not making that call for you. I know what it means for both of you. But I'm not doing any more damn testing, and I'm already tired of wearing black suits and dumbass ties. I have to do the right thing for me."

"Now there's a concept. Can you handle the consequences?" asked Barb, her voice steady.

"I'll have to. No one said life would be easy," said Josh, meeting her gaze.

Alex slid off from the bed, walked to the closet, and removed his clothes, scrambling to cover a naked, chunky left cheek when the rear of the gown suddenly flopped open.

Josh laughed. "Need a picture of that for Sophie."

Alex snorted and grinned. "How long before we get to Vegas?"

CHAPTER-47

Manny raised his hand. "No. Not yet."

"What? Why not?" asked Agent Wilkins. "The video footage on these discs might blow this thing wide open."

"Maybe. But I think it's what he wants. This killer is no idiot. He wants us confused and off track. That's exactly what will happen unless we do this right."

Wilkins looked at the forensics tech and motioned for her to stop loading the first disc into the computer that would project onto the white screen located at the front of the conference room.

"Okay. Tell us what that means, Manny. To this juncture, you've not told me shit, and it's time."

Agent Wilkins had made two good points. The anger in her voice told him that he needed to address them. It also told him *she* was ready to give *him* details.

"Fair enough. We need to revisit the mummy situation at the hotel, discuss what Dean discovered, talk about what Sophie and I found by speaking to a barmaid, and most importantly, have *you* tell us what you saw in the unsub who demanded that you take a good look," said Manny.

"Why not just cut to the chase?" asked Sophie.

"Because there's an order here. I didn't see it at first, even when we were talking at the Egyptian, but it's clear now. This killer has done things in order. He's planned each detail. If we want to see where that's leading, we've got to follow his order."

"I agree with Sophie: why?" said Agent Wilkins.

Shifting in his seat, Manny leaned forward. "It's like a giant jigsaw puzzle. You can't put one piece in and connect it until the others are there. We'll miss something unless we see the progression of where he's going, and, in the process, we won't be able to get a step on him. We have to get ahead so people don't die and he wears cuffs or eats a bullet or two."

"So that's what's going on when you do your profiling trip?" said Sophie.

"Most of it. It's logic, but sometimes. . . "

"You get a feeling. We've seen that," said Sophie.

"Listen. There's a pattern in almost anything or anyone. We're creatures of habit, and in case you haven't noticed, almost everything around us has symmetry. Whether people believe it or not, they're incredibly predictable. All of us. So if we take a short cut, as much as I would like to, we're going to miss something."

There it was again. As he finished speaking, the sense of how screwed up this whole thing appeared, charged him. So like Argyle. And so not. So brazen, arrogant, but slightly disorganized. It was as if the killer was flying by the seat of his pants, but wasn't. Manny found himself believing just that much more in what he'd just said: they couldn't afford to miss a thing. Not one.

Agent Wilkins stood, subconsciously touching the dark bruising just below her jaw, nodding.

"Good reasoning, Manny, but we're not going down investigation lane until I know who or what truly brought you out here. And forget the phone calls and text."

He exhaled. "We talked to a barmaid in the Egyptian who gave us the first name of a man, or demon, depending on your perspective, that sounded like he could be our unsub. The name is Fredrick."

She shrugged. "Okay."

"Have you heard of the serial killer, Doctor Fredrick Argyle?"

Her look went blank, then back to focus. "Who in the Bureau hasn't? He killed, what, fifty or more people? You ended him in Scotland or Ireland a year or so ago, right?"

"That's the one. The thing is. . .we're not sure I did end him, as you say."

Manny, with the help of Sophie and Dean, went through everything that had happened from Max Tucker's death in North Carolina to the empty graves in Lansing to the texts Manny had sent announcing Chloe's pregnancy, her subsequent return text, and the phone call to

Gavin. They detailed the cult-growing charm and power Argyle possessed, and Dean filled her in on just enough forensic evidence to cause her eyes to widen.

"That's why we're here, Agent Wilkins," finished Manny. "The man that died on that boat in Ireland could have been someone other than Argyle."

Waiting for the conversation to sink in as much as possible under the circumstances, Manny watched Agent Wilkins grapple with the truth that was far from believable.

Finally, she looked up from the table. "Okay. We get paid for figuring this crap out, so let's get to it."

Looking at his watch, Manny got the sense that time was running short.

"When you and Agent Frost picked us up from the airport, we drove the most common route toward the office, right?" asked Manny.

"We did. It's the fastest way here," answered Agent Wilkins.

"So the route would be fairly common knowledge, and those SUVs aren't exactly the kind of vehicles that go unnoticed, especially if you're looking for one."

"Yes, that's true."

"All right. Think back, and this is for all of us. Did you see anything on the way to the intersection that seemed unusual or got your attention?"

"We did this before. Do you want us to close our eyes and shit?" asked Sophie.

"If it helps," said Manny. "And that's a good idea."

After a few moments, Sophie spoke again. "You know, I have to admit I had stars in my eyes and was sort of preoccupied with Kim and Dean's history. Of course, that brought out the snippy-bitch syndrome. I don't remember anything that seemed off color to me. But then again, this isn't like home, so I don't know what's truly out of the ordinary."

Manny nodded. "I keep thinking the same thing. I was a little starry-eyed as well. I've not been here enough to know what normal is."

"For the time of day and the route down Las Vegas Boulevard, then to the intersection, it was pretty typical. People flock to the streets when the temperature is around eighty or so. It wasn't unusual to see people of all walks out and about, if that helps."

More silence.

"I can't think of anything except when Agent Frost changed lanes to let that green Jaguar pass by us. Not that unusual, I guess, but it was the only thing that stood out for me," said Dean. "Other than Sophie and Kim's conversation. That was pretty cool."

"Don't flatter yourself, Mikus. We were simply getting to know each other," said Sophie.

Writing on his white tablet, Manny nodded. "That could be something, Dean. Let's find out."

"How?" said Agent Wilkins.

"We're waiting for more forensics and to see the surveillance video, but maybe that car, or another vehicle we *didn't* notice, went past us and then came back to that particular intersection, and waited to take the shot," said Manny.

"Makes sense, but risky," said Sophie.

"It was . . . just one more thing that makes this profile a little different than I'd expect," said Manny.

"What does that mean?" asked Sophie.

"I'm not sure. Yet. Let's keep going with the mummy in the room at the Egyptian. Dean?"

Reaching up to stroke his beard, Dean then adjusted his paisley driver's hat. "The forensic info was pretty slim. He did a good job of not leaving much, if anything, unintentionally. It kind of reminded me of the casket back home. A few things, but nothing that made me want to dance the tango."

"Oh, that I'd like to see," said Sophie.

"Me too," said Agent Wilkins.

"Not me," said Manny. "What else?"

"We can do more things on the spot than we used to, thanks to the new databases we've set up. I hadn't had a chance to discuss this with Manny and Sophie because we were called here, but like I said, there wasn't much. I researched the gauze via its number stamped into the ending of each roll. You can buy it anywhere and in several department stores. I also was able to take great pictures of the five Canopic jars and send them to our database with instructions to forward them to local authorities all over the country. Maybe someone will recognize the work or something."

"Good thinking," said Manny.

"It's a long shot, but you never know if someone might recognize the craftsmanship. Maybe we get a link to the killer from it."

"I also took pictures of the grooves around the edges of the incision and the drill hole. Like I said, we're putting new databases together almost daily, so hopefully the guys in the home office will come up with a match to the drill tip and type."

"Isn't this all a bit ridiculous?" asked Agent Wilkins.

Manny could tell frustration and impatience were beginning to get the best of her.

"For crying out loud. We know what the man looks like. It's right here on video, and I got a bird's eye view. Face to face. Up close and personal. Ass to eye. Whatever damn way you want to say it."

"Did you?" asked Manny. "How do you know it's not just the look he *wanted* you to see?"

Agent Wilkins blinked and then bit her lip. "I . . . well, I don't. Awww shit. Didn't I?"

"We'll find out, just stay with us. What else, Dean?"

"The usual fibers, hairs, and stain routine. I used the UV light to see if there had been any recent sexual activity. There hadn't been. There wasn't any reason to use Luminol because the blood loss was contained, and surprisingly, not that much."

"That could mean she was killed somewhere else," said Sophie.

Dean shook his head. "Normally, I'd agree with you. But I don't think so. It would have been difficult to get her into her room unseen for one thing, and the other is the precision of the wounds, particularly on the side of her head. He missed the big arteries."

"Cause of death?" asked Manny, wondering if there might be another angle here. He suspected there was.

Raising his eyebrows, Dean answered. "Good question. I'm not totally sure. The ME will have to make that call. Each of the injuries could have killed her. But, if you're inferring that he could have killed her a different way, which might also account for the lack of blood, then that's possible. I did draw blood for toxicology reports, as usual, so we'll see when we get the results."

"What about the contents in the jars," asked Manny, pretty sure his first evaluation was the right one.

"Like you thought, the first four smaller jars had sections of human organs. Liver, lung, stomach, and large intestine. The large jar on her midsection had a large part of her brain, I'm pretty sure it was her brain and not someone else's, that is," said Dean, his voice growing quieter.

Manny made another note on his tablet, his internal scowl growing.

close, personal, to actually watch his victims die. I'm not sure he could have resisted the opportunity to do that."

"You're right about that, but again, maybe he decided to throw us off track," said Sophie.

"Maybe, but I simply don't buy it. He can't control that part of his ego. And do you think a tiger changes his stripes?"

Sophie sighed. "No, not really."

"In Agent Wilkins's description, she said he was over six feet but not 'tall.' Argyle was all of six-four. Subtle difference, but significant in this case, because people tend to notice when folks are unusually tall or short. Agent Wilkins also said he was stocky. Argyle was strong as hell—I can attest to that personally—and well built, but not stocky."

"Okay, that's a little distinctive, but you and I both know that two people can look at an identical situation and, like a car accident or someone falling on their ass stone-cold drunk, get almost totally different pictures of what happened," said Sophie, returning to her chair.

"That's true, but at least part of the descriptions will overlap usually in those situations. Do you remember when Argyle got into it with one of his patients and the guy used a toothbrush for a shank?"

"Yep. I do—"

Sophie stopped, stared at the marble-topped table, and then looked to Manny.

"He got that scar on the left side of his face, on his cheek. And was proud of it," she said. "No one's mentioned seeing that."

Agent Kim Wilkins shook her head slowly. "There wasn't any scar. I would have noticed. Even if he'd tried to cover it up. A woman can see a bad makeup job from a mile away and a good one from a few feet. He had nothing. If the scar was that noticeable, then this supports your theory that this isn't Argyle."

"It would seem so, at least for now. If we are right, that leads us to the most obvious and maybe more disturbing question: who is this sick prick and why is he doing this?" said Manny.

"Where do you want to start looking for that answer?" asked Sophie.

"I have a couple of ideas. We should be getting some more updated reports from the labs here and in Lansing. Alex's advice to run the three hairs separately could be a hell of a clue. But first things first. We need to look at those videos."

"About damn time," said Agent Wilkins. "Before we do, though, I need a break. I have to make a call and powder my nose."

Right then, Manny's phone began to vibrate, and he saw that Josh was calling. "Okay. Five minutes for all of us, then we get back to the videos. I need to take this call, and I have to check in with Chloe before she calls the National Guard."

"Yeah, well, I like the bathroom idea," said Sophie.

"Me too," said Dean.

Fingering his phone as the others left the room, Manny pushed the speaker button.

"Hey, Josh. I thought you were still in those brown-nosing sessions."

"Funny, Williams. I'm not going to be doing those anymore, but more on that later."

The sound of the jet was low but noticeable.

"Why are you on the jet?"

"That's why we called. There's been a change of plans, and Alex and I are on the way out. We're probably three hours away or so."

Manny didn't care for how that sounded and just who was we? He supposed he already knew.

"Alex and you?"

"Yes."

"What happened to his surgery?"

"Again, we'll fill you in. I just wanted to let you know we'll be in town and ready to dive in, if you don't already have it all handled."

Handled? He felt his doubt rise to another level. He prayed the members of the BAU weren't the ones going to be handled. Taking Argyle out of the equation made it more unpredictable and more dangerous in Manny's eyes.

"Let's just say we could use the help."

Josh hesitated. "That wasn't exactly a ringing endorsement for solving this thing."

"It's not. We'll explain everything when you get here, if all hell hasn't broken loose by then."

"We'll hurry. And hold back those gates of hell for a bit. Okay?"

He started to answer when Josh's phone cut out and the connection went dead. It wasn't unusual to lose the signal flying at thirty thousand feet, and it could be a while before the signal was strong enough again. It didn't matter really. They both knew what was happening on each other's end. That would have to do for now.

Dialing Chloe's number, he waited for her to answer.

She didn't.

He glanced at the phone to make sure he'd hit the right speed-dial number. Chloe's name stared back at him. He called again, same result. He tried to ignore the sense of uneasiness. He could count on one hand the times she hadn't answered when he called over the last few months.

Maybe she was in the shower or her phone was dead. Or—

The text screen popped up, and Chloe's message with it.

Sorry. I'm in the library doing research. Text me that you're okay and I'll call later. I love you.

He smiled. She was already working hard. No surprise there. What was surprising was how much relief he'd felt when the text came in. Next to love, worry was the number one emotion most people felt. He'd vouch for that. The Guardian of the Universe was an expert on worry.

He typed that he was all right and he'd call when he could. Then he sat down at the table and waited. He wasn't sure what was going on with Josh and Alex, but he knew they had good reasons for leaving DC and coming to Vegas. And they could use the help.

Looking down at the table, he pulled Dean's drawing closer, studying it. He then flipped open the first murder file and began to go over the details of the man's body found in the garbage bin near the Egyptian. The images were, at best, gruesome. The killer had no qualms about what he was doing and how. He looked at the next folder with the young woman, Paige Madison. Her death had been less violent and more staged. He guessed it was to make sure the phone was the focus. He then went over what they had on the woman found as a modern-day mummy— whatever limited amount of information was there, that is. He shook his head. Again, not as frenzied, in a sense, but the message was far more pronounced than either of the others—with the exception of the two bodies in the casket in Michigan.

The killer was all over the place. Smart, sloppy, brazen, covert, careful, and unpredictable. Each description covered at least one aspect of his spree.

The idea that the killer was trying to be caught came to him again. But that was rare for killers of this nature. "Who are you and what are you doing?" he whispered.

CHAPTER-49

Entering the open balcony gave him a fresh, clean taste of the early-morning desert air. The arid environment served to clear his head a bit more, and he welcomed it. Today would be a day of days, and he'd waited long enough for the culmination of his efforts to come to fruition.

Patience was many things, but a virtue? He didn't think so. No matter. Today would end the way he'd dreamed it would.

After another deep breath, he stepped the rest of the way through the tinted glass door and stood near the railing, glancing down to the street some twenty stories below. The people moving on both sides looked like ants and he thought that appropriate. Piss ants, to be exact. They all deserved to receive what they'd earned, literally and figuratively; shitty lives and slavery to some meaningless job for years on end. For what? To simply live a few more years in pain and misery, riding the wave of medications designed to help them fight any assortment of maladies.

Damn fools. Most people had the power to exercise a new future for themselves, but would never realize it, as he had. Instead, they'd follow the trail of their peers and predecessors.

So be it.

"As they say, more for me," he said out loud.

Moving back inside his room, he sat in one of the high-backed chairs that resembled an Egyptian throne and began, again, to go over the day's "activities."

He suspected that the rest of the BAU was on the way west. Frankly, he was surprised it had taken this long. Each member of that unit had a loyalty button molded in the shape of Agent Williams's face and was easily pushed. Corner and Downs simply couldn't help themselves. He had a contingency plan in the event he was mistaken, but he didn't think he'd need it. After all, men like him weren't wrong often, particularly when it came to human nature.

The scent of his dark-roast coffee demanded his attention, and he lifted the cup from the ornate glass coffee table and indulged, nodding his approval.

No doubt, by now, Williams had drawn some obvious conclusions, and some not so obvious. There were too many inconsistencies in the FBI's view of this case to ignore. He supposed if they had already gotten a look at the video footage Williams would suspect that Doctor Fredrick Argyle wasn't part of this frolic in Vegas.

All of the evidence would contradict any other conclusion. After all, one's senses are unfailing and in a real truth, don't lie, right?

Careful little eyes what you see. Careful little ears what you hear. Careful little minds what you think.

He laughed loudly.

"You may need to rethink that one, Special Agent Williams. Rethink it indeed."

Setting the coffee cup on the table, he gazed at the other man scated in the chair opposite him.

He appeared to be a little under the weather, perhaps a little worn out, yet his inspiration, his mentor, his counsel had offered him far more than most men deserved. He was grateful for that.

Taking another draw from his cup, he lifted it and toasted the man sitting opposite him. "Thank you for your help," he said.

The silent, powerful grin was brilliant. And all of the encouragement he needed to finish what he'd started.

Finally.

CHAPTER-50

The forensics tech switched off the video feed spilling from the computer, controlling what Manny, Sophie, Dean, and Agent Wilkins had watched for the fourth time. She moved to the wall and switched the lights on, leaving the room.

"I think you pissed her off, Williams. My God, man, how many times do you need to see something before you get it?" asked Sophie.

She was being a smartass to cover her discomfort with what they'd seen on the three DVDs . . . well, on at least two of them. Manny wouldn't have expected anything different.

He managed a smile. "You know how visual men are, right?"

"Yeah, I get that. But usually it has to do with some woman's ass or a set of killer knockers like mine. Not surveillance videos."

His smile became more genuine. "You know, I don't think you should sugarcoat things. Just tell me what you think, okay?"

Her eyes darted in Dean's direction, over to Wilkins, and then back to Manny. She returned his grin. "Good one, Williams. I'm not the only smartass in the room."

"Maybe, but I had to be sure what we were seeing. And I'm still not."

"Me either," said Agent Wilkins.

Dean was nodding. "I don't think the video at the street corner helped much. It was too grainy and dark. The only thing we can say for sure was that a car similar to the green Jaguar went south when we were going north at approximately the same moment Agent Frost was shot. That's my take."

"But that new software program can clean that up, right?" asked Manny.

"It can," said Dean. "But I think it would be a miracle to clear it up so much as to give us a definitive look at the driver. We'll get a better look at the plate, but—"

"The plate and the car are probably stolen anyway, at least that's how I'd do it," said Sophie.

"Good point. We'll get Agent Wilkin's staff on it anyway," said Manny.

Manny bowed his head, closed his eyes, and went over the other two security videos in his mind one last time before they discussed what was there, or what they assumed was there. He thought he knew what he saw, what was said, but he wanted to be completely sure of himself before he asked someone else to do the same.

The video from the FBI's office had confirmed what Agent Wilkins and Detective Teachout had said about their attacker. While it was difficult to ferret out things like weight and height from a video, perspective with other objects in the hallway and office helped tremendously. But he hadn't needed any of those things. He'd never forget Argyle's gait, his swagger, his arrogance reflected in every step he took. The man in this video had some of that, but as Manny had suspected, the man was shorter and more bulky. Manny also couldn't put a finger on his walk or any other mannerisms this killer might subconsciously expose to a profiler. He probably had done it on purpose. Manny would have.

He wasn't Argyle, but he could be as dangerous because of his unpredictability.

The video in the Egyptian was far more unsettling and, as fate would have it, more difficult to unravel. That made his stomach clench. He just couldn't rule Argyle out of that one, at least right now. The close-up of the man's face said he could be the Good Doctor, or it had been a hell of a makeup job. What he'd mouthed directly into the camera forced that possibility.

Looking up, he saw three sets of eyes pointed in his direction. It occurred to him, once again, how the eyes were sometimes better at expressing questions than the mouth.

"Sorry. Just getting ready for your input on the other two videos. I need to make sure I saw what I saw," he explained.

". . . and we saw what we saw," said Sophie.

"That's right. So have at it. Let's talk about the one here in this office," said Manny. "Agent Wilkins?"

"I've never met Fredrick Argyle, so I'm worthless regarding that. All I know is that the guy on this video is the man who walked into my office and screwed up my morning. There's just nothing there that changes that or adds to what I saw. He walked in like he was God and it seems he left the same way," she said, her voice growing louder.

Manny suspected it may be a while before the vivid memory of her attacker would fade enough to allow her a good night's sleep.

He knew that one.

"Thanks. Dean?"

He shrugged. "I have even less input than Kim. I only see what's on the video. But I will say that I'm sure he's wearing a disguise. The hat is low, causing his wig to pull up around the back of his neck. His mustache and sideburns are a little much too. They just didn't seem to fit the color or the shape of his face."

"Anything else?"

"Not until we get an analysis of any fibers or hair the forensics staff may have located," said Dean.

"Okay, Sophie, it's you and me. Fire away," said Manny.

"Nice choice of words, Williams. I'd love to take this bastard out. Anyway, I think, judging by his walk and mannerisms that I agree with you. This isn't Argyle. As much as I was convinced it had to be, I know it's not. So I got past that and tried to see if there was anything else about this unsub that I recognized. There wasn't really," said Sophie. "He's right-handed, even though he backhanded Detective Teachout with his left. I—" Throwing up her hands, she sat back in her chair. "I tried Manny, I just don't see anything else."

"I'm almost at that stage. He was all the things we talked of regarding his arrogance, etcetera, and I didn't see anything about his appearance that made me think it was Argyle. I like what Dean said about his disguise. Not much doubt there. I will say that I think he walked a bit slower than Argyle. Either wasn't in a hurry or maybe he had something wrong with his leg."

"Or he wanted us to think that," said Agent Wilkins.

"That's true. So I think we can agree on ruling out one suspect—Argyle—which of course puts us back at square one with who and why," said Manny. "But we *can* clear up the why."

"Please enlighten us, Special Agent. Because the only reason I can think of is to make sure you got a good look at his puss and that I backed it up with an eyewitness account," said Agent Wilkins.

Turning his hands over and laying them flat on the table, Manny nodded slowly. "I'm afraid that's the only reason I can think of as well, Agent Wilkins. It wasn't just that he could do what he did, he wanted to make sure you could describe him."

"But wouldn't the damn video be enough?" asked Sophie.

"That's what I was thinking," said Dean. "Why make sure Kim can verify everything about him?"

"I have a thought, but let's talk of the footage from the casino first," said Manny.

"I'll go. Looks like the same guy who attacked me," said Agent Wilkins. "Everything about his face, although the video quality isn't quite as good . . . I'd say it was him."

"I'd agree," said Dean.

"Me too," said Sophie. "The only difference I see is the angle of the camera. He was looking almost straight up in the casino, and it's more like just above eye level in this building."

Manny glanced down at his notes and drew a ring around the last word in the last sentence. They were right, almost. He believed he saw a little more than that, something a tinge different. Then again, his old baby blues could be playing tricks on him. Or maybe the camera was just unfocused enough.

"Agent Wilkins, can you call the tech back in? I want to see location twelve fifty-five on that video."

Dean stood up. "I can get us there. This is like the equipment we had in Los Angeles. The question is why?"

"I'll show you when you get there, but I think I saw something else. I'll let you decide."

"Damn, Williams. Did we miss something?" asked Sophie.

"Maybe not. I just want to make sure. I was looking for it so that might be the reason I saw it, or assumed I did. I'd tell you but I want you without prejudice when you look for yourselves."

"Without prejudice, huh? That's just funny when it comes to you and this job," said Sophie.

He raised his eyebrows. "What? Why?"

"Because you're my hero, and I believe everything you say," she said, grinning and then batting her eyes.

"Okay, smartass, pay attention. I've been wrong far more than you think and I'm not getting any younger, so it could be anything," he said, returning her grin.

"I'm almost there," said Dean.

A moment later, the screen flashed an image they'd seen several times before—the killer mouthing his message. Then Dean stopped it at twelve fifty-five to display a still-life image.

"First things first: we're in agreement with what he is mouthing here, right?"

"I got 'One never knows, Agent Williams,'" said Agent Wilkins.

Dean and Sophie nodded their agreement.

"Okay. I'm getting a little sick of hearing that because this guy's full of shit. I'm tired of hearing that line. One does know, I think that's right. I also think it's overkill and Argyle would have come up with something else more personal by this time."

"Okay. Then why are we here at this spot in the video again?" asked Sophie.

"Look closely at the image. Focus on his left cheek. Do you see that?"

At first, no one said anything. Then Sophie, followed by Dean, moved away from the table, and Sophie reached out and touched the screen.

It was hard to ignore the crescent-shaped shadow on the left side of the killer's face.

CHAPTER-51

"Shit, Manny. Is that a scar?" asked Sophie, stepping back from the screen.

"You tell me," he said.

"It looks like it might be, but it could also be a shadow or a piece of dust on the lens of the casino's camera," said Dean.

"I don't think so, Dean. It looks like it's on his face," said Agent Wilkins. "I can tell you this, he had no such mark when we had our prayer meeting. It could be a fake."

"It could be," whispered Manny.

Staring at the half-moon located on the killer's face, Manny let his mind shift gears and run crazy.

All along, this man had been messing with them, intentionally for the most part, but at other times, Manny didn't think so. Both types of actions were a byproduct of this man's personality, his profile. Consistency sandwiched within inconsistency.

He moved to the screen and ran his finger along the scar. It fit and didn't fit. He stepped back and was struck with an odd memory.

When Jen had been four, she'd discovered that she could tell Louise one thing and do another by going to Manny and telling him momma said it was okay. Thus telling the truth that Momma had said it was okay, but her version wasn't quite the same. At one point, after that had happened a few times, she came to Manny and had said that Louise had told her she could go play in the snow by herself because she was becoming a big girl. He'd thought it odd, so Manny had taken her by the hand and sought out Louise, believing a four-year-old was too young to be out alone.

What Louise had told her was that it was okay to go outside *with* Daddy and that she could dress herself because she was becoming a big girl.

After educating Jen on the virtues of telling the complete truth, he and Louise had one of those *twinkle in the eye* moments that parents have when their child is caught doing something wrong, but it's funny at the same time.

This whole thing had that feel. There was a truth in all of this, yet it was hidden because of the games and the idiosyncrasies of the killer's actions and perceptions. He racked his brain for a pattern, any kind of order that would give him insight to this bastard's end game, and, for that matter, his beginnings.

The bodies in the casket, the phone, Agent Frost's pointless murder, the videos, the brazen attack on the Bureau office, the modern-day mummy in the hotel, the text, the Canopic jars, and the seeming obsession with Egyptian culture all hid a truth, a take on the killer's reality that went everywhere and then nowhere. It was almost like the killer wasn't sure how to get to the end of his journey and needed help.

But where in God's name was the end of his journey? All Manny knew for sure was that the killer's destination would be dark, violent, and deadly. He had already displayed sick glimpses of those traits, and his grand finale would encompass a huge dose of all three. Now *that* was something Manny would take to the bank.

He suddenly felt more unease than at any point since they'd reached Vegas. That emotion reminded him that the *hows* and *whats* of a killer's method, while crucial, were only a means to accomplish the end the killer desired; the *why*. He'd do well to remember that this man had drawn the BAU to Sin City for a specific purpose. He was pretty sure it wasn't for dinner and a show.

Come on, Williams, what does he want?

"What's going on inside there?" asked Sophie, touching Manny's head.

He sighed, running his hand through his hair. "I don't really know, Sophie. It's just not coming to me. I hate to say it, but it's one of those times that I simply don't see the rhythm of our boy's world. I can give a basic profile. You know, white male, thirty to fifty, tall, strong, smart, bent on vengeance, without strange sexual—That's it, right? That's something I've missed. Damn it, Williams."

"What is it?" asked Dean.

Manny turned to him. "Have you seen any indications of sexual abuse or some sick-ass defilement of the corpses? I mean . . . we have the mother's hand on the son's crotch, but nothing else for this guy, right?"

Dean shrugged. "You're right. Nothing about, on, or in the other victims have shown sexual contact. No abuse, postmortem or antemortem, or any indication that he'd gone there."

"Highly unlikely for a serial killer," said Manny. "Sexual gratification, like we discussed earlier, is usually a huge motivation, no matter the act."

"He could be recording the actions or killings for self-gratification later," said Agent Wilkins.

"But there was no indication of that on the video in the FBI office, and coming into the building and swatting a few cops around had to give him a major hard-on, if he were capable or interested," said Sophie. "So he's not interested in sex here? I'm not buying that totally. He's a man, for crying out loud."

"I think it's not a primary motivation at all. He could have slept with Grace before he killed her and wrapped her the way he did. It's almost like he's avoiding it," said Manny.

"Men avoiding sex? What the hell is this world coming to?" said Sophie.

"I see your point, Sophie, but he's not interested. Remember when we talked about trying to apply conventional reasoning to insane

actions? We have to think differently. The lack of
sexual references or actions makes him some type
of visionary killer, but his psychology isn't
consistent. There's not been one mention of voices,
demons, or even that God told him what to do.
Just a few messages for us to follow and trip over
along the way," said Manny.

Sophie plopped back in her chair.

"So what does that mean?"

Manny abruptly knew what that meant.
"Listen. We've been running behind this guy for a
while. He leads, we follow. He throws us a few
crumbs, we search for more. In that way, he is
much like Argyle. I think he thinks he has us right
where he wants us, and in almost every way. I
think it's our turn."

"Our turn? To do what?" asked Sophie.

"Think about it. What's the thing that he'd
most expect from us?"

Agent Wilkins nodded. "He'd expect us to react
to his next act. And depending what that is, he
will have us deeper in the trap, so to speak."

"Right. Now what's the least thing he'd
expect?" asked Manny.

"Oh, oh, I have an idea," said Sophie, her eyes
alive. "Since this guy isn't about the sex, why don't
I dress up like a hooker and run through the
casino calling out Argyle's name and offering oral
sex?"

Walking around the table, Manny pulled
Sophie from her chair and hugged her.

"You know, girl, that's just brilliant."

CHAPTER-52

Scrolling down, Chloe reached the end of the microfilm, and then slapped the side of the antiquated projector with an open hand. She'd missed the date she wanted to read by one stinking day. Although the microfilm box said it was here, it was inaccurate. One day. Her frustration wasn't just with the process of loading and threading the old microfilm, but with the fact that many of the boxes had been mislabeled and misfiled over the years. In a day and age when almost everything pertinent to anything had been transferred from this archaic example of a manual, inefficient system to a navigable website, she was amazed that the City of Lansing hadn't followed suit. She understood budgets, but this was ridiculous.

Added to that was the fact that she was exasperated and delayed in finishing research on Alan Gordon's murder. One thing she'd learned, and learned over time, was that local stories and information dealing with a specific historical event had better insight, at times, than the cops.

Most reporters had their sources, even the bad ones, and speculated far more than law enforcement.

Admittedly, journalism had evolved to the point that most of it was irresponsible and codeless. In the past, reporters tried to protect the subjects of their articles as much as possible. Not in this day and age. Reporting had become *blood in the water, let the sharks loose, and to hell with the consequences* sensationalism with an almost intentional disregard for the total truth. Another reason she'd almost completely stopped reading newspapers.

But what she was seeking was far more personal than the current-day definition of journalistic reporting.

There was more information somewhere, and her experience, if not her intuition, whispered that it was so. She simply had to find it. That was why she was going through this total *pain in the ass* method of searching old newspapers. She wanted to see what the locals had written about the horrible murder. Maybe some local reporter had had better luck than the cops turning up *something.*

With another sigh, Chloe took out the next microfilm from the dilapidated, discolored box, looked at the date on the roll, and loaded it into the wobbly reader's feeding slot. She turned the black knob and watched the header go up the screen until wonder of all wonders materialized. The screaming headline told her she'd hit pay dirt.

Her elation was quickly exchanged for a creepy, disconcerting reality.

LOCAL STUDENT FOUND VICIOUSLY MURDERED

Funny. She'd read a thousand headlines and not many had struck her with its pure authenticity like this one. Behind this headline was far more than print and yellowing paper, but a young man whose promising future had been stolen from him. Alan Gordon may have lived a simple life, raising a family and growing old with the woman of his dreams. That was probably likely, on some level. He would probably have experienced his fifteen minutes of fame, but chances are, nothing more, at least as the world sees fame. Yet, what if that wasn't true? What if he'd been the one that God had designated to cure cancer or bring about a world of peace or discover the way to visit other galaxies with the flip of a switch?

She continued to stare at the screen. Manny's voice quietly added to her own. She could imagine him saying that hundreds of kids die each day and any or all of them could change the way the world does business. But we can only help the ones who let us. Nothing more, nothing less.

Chloe shook her head, bit her lip, and scrolled down to the main story, praying that stories like this one would eventually disappear, for eternity.

The reporter was a name she recognized. Eric Hayes was the reporter from the Lansing paper that Argyle had killed on a cruise ship just before they'd captured him two-years ago, or maybe he'd captured them. At any rate, she wouldn't have remembered except for the terrible crime scene pictures of the long, bloodied knife sticking through one side of Hayes' neck.

Great. More pleasant memories strolling down serial-killer lane.

Reaching the main article, she dissected each word. Hayes had written a decent piece. His facts were close, with the usual small, detailed inaccuracies of getting information secondhand or from the infamous "source," but he did the story justice. He'd even thrown in a few quotes from first responders to the scene.

Turning the knob, the next frame came into view.

Chloe frowned. Below the end of Hayes' story was an editorial with the caption: COPS FAIL TO STOP VIOLENCE.

It was written by a staff reporter. Generally, when the term staff reporter was on the tagline, the commentary was written by someone who didn't want to be named or a newbie who was being given the opportunity to dip into the world of reporting.

She leaned closer to the dim screen and began reading. There was no question that this person had a proverbial hard-on for the LPD. The writer used the terms incompetence and favoritism, and even claimed the police in Lansing had been instructed to ignore certain complaints coming from rich-bitch areas of town that contributed heavily to political concerns on the force.

The commentary seemed to be an angry rant, and she was about to go back to Hayes' story to see if she'd missed anything when the next line of the editorial forced her to read on.

. . . Take the murder of poor Alan Gordon. This reporter interviewed several bystanders and subsequently the two people who'd found his body. They were visibly shaken by what they'd stumbled upon, yet were also puzzled by the LPD's lack of interest in what they had to say. When they began to offer information, including the fact they'd heard a motorcycle roar down the street opposite the park just as they stumbled upon the body, a detective, later identified as Gavin Crosby, asked the woman to stop speaking and set up an appointment to come down to the station. He told her to get her story straight then come and see him. She said he then walked away, talking with another detective about how many kids he knew with motorcycles without even asking her name. Good citizens of Ingham County, this is what I'm . . .

The article finished how it started with almost incoherent ranting, yet Chloe had gotten something. Something she hadn't counted on. Something Gavin had said.

She reread the part of the article that portrayed Gavin walking away. The alleged quote by Gavin bothered her. One key word more than the rest.

Why would Gavin say what he said regarding how many *kids* he knew with motorcycles?

Kids? Why not just people? Was it just a generalization? A slip of the tongue? Or had he known something else?

There was only one way to find out.

After she packed up her bag, she turned off the machine and headed for the door. Chloe felt her anger grow, even though she was trying to control it. She felt betrayed with the lack of Gavin's total honesty, as she saw it.

Her Irish ire wasn't going to let this one rest. There was no mistaking in her mind that Gavin had more knowledge about this case. It was time to find out what.

As she reached the front door of the library, she walked outside, pulled out her phone, and dialed.

It was time for another talk with her boss, and this time, she wanted the truth.

*****

Gavin's phone vibrated, and he took it from his suit-coat pocket, expecting it to be from someone in the office. He was almost right. Chloe Williams's number flashed on the bright screen, begging him to answer, it seemed.

He'd been right to turn her loose on this file. Manny would say it was to resolve a deep-seated injustice and to help him reconcile a sense of guilt. He'd be half right. The injustice was never very deep, never far from his thoughts, even when it should have been, but he did want to set the record straight. No, he *needed* to set it straight.

Watching the screen, he reached out his forefinger, hesitated, and then declined the call. He switched off the phone, sat back in his chair, and waited. He had never been particularly philosophical; he just simply did what it took to get the job done over the years. Yet, if he'd learned anything during his life as an officer, he'd learned that escaping what was rightfully yours, what your actions truly owned, was impossible. Karma could be a bitch, as they say, but it was far more than that. He supposed there were other words for Karma, but in the end they all meant the same thing.

Fate, destiny, truth, even God's will were all in the mix for what the next few hours held, and he was accepting of that.

Chloe's work had made that easier.

Picking up his briefcase, he left the room.

CHAPTER-53

"No. Don't do anything. Let him go for now. I'll be in touch when a final decision is made."

Assistant Director John Dickman hung up the phone and watched as the number on the LED display faded to gray, then reappeared showing only his last name and extension. The exchange on the mini-screen was almost a microcosm of his professional life. Names changed as personnel changed but one name, his, always came back when the day's business was over. Someone had to be the constant, the rock, the man everyone could count on. And, for the last twelve years, he'd filled that role. No questions asked, no hesitation. He always did what it took—men like him were rare commodities. Locating a suitable replacement, in this era of political correctness and human rights first, would be difficult at best.

Moving around the front of his desk, he sat in one of the plush, black leather chairs and crossed his legs. He then took out his pack of cigarettes, lit up, and blew a slow, steel-gray ring that floated aimlessly toward the chandelier guarding the high ceiling.

Dickman had interviewed six candidates to take his place and selected three for subsequent testing. Two, one woman and one man, had performed impressively. Their test scores were off the charts, their intellect infallible, and their ability to size up a situation and act accordingly had surpassed expectations. Both were going to make fine assistant directors for the Bureau . . . hell, maybe even run the damn place.

Drawing another drag, he then put the cancer stick out in his imported ashtray. Then there was Agent Joshua Corner. The young man that ran his BAU and had answered to him for the last three years was as talented as the other two, perhaps more. He was smart. And his field experience made him a perfect potential candidate. But that's where the potential, compared to the others, became an albatross around his young protégé's neck.

He was almost the polar opposite of the other two when it came to taking orders. In fact, Corner fought him on almost every move over the last two years.

For instance, Corner added Chloe Franson to his unit. Despite Dickman's warning regarding some of her anger tendencies—and there were concerns how she would recover from being shot in the bust in New York. Corner told him they could use some emotion and that the gunshot, according to her psych report, would make her even more determined to do her job. He was right, to a point, and she proved extremely valuable in hunting down Argyle. Corner used his intuition and ignored advice from his superiors. That didn't go unnoticed. Chloe's subsequent resignation, as a result of her marriage to another member of the BAU, also had gone under the negative side of the slate.

Bringing in Manny Williams and his crew was also a calculated risk, yet, in that instance, the FBI had already been monitoring Williams before Corner had worked with him on the cruise ship. True profilers were rare by any standards and to land him without wrangling through much difficulty had been a bit of a coup.

But even hiring Manny Williams wasn't as open and shut as it ought to have been, given his advice to Corner.

Corner initially admitted, based on the testing, that he may not have hired Williams because he was sometimes too emotional based on the psychological examinations conducted by the Bureau. But ten minutes in a room with Williams and watching him work was all Corner needed to be swayed to hire him.

Again, Corner had exhibited great instincts, flexibility, and street smarts.

He got up from the chair and went to his personal coffee machine and poured a second cup, then wandered back to his desk.

Smarts.

Maybe too smart. Corner had dug into areas that were way out of his league and pay grade, and he'd done it more than once. Even after being warned that a repeat performance would carry consequences, he simply did what he thought was the right thing to do—orders be damned.

"Dangerous, my young friend," he whispered.

Brash, loyal to a fault, unimpressed with authority, putting his nose into places where he had no business being, and now this final incomprehensible stunt. The man had left the most important three days of his professional life, taking a top candidate for government research in the area of cyber-prosthetic work with him.

Reckless. And for what? Some sense of warped loyalty involving his unit and ignoring the bigger picture in the process?

Pulling Corner's file from his top drawer, he tossed it on the right corner of the desk.

"Your time with the BAU is almost over, Josh Corner, in more ways than one."

He reached for the phone and dialed another extension.

The day of reckoning had arrived for Special Agent Joshua Corner.

CHAPTER-54

Looking around the wooden table in the Egyptian's main conference room, Manny counted the faces involved in the next, unorthodox step in this investigation. He didn't just *count* the faces, however—he wanted to see what was going on in each of their minds. Five cops from the LVPD and seven more FBI agents, not to mention at least six resort security agents, were about to embark on one of the rarest of surveillance assignments in the history of law enforcement. They needed to be ready for anything. And he meant anything.

Added to that, Josh and Alex were on their way from the airport and would be arriving shortly to increase the force. He was grateful for that.

Scanning the crowd again as most of the cops engaged in small talk waiting for the meeting to begin, he heard the small, intense voice of discomfort nudge him. He was used to small teams and the flexibility they offered. Taking charge of a group of over twenty, and making sure they knew their assignments, was a bit out of his security zone, but then again, this plan was as well. The worst thing was not knowing if the plan would work. What if the killer wasn't even in the building? What if Manny had made a mistake and coming back here wasn't on the madman's agenda at all? What if he'd totally mis-profiled this psycho? What if . . .

He shook his head. Coming here was in this killer's makeup, wasn't it? Killers like him, while unpredictable in some of their advanced behavior, had basic needs that proved virtually impossible to resist over time. One of those base behaviors was the uncontrollable urge and compulsion to watch the results of their activity after they'd created chaos. No matter what the variables were, Manny was at least sure of that.

He frowned. Was he? Going back over everything he could draw on from the killer's actions thus far, especially the attack at the FBI building which doubled as a taunt at Williams, he came to the same conclusion—for a third time now. Yes, he was sure he was right. Moving closer to the door, he peered through the small, wired window looking for the rest of his team, especially Sophie.

No show yet.

Manny continued to stare through the glass as he ran his hand through his hair.

The killer would have to think that after what had happened—what he did and how he did it in the FBI's Vegas office—Manny and Sophie and Dean would come back to the hotel to clean up and then have another meeting with LVPD and the FBI's local crew on what to do next. His delusional sense of power wouldn't let him travel any other road. Manny knew if he were in the killer's shoes that's exactly what he would do. He'd want to watch the moronic law enforcement react to him, but that wasn't all. This situation was racing toward an end game, one the killer needed to control.

There was the feeling of uneasiness again. That vein of doubt that spoke softly of a haunting unpredictability continued to tease him. So be it. They had a trick or two up their sleeves as well, Sophie's idea had sealed that notion.

Never before had he gone in this direction. Inviting attention from a serial killer was never a great move, but if this worked, it might throw him off his game just enough to make a mistake and, with nearly two dozen cops in the building, they'd end this amusement once and for all.

Just then, the door burst open, and Josh and Alex walked in, followed by Dean. Manny felt his spirits rise immediately. It was good to see his friends and to have two more good cops in the mix.

"About time. Where have you been?" he asked, grinning.

Josh reached out his hand. "That westerly wind is a bitch, besides, getting in deep trouble with the AD takes a little time, not to mention, Alex was dinking around in that hospital bed."

"Yeah, he always blames the one-handed guy. Never fails," said Alex, returning Manny's smile and shaking his hand as well.

"Don't get me wrong, it's great to have you here . . . but what happened back east?" asked Manny.

"We'll talk later," said Josh, his smile disappearing. "We did what we should have done two days ago."

Scanning Josh's face, then Alex's, Manny finally nodded. "All right. Later, if we're able."

Josh frowned. "What the hell does that mean?"

Manny began to answer, but before he could, he stopped, mouth dropping wide open as Sophie walked into the room.

More like strutted.

Her appearance must have had the same effect on every cop in the room because the small-talk buzz stopped abruptly, all eyes on his partner. He'd seen her in every situation possible, he'd thought. Amazing how often he could be wrong.

After a moment of stunned quiet, someone released a slow, tantalizing whistle which reflected what every man and woman in the room was thinking: Sophie Lee, FBI special agent, might have missed her calling. She was absolutely stunning.

A short, red dress fitted with hundreds of sparkling sequins running in contrasting swirling patterns accented every curve the woman possessed. The plunging neckline showed her enhanced cleavage, leaving no choice but to stare.

Add in the matching four-inch pumps, a sparkling black handbag slung over her shoulder, and enough jewelry around her wrists to drown a good-sized man, and she was ready to blow the top off the building. That wasn't all.

She'd dyed her hair with several bright red streaks running the full length of her long black locks, topped off with a wide-brimmed hat matching her handbag. No hooker in Vegas had ever looked more appealing or perfect than Sophie Lee did at that moment. Hell, maybe none on the planet.

Stunning was the wrong word; mesmerizing was better.

A protective, older brother attitude quickly stepped into his mind. She was Sophie, always had been, but he suddenly didn't care for how the men in the room were looking at her. She'd think that funny.

Dean was excluded from Manny's pseudo-condemnation of the other cops.

He glanced at the CSI and felt his smile return. Dean was flushed, his eyes as wide as some surprised cartoon character. He tried to speak, but nothing came out. He swallowed hard, and, for a moment, Manny wondered if the man was going to faint.

Slowly scrutinizing the cops in the room, Sophie spoke, hands on her hips, smiling. "What the hell are you all looking at? And wipe the drool from your chin, Mikus. It's embarrassing."

Quickly pulling off his teal paisley driver's hat, Dean took a step closer. "How much?"

Laughter rippled through the room, and Sophie took advantage of the moment.

"How much you got, big boy?" she answered in her best Marilyn Monroe impression.

Taking the billfold out of his back pocket, he handed it to her.

"All I have," he said, his eyes growing serious.

Manny doubted that few, if any, in the room caught his double meaning. She could have all of him, and that had been true from the beginning, hadn't it?

Her smile left and then returned in a split second. His gregarious partner had heard him, really heard Dean, but did her best to stay in the moment.

She flipped the wallet back to him. "I only take cash, and I don't do cops."

More laughter echoed around the room. Manny hoped they would all still be laughing in a few hours.

Stepping to the front of the gathering, he motioned for people to settle down.

"Okay. Enough of the show-time. Let's go over what we need to do. No screw-ups. Sophie will be a target, so we have to be on the same page here. If I'm right, we could end this killer's run."

"What if you're wrong?" came a voice from the back.

For the second time in three minutes, the room grew eerily silent.

Looking at the ceiling, Manny thought about the question. His answer was the best he had. "Pray I'm not," he said. "Pray I'm not."

*****

Standing near the railing on the fourth floor, looking down at the entrance of the conference room, he watched as Sophie Lee disappeared through the door, dressed like the slut he'd always known she was. Her entrance, combined with the expected arrival of Corner and Downs, had put the finishing touches on his day's anticipated activities.

Everything was set. All that was left was to bait the trap, and then Williams and his tribe of morons was just about to hand him who he needed to finish what he'd started.

His smile grew as he walked away from the railing and headed for the casino floor.

CHAPTER-55

The tiny microphone attached to the strap of Sophie's dress was so powerful she didn't have to lean toward it to be heard. The ear bud wasn't quite as undetectable, but one had to look for it.

"You boys hear me?" she whispered.

"Loud and clear," said Manny.

"Got you, Princess," said Dean.

"Yep," said Josh.

"I've got a good signal, Lee," said Alex. "Just don't get carried away and try to make a quick hundred, okay?"

"Bite me, Dough Boy. At least I could. We'd better be watching you to make sure you're not on the other end of one of those propositions."

"Really? I bet if I wore a red dress that showed my ass and had my boobs, my fake boobs, hanging out like that, I'd get an offer or two," said Alex.

She smiled. She heard the concern in his voice in spite of giving her shit, as usual.

"Yeah, but it'd be from the guys who just got out of prison," she answered. "And don't worry, we've got this."

"Prison. Whatever, wench. And I'm not worried. Just be careful. If something happens, Josh's paperwork will be a bitch. And . . . and I'd have to break in someone else to give me a hard go. I don't have time for that. Okay?"

"Got it, Dough Boy," she answered, doing her best to keep her emotions out of her response. It was nice to have more than one big brother.

"Now that we've got that out of the way, let's get this shindig rolling," said Josh.

"We've got you Sophie, so it's all yours," said Manny.

Funny how his voice still had a calming effect on her, even now.

Climbing on the self-propelled carpet-cleaning machine, which resembled a hockey rink's Zamboni, as gracefully as possible wearing a skirt that begged to show her butt-cheeks, Sophie tossed her bag around her shoulder, grabbed the controls, and began maneuvering down the middle of the casino floor.

Driving anything with wheels had always been easy for her, and this machine was no exception. She turned down the main isle of the busy table-gaming section and began waving to anyone who looked her way, yelling greetings to everyone.

She could count on one hand the times she'd felt self-conscious in her adult life, and this was getting close to another one. Yet, it really wasn't. She'd shut out virtually all concerns of self-consciousness after her first divorce.

What people thought of her carried no real value toward who she was inside, so why sweat it? Manny taught her that with the way he simply accepted her for her . . . that and a few lessons from the school of hard knocks.

Her changed attitude over the years had made her a perfect candidate for this almost-undercover action. Besides, she got to wear one of the hottest outfits on the planet and charge it to the FBI. That was having and eating your cake at the same party. Everyone should have that happen to them every once in a while.

Glancing down at her dress as she steered the carpet machine around a gentle curve and paced into the very heart of the casino, she was struck with another enlightenment: if most women were honest with themselves, they wanted to wear something like this just once. She'd seen it here in Vegas. And why not? Life was short—try everything.

She knew she wanted to.

Sophie kept waving, yelling, and drawing attention to herself as she moved along the aisle, but her eyes were working, taking in whatever and whoever she could. She was comfortable with what she was doing, but she wasn't going be stupid either.

She'd located a few of the agents and cops, and of course, knew exactly where Manny, Josh, Dean, and Alex were located in the casino, but hadn't seen who they were looking for yet.

He was going to make an entrance, no doubt in her mind. She wanted to see him first, however.

That abruptly made her a little uneasy as she thought back to the cruise ship and how Eli Jenkins had almost been the end of her. Only that was different. She had a posse watching over her this time, and no matter how this demented bastard reacted to her taking the spotlight, his spotlight, they were ready for him.

She kept waving and yelling as more and more people came her way. It was working. She was disrupting the whole casino, and that was the complete idea.

Manny had a theory, and she and the other's had agreed, that by her drawing attention to herself in such a big way, the killer may not be able to balance the diversion of attention to the desired outcome for these murders and the warped game he was playing. It was as if they'd be ignoring him. For a killer like this, that would never do. Sophie's parade could cause a major short-circuit in the narcissistic realm the killer lived in and his anger would take over, causing him to react in a brash and uncontrolled way, and to ultimately show himself. That would be a perfect reaction.

Even if he were able to restrain himself in reaction to Sophie's hooker carnival, and if it were Argyle, he'd be able to contain himself to some extent, this unexpected step by the Feds would be out of his control and the pattern he'd tried to establish.

As bright as this psychopath was, he was still a psychopath. Taking control away from him could drive him to do something impulsive and that meant showing himself. The trick was to make sure no one got hurt in the event he went ape shit. That worked for Sophie. She liked the idea of seeing another sunrise.

Slowing down as the mass congregated closer to her, Sophie saw the guests looking at her, smiling, laughing, and pressing closer to the machine. She began tossing out some hastily made business cards, asking people to call a fictitious number for a good time. The crowd buzzed even more.

She stood up, put her hands on her hips, and began to gyrate to the music echoing through the casino. The mob grew ever louder, pressing closer. She raised her hands in the air, scanning the crowd as best she could. She saw Manny standing on the fringe of the Tiki bar some thirty feet to her left, watching her and searching the crowd at the same time.

"Okay, you losers. Do you want to have a really good time? Well, do you?"

The throng that had gathered, maybe a hundred strong, voiced their reply with a boisterous *hell yeah*.

"That was your best response?" she hollered.

The next sound from the floor was like a cannon exploding as the deafening retort seemed to shake the very casino. By now, folks were pressing so close she could smell expensive perfume mixed with smoke and spilled beer.

Raising her arms higher, she motioned for them to get louder.

They did.

"You still doing okay?" said Manny.

His voice almost surprised her. She wasn't used to the wire setup, but recovered.

She started to speak, then remembered she was supposed to nod whenever possible to avoid breaking character. She gave a slight nod that she was fine. The closeness of the patrons wasn't a concern for her. Not being able to see much beyond them was.

Still, looking through the swarm of people, she did see more cops and agents, but no killer. Or anyone that looked like him.

Picking up another stack of cards, she flung them in two directions, then turned slightly to toss a bundle behind her.

"How about some free drinks?" she bellowed.

Another rousing roar as people scrambled for the coupons.

The slight break of attention allowed her to check behind her.

Nothing out of the ordinary, if there was such a thing in Vegas and in this situation.

Josh was standing at the edge of the closest bank of slots, Alex on the opposite side of the isle, both appearing to be casual observers of Sophie's show.

Glancing up to the second-floor balcony that led toward the show theaters and the food court, she expected to see Dean.

He wasn't where he should have been.

She looked again.

Still no Dean.

Knowing she wasn't supposed to do it held no power in her next action.

"Dean? Where in hell are you?" she whispered, doing her best to hide what she was doing.

Waiting for him to respond, her imagination careened out of control. What if—? Her earphone greeted her with static. What came next caused her stomach to fill her gorge.

"Don't worry, Princess, Special Agent Dean Mikus is in good hands."

"Who is this?" she yelled.

"Don't you know, Agent Lee? Don't you know?"

She jumped from the machine, plowed through the crowd, and sprinted toward the escalator leading to the balcony, her veins turning to ice and that voice ringing in her head.

Sophie *did* know.

CHAPTER-56

Lifting the bottle of water to his lips, he finished it off and tossed the container in the trash. He was doing his best to be patient. He needed the information he'd requested and, in his mind, it was taking far too long. He didn't understand all of the technology that ran amok these days, but he knew there shouldn't be any trouble with this request.

He sat back down, placed the phone on the table, and watched it.

She'd told him it could be a couple of hours. It had been four. What came next, for him, hinged on getting that information. He'd made that incredibly clear. She told him she understood, but she could only do her part, the rest was contingent on a speedy response on the other end.

Hell, he understood that, he supposed, but why now?

He rolled his fingers on the table, watching the people walk past the window.

Just once in his miserable life, he wished something could go right, especially this close to the end.

The end.

That's what this was, wasn't it?

Oddly, there was some comfort in that. Once everything was out in the open, his chance of survival was akin to shit not stinking. But he'd known that from the time he'd decided to walk down this road.

Shifting in his seat, he glanced at the phone for the hundredth time, and the last painful look was greeted with the message he'd been waiting for.

"I don't know how you knew that, Sir, but you're right. He's not where he's supposed to be. Here's the address, according to the last GPS search. It was kind of tricky getting it because it looks like the main phone GPS chip was disabled. I don't think he knows about the other one, the one hidden in the battery compartment. Anyway, that's how we located him. I hope that helped."

"More than you realize," he said to himself.

With that, he memorized the address and started to put the phone in his pocket, thought again, and wrote out a lengthy text without pressing the send button.

When the time was right, he'd send it. It was the least he could do, under the circumstance, providing he'd get the chance.

After all, death and dying had a way of screwing up the most pointed of plans.

CHAPTER-57

"Stop. All of you. If you want to see Agent Mikus alive again, you'll all stay exactly where you are. I know that you can hear me, so please don't be so foolish as to assume I'm unaware of that fact."

Halting in his steps, Manny glanced to his left then quickly to his right. Sophie had stopped on a dime and Josh had followed suit. The agents and LVPD officers that he could see had also followed suit.

The command by the killer wasn't the only reason Manny had put on the breaks. He'd recognized the deep resonance filtering through Dean's mouthpiece.

How could he not? He'd heard it a million times in his head.

Argyle's voice was unmistakable. It had been from the first time he'd heard him. But how could it be him? Manny had already determined that this killer couldn't be Fredrick Argyle, yet the sound of him speaking said he was wrong.

He turned toward Sophie again and saw she was staring at him. Even at forty feet, he could see her own unanswered questions on her face. That seemed to be going around.

Argyle's voice wasn't her only concern. Dean's obvious capture was taking precedent in Sophie's world, and he understood. Only too well. But they had to keep their heads and go with what they knew. Dean's life, and maybe theirs, depended on it.

He raised his hand in a gesture designed to help her calm down. She waited to respond, then finally took a deep breath and nodded toward him.

The killer spoke again. "That's better. It's good to see that law enforcement can understand a simple command."

The full game was on. He could tell by the killer's voice that he was excited, almost geeked. That meant he was ready for the climax of his charade. Whatever the hell that was boiling down to mean.

Gathering his wits, he concentrated on the coming conversation.

"What do you want, you warped prick?" asked Manny softly.

"Come, come, Agent Williams, is that any way to talk to an old friend? As for what I want, we'll get to that."

"We're not friends. You're a twisted murderer, and people like me are here to end you."

"Ahh. The classic good-versus-evil. Is that right, Agent?"

Manny put his hand to his earpiece. It was delicate, almost unperceivable, but he'd heard something different in the would-be Argyle's voice.

"You finally get it," answered Manny.

"Oh, I get it. The trick is in the perspective, Agent. I've learned this is always the case."

There it was again. He frowned.

"I'm sure you're not here to debate morality and what that means, so I'll ask again. What do you want?"

"Stop!"

Manny jumped, then realized what had happened. He scanned the room. One of the agents had begun to move toward the stairs leading to the upper level. The killer had somehow seen it.

How? Where was he?

"I'm not one prone to give a second warning. If any of you move before I tell you to, the next message you receive will tell you where to find Agent Mikus's head. Are we clear?"

"We get it," said Manny.

"Good. I'd hate to spoil the upcoming party."

Before Manny could respond, Sophie did.

"Listen, you son of a bitch, if you harm him, hell won't be safe for you. Do you get me?"

Her tone was controlled but intense.

"Agent Lee. I see the rumors are true. You have a special place for Agent Mikus in your heart, yes?"

"That's none of your damned business, you freak," she answered.

"I think perhaps it is. But we can discuss that in, let's say, two hours. That's all the time you'll have."

"What does that mean?" asked Manny.

A moment later, his phone beeped with a text message from Dean's phone. He looked down and saw an address in North Las Vegas scroll across his screen.

"No more talking. No more questions here. The address you've received is where you and the rest of the BAU will join me. Only the four of you are invited and you will come alone, unarmed, no phones or any other GPS devices. Oh, and no companions from the LVPD or the FBI are allowed. This party is by special invitation only. If I sense anyone other than your sad team . . . well, you can guess what Agent Mikus might look like when you finally recover all of his parts. Are we clear?"

"Perfectly. We'll be there," said Manny.

"Oh. I know you will, Agent Williams. I know you will. I want to thank you for finding a way for us to meet. I so enjoyed the opportunity you afforded with this ridiculous attempt to, how do you say it, draw me out? Oh, and one more thing. If anyone leaves their current positions in the next five minutes, I'll know and be forced to end Agent Mikus's life. So, please stay put."

"We will."

The next sound he heard was a grinding crunch as the killer crushed Dean's microphone.

As he stood his ground, helplessly, Manny looked at the address again, the killer's voice echoing in his head.

Manny had been wrong. Dean was now in the killer's grasp, and they'd played right into his hands. Manny's plan hadn't worked and now they were all in danger of never seeing home again.

As guilt and frustration simmered during the last seconds of the killer's instructed imprisonment, Manny wondered how he could have been so wrong.

CHAPTER-58

Dean felt the leather strap close around his left leg and felt the cold buckle as it was drawn tight. It was the last of his limbs to be bound after he was forced to sit in the hard chair. The tight gag had been removed, but the dark blindfold was still in place. He had no idea where he was. Not that it would matter much. It wasn't like Las Vegas was a town he knew well.

His current surroundings did seem a bit cooler than the ride and offered a smell much like a cement slab in a basement or warehouse. He wasn't in any sort of mainstream building, of that he was sure. He found little comfort in that, however. Secluded like he feared he was could never be good.

For the hundredth time, he wondered how he could have been caught so unaware of his surroundings. One moment, he was watching Sophie put the casino crowd into the palm of her hand from his perch on the balcony; the next, he felt the gun on the back of his neck.

"Do exactly what I say if you want to live," his kidnapper had said. Dean complied. He didn't want today to be the day he died.

He'd then been bound, had his microphone and earpiece removed along with his power pack, forced into the green laundry cart, and covered with dirty, smelly linens. Ten minutes later, he was wheeled into the back of a van or truck and driven to this location, wherever that was.

His captor had not only managed to terrify him into silence, which seemed prudent with a gun at your head, but had also exposed him to his only real phobia.

Dean could only imagine the millions of germs that were at work on his skin and hair at that very moment.

He shivered.

If the killer didn't end his life, the microbial assassins he'd been exposed to most assuredly would.

The only noise he'd really heard, once relegated to the cart, were the sounds of the road and some traffic. He'd actually felt them more than heard those sounds because of the position of the blindfold wrapped around his eyes and head. The cloth had covered his ears as well.

It was a good move, and he'd have done the same thing.

Good God, he was thinking like a serial killer.

The hand on his shoulder caused Dean's stomach to clench with surprise and jolt in agony at the same time. The pain from the man's grip was brilliant. He felt like his collarbone had been crushed.

"Welcome, Agent Mikus, to my humble abode. I trust you'll find the accommodations acceptable."

"Would it matter if I complained to the manager?" he gritted through his teeth, determined not to let the killer see him sweat.

The man laughed as his grip eased. "No, I suppose it wouldn't. But I appreciate your concerns."

"Do you?" asked Dean.

"Of course. This isn't, as they say, my first rodeo, Agent. I'm fully aware of your position. The question is, it seems, are you? Do you know what your future holds?"

"Not entirely. But I'd venture a guess that you think you do, right?"

"I don't think, Agent. I know."

Dean felt the killer's breath on his face. "You and the other people who've caused my life to be the most miserable existence on this God forsaken rock are going to pay for what you've done. I've had no real peace, and before that can ever happen, you must all die—and die in what many would consider a horrible death."

"That end will satisfy you? It will fix whatever wrong you think you've suffered? Is that right?" asked Dean. His anger was rising along with his fear. Not just for him, but at the horrible contemplation of Sophie dying gruesomely.

"Oh yes. It will. Then I'll be free from my own personal demons, as Agent Williams would say."

Slowly, Dean had been putting pressure against his bindings. Breaking them would be an effort in futility, so he stopped.

"What demons would those be?"

"Do you care, Agent? Would it matter to you?"

"No, I guess not, but I'm curious as to what turned you into what you are."

The crushing grip returned, this time to both shoulders. Dean cried out. He had not felt pain like this. He wondered if he might pass out.

The next second, the killer was at his ear again, squeezing harder. "Oh, you'll find out, Agent. You'll find out."

Suddenly, the pressure eased from his shoulders. Before Dean could fully grasp why, he felt something strike the side of his head, and then Dean's world went dark.

CHAPTER-59

"We're ready to wrap this up, Chloe. I'll call soon. I promise."

Manny hesitated, then sent the text. He hated not telling her what was going on, but it would only worry her more.

Watching to make sure the text went, he then handed his phone to Agent Kim Wilkins. She nodded without speaking, only her eyes had no such compunction. Her disapproval of the BAU's next action was off the charts. He understood why, but this was Dean. He was one of their own. They had to go to him, no matter the risk. Besides, if they refused, the killer wouldn't stop with killing Dean. More innocent people would die until he got what he wanted. He'd simply find another way to get the rest of the BAU where he desired.

To hell with regulations. It was time for this to end. It helped that Sophie, Josh, and Alex were all in agreement.

He moved aside as the other three handed their weapons and phones to Agent Wilkins, then they stood in a semi-circle, facing each other.

His gaze lingered on Sophie's face. His ex-partner was doing an uncanny job of holding her emotions in check. Her face was stoic, alert, and then he saw something else. She was pissed. Her anger issues had been well documented over the years, but this was different. She hadn't wanted to delve into a relationship with Dean because she wasn't ready and the memories, if not the pain, of her first two broken marriages had forced her into a cautious approach to anything that resembled a relationship. Yet, Manny knew that her heart had been Dean's for the taking, almost from the beginning. Now she was faced with a different kind of breakup.

That might not bode well for his kidnapper, if she got a chance to express her displeasure. But it could work in reverse if she didn't keep it together.

"You're okay, right?"

She looked at him, took a deep breath, and nodded.

Alex and Josh, almost on cue, did the same.

Brave people.

He'd read once that bravery isn't the absence of fear, but the ability to overcome it. Manny wasn't sure about the others, but fear and he were having a conversation.

Well, if this is the day you die, Williams, I can't think of a better group to do it with.

Turning to Agent Wilkins, he caught her full attention with his eyes. "Kim, I must have your word that no one follows us or tracks us in anyway. This maniac has technology enough to scramble the source of phone messages and calls, so that makes camera security child's play. He'll know if we try something that he ordered us not to do. Got it?"

"Manny. You know what the manual says about what you're doing. I mean how many more times do I—"

"I don't give a rat's ass about the manual," said Josh, pointing at her. "This is my damned unit, for now anyway, and we're doing it this way. So don't interfere. Just do what you're told."

Agent Wilkins put her hand on her hips, scanning the four people standing in front of her. Manny saw that she was going to object again, but instead she stopped, turned on her heel, and headed for her SUV.

As she opened the door, she whirled toward Manny. "You've got three hours. That's it. And Josh, I don't give a shit if you are in charge. I'll do what I have to. And in the event you think I'm being a complete company dweeb, don't forget that Dean and I have a hell of lot more history than I have with any of you. Do *you* get *that*?"

Josh looked Manny's way, then he nodded to Agent Wilkins. "Fair enough," he said.

"I just hope you know what the hell you're doing." She climbed into her vehicle, started it, and then drove to the other end of the parking lot, where she parked facing away from them.

"Guess she doesn't like our plan," said Alex.

"We have a plan?" asked Josh, showing a tight smile.

"As ill-conceived as it is," said Manny.

"Anything we need to talk about?" asked Josh.

"I have one more thing," said Alex. "I got one more email from the lab in Lansing about the hairs we found in the casket back home. Not just the one, but all three."

"And?" asked Manny.

Alex stroked his chin. "I just wanted to tell you I was wrong. The DNA from them wasn't in the database."

"What in the hell are you bringing that up for now?" asked Josh.

"I'm not sure. Other than to tell you this killer hasn't made any mistakes, so we need to walk into this with our eyes wide open, okay?" said Alex quietly.

"And you're nervous, right, Dough Boy? Don't worry. I've got your ass," said Sophie, trying to smile.

"Yeah, there's that. And you'd better."

Reaching over with his right hand, he gave her arm a squeeze. "All for one, right?"

She nodded. "Something like that."

"Anything else?" asked Josh.

"Yeah. I want to remind you that no matter what you heard at the hotel when Dean was taken, this isn't Argyle. He wants us to think that he is. When we talked about the copycat situation back in Michigan, we weren't really sure. And there are still questions about why the killer is doing this the way he is, but it's *not Argyle*. The videos we've seen, the fact he didn't kill the two detectives at the FBI building, and the way his voice is a little different proves it," said Manny.

"You're sure, right?" said Josh.

"I am. He's just too different in his approach. His mission is much more defined. If we go in getting that confused, we could have a very short visit."

"Sort of like the devil you know is better than the one you don't," stated Alex.

Shifting her feet, Sophie stared at the ground, her hands clasped in front of her so tightly her knuckles were turning white.

"Again, are you okay?" Manny asked.

"Hell no. I know you think we need this information, except I don't. I don't care who this prick is. I'm going to take him out," she said through her teeth.

"You'd better care who he is, Sophie. You'd better. If you go in there with your emotion running your motivation, Dean's as good as dead and so are we, get me?" he snapped.

She answered without looking up. "I freaking get you. It's just not that easy for me. I'll be fine. Okay?"

"We all feel the same way, Sophie. We do," said Manny.

"I doubt it. But like I said, I understand. So, can we do this?"

"Okay. You're right. Enough talk. We've gone over everything. We're as ready as we're going to be," said Manny, trying to sound confident.

He wasn't sure it worked, not even for him.

"Then let's get to it," said Sophie.

She led them to the other black FBI-issue SUV. They stepped inside, then Sophie brought the engine to a roar and sped out of the lot, heading north.

While they made the drive in silence, he watched as the dark cloud that had rolled in from the west suddenly released its contents.

Sophie turned on the wipers, flipping the moisture away.

As he watched the Vegas rain hit the windshield, it was impossible for Manny's mind, no matter how hard he tried, to escape the notion that death was going to touch the BAU.

And more than once.

CHAPTER-60

Fifteen minutes later Manny, Josh, Alex, and Sophie stood at the front door of the office of a rundown building that doubled as an entrance to an outdated warehouse stretching back toward an older subdivision some three hundred feet.

On the right door was taped a handwritten, four-line note.

DEAN AND I ARE GLAD YOU SHOWED. ESPECIALLY DEAN. TAKE OFF YOUR SHOES AND SOCKS AND ALL OF YOUR JEWLERY, THEN COME TO THE BACK OF THE BUILDING. WE HAVE ACCOMODATIONS FOR EACH OF YOU.

Manny exhaled and glanced at the others. "Metal detector, like we suspected. Just do it."

Alex was the last to bare his feet.

He stood and nodded he was ready.

"Into the lion's den. Shall we?" said Manny.

He didn't wait for an answer. Pulling open the door, he walked through the virtually vacant office, the smell of must and mold replacing any odor that may have given the area a sense of its original purpose.

Reaching the double-steel door marked WAREHOUSE in faded red, he stopped. Sophie moved up to his left, Josh to his right, and Alex a step to Sophie's left. He was pretty sure none of them were all that eager to go through with the next step.

Although he knew the reason they were standing here, and that Dean was in the clutches of a madman, wasn't his fault, he wondered, again, if his plan to flush this killer out into the open would have been better as a last resort.

He shook it off. It didn't matter at this point. Guilt and second guessing would only distract him and God knew he needed all he had.

Reaching out to push the door open, he pulled his hand back. Maybe this was wrong, maybe they should leave. Maybe . . .

"We got this, one way or the other," said Sophie, without looking his way.

She was right. They'd gone too far to turn back now.

But that couldn't stop his heart from racing at the thought of what they might encounter in the next room.

As if the killer knew what he was thinking, the intercom system filled with static then boomed.

"Come now, don't be shy. Your destinies lie behind those doors."

The voice was once again unmistakable. It was the same one from the casino. No doubt about that. That meant Dean was somewhere in the building, which was reason enough to continue.

Manny pushed open both doors and took several cautious steps inside and then, as if he were hit with an invisible wall, stopped in his footsteps. He wasn't sure what he'd expected, but what lay before him hadn't entered his brain.

By the way Sophie, Alex, and Josh reacted, they were all in the same boat.

Disbelief covered them all.

In the back of the room were five large, high-backed chairs. One in the center and four others branched away from it into what appeared to be the west, north, south, and east. The four peripheral seats were covered with blue velvet while the one in the middle was decorated in red. Each of the four directional chairs had two thick cables running from it, leading to the three-foot platform that supported the larger chair in the center. Directly next to the center chair's right was a tarp covering something long, fairly wide, and two feet high.

That wasn't all. Far from it.

Each of the chairs had a large carving resting on the pinnacle of each chair back. They were replicas of the Canopic jars they'd seen in the room where Grace was turned into a twenty-first-century mummy.

The resemblance for the situation was unreal. And the eerie symbolism wasn't lost on Manny. He suddenly knew why the Canopic jars had been placed the way they were and why there had been a fifth. It was no coincidence that there were five members of the BAU and that each of them played a role within the group. The killer knew that and was about to define those roles further.

He had not left any detail untouched. Not good.

Manny felt his dread reach deeper into the stratosphere when he realized that the chair facing the west was occupied.

Dean Mikus sat bound by leather straps to his forearms and lower legs, head resting on his chest. Manny could see the trail of blood running down the side of his face and fought more panic.

Seeing what he saw, Sophie swore under her breath and took two steps before Manny could grab her arm.

The killer was right on cue.

"Stay where you're at until I tell you to move. And no, Agent Mikus isn't dead—yet—but he will die quickly if any of you do anything rash."

His voice had changed again. Less Argyle-like and closer to what Manny suspected were his normal conversational inflexions. The voice was still a disguise, but the facade was melting away as the killer's plan came closer to its climax. Manny heard no panic or even excitement in that voice. He almost wished he could. This man was in complete control of himself.

"All right. I want Agents Lee, Corner, and Downs to sit in the seats I tell you to sit in. Agent Lee, to the left of Agent Mikus. Agent Downs to her left, and Agent Corner left of him. Once you're in your proper place, Agent Williams will make sure everyone stays put tightening your restraints.

Then he'll join you by taking his place in the middle."

"You'll have two minutes to complete what I just instructed you to do. Again, don't test me. Oh by the way, Agent Williams, I'll know if you've not tightened the shackles sufficiently. The chairs are equipped with sensors that will tell me when you've done your job."

"What the hell is this all about?" asked Manny, keeping calm.

"I ask the questions. You simply do what you're told. You'll see your truths soon enough."

Disconcerting how steady his voice remained.

"What if we end this right now? What if we leave?"

The laughter was genuine. Crazy but genuine.

"You have no weapons. I know that because of the metal detector you walked through when you entered the building, and I assure you that if you morons touch any of the doors from inside, you'll set off pressure locks that seal this place like Fort Knox. It would be like shooting fish in a barrel. Follow my instructions, and maybe, just maybe, one of you will make it out of here."

As he talked, Manny searched the area, as the others had been doing, trying to locate their twisted host. Nothing.

"Come out. Let's talk—"

"Oh. We'll have a conversation, Agent Williams, as you might imagine. Now go, agents, go. You have one hundred twenty seconds.

The four of them looked at each other. Manny nodded, and they each hurried toward the hellish setup that would eventually imprison them.

Josh reached his chair first. Manny did what he was told and strapped his boss in. Their eyes met briefly. Then he went to Alex's chair and repeated his assignment.

This better work, Williams.

Sophie was last. She was late getting into her chair because she'd stopped to kiss Dean on the head.

Hell, he didn't blame her. He would have done the same thing.

Besides, this maniac had gone too far to let a few seconds spoil his fun.

He tightened her restraints, making sure her right wrist and hand were at the angle she needed, gave her a quick look, and then walked over to his chair and stood beside it, waiting.

"Well done, agents. Who said you Feds couldn't follow directions? Now sit in the chair, Manny. Do it now."

The voice had changed again, and it was almost familiar. The intercom distorted his words, but at that moment the killer seemed to shed any concern for concealment.

"I think not. Come make me, you cowardly piece of shit," Manny yelled.

A door flew open some twenty-five feet to his left. Manny watched as the killer stood in the doorway. He was dressed in a black trench coat, a black Fedora, and his face was fully covered in facial hair. His disguise was topped off by wide, dark sunglasses.

"Sit down, Manny. Do it now or I'll kill everyone. You have ten seconds."

This time the killer was close to losing it. Manny had pushed the button he'd hoped for.

"No. And why are you calling me Manny instead of—"

Maybe it was the heightened state of Manny's emotions or maybe a sense of impending doom, or maybe he had subconsciously simply put all of the facts in the right order. He didn't know and didn't care. As hard as it was for him to believe, the use of his name, disguised voice or not, made the killer's true identity leap into his mind.

He stood paralyzed in disbelief.

Tilting his head, the man Manny had known for over fifteen years allowed the black coat to slip to the floor.

"I see you've finally figured it out, Manny."

Slowly, the killer removed the facial hair and hat, casting them aside.

Behind him, Manny heard Alex Downs swear in disbelief.

Mike Crosby, Gavin's son, walked toward them, wearing the grin of a madman and holding a Glock 22 in his hand.

CHAPTER-61

Over the years, Manny's ability to compartmentalize had served him well. He needed that ability now. He'd known Mike Crosby since he was a teen. But apparently he hadn't known him as well as he assumed. All of them now needed to block out who Mike Crosby was and concentrate on getting out of this.

Manny's stomach dropped. That was going to be a trick.

"Mike. What the hell are you doing?" asked Manny.

Taking a few more steps, Mike raised the gun, reached into his pocket, and took out a cell phone.

"What I should have done after Lexy and my Mom died. Getting rid of the real problems: you and this bunch of losers. Now sit your ass down or I swear I'll start killing each one of these people."

Manny was over the shock as much as could be expected. Survival mode ensured that.

"Why this? Why all of this?" asked Manny.

"I told you to sit down. No more questions. I'm here to do what is necessary. What has to be done."

"But Mike—"

The younger Crosby's face twisted into something evil, and he raised his weapon toward Josh Corner, then fired.

The sound of the gunshot was the most awful sound Manny had ever endured. Josh's subsequent mind-bending scream was worse.

Manny spun toward Josh and saw the blood gushing from his left shoulder. The pain and disbelief in his boss's eyes were hard to separate. Neither belonged.

"Get into the damned chair Williams, or Lee is next and it won't be in the shoulder," snarled Mike.

The gun barrel's heat next to his ear told Manny that Mike had moved close.

Can I get him now?

No. It would be suicide to try anything.

Manny did the only thing he could do. He sat in the padded chair.

He immediately felt the vibration of something powerful under his seat and wondered what it was and how it fit into Mike's fantasy. He was almost glad when Sophie interrupted his thoughts.

"You son of a bitch, Mike. I don't care why you're doing what you're doing, but I'm going to take you into the next world," she screamed.

Mike ignored her and, while holding the gun to Manny's face, clamped the metal bindings over each of Manny's forearms. The first one clicked into place, the second followed suit. Manny wasn't sure why his bindings were different, but he was sure Mike would clue him in, one way or the other.

Manny shot a look toward Josh and saw that the blood flow was steady, but not the worst he'd seen. Still, Josh wouldn't last long if it wasn't stopped.

Mike backed away from Manny, pointing to all of them as he swung around in a full circle.

"Get a good look. All of you. I want you all to feel my pain. My loss. It's your fault that I'm alone, and soon one of you will know what that feels like."

"We can talk about this, Mike. You can stop what you're doing. It's not too late," said Manny, trying to reason with him.

"Oh, it's too late Manny. For you. You lost Louise and I believed it right. Fair. You should have caught Argyle before he killed Lexy. You should have helped my mother before she was killed. But I thought you would continue to be miserable and pay for your sins so I coped with losing them the best that I could. But then you married that Irish bitch and you were back in the saddle. Finding happiness, and I was still in hell. And these poor excuses for human beings helped you get there."

"Mike, I loved Lexy and your mom. We did our best to—"

The blow came fast, and Manny's head jerked to the right, stars doing a temporary dance in front of his eyes.

"Don't mention them. You don't have the right," he said, venom in his eyes.

"Big brave man hitting people when they're strapped to a chair. Let me loose. I dare you," said Sophie, her expression full of rage.

"No. My turn first."

Looking quickly toward Dean, Manny saw that he was awake. Weak, hurt, but awake.

"No, me," said Alex.

Josh chimed in. "Hell, I'm shot, and I could kick your ass."

Mike stood his ground, looking at each of them in turn without speaking.

He finally nodded, then stepped toward Manny and put his hand on the tarp covering the long, oblong shape to his side.

When he spoke, he sounded like the Mike Crosby he'd known for the last two decades. It was so damn bizarre, no matter how many times he witnessed it. Manny would never get used to psychopaths careening in and out of worlds and realities belonging only to them without so much as a thought. He supposed that was a good thing.

"This *cover each other's ass* mentality was why I knew I could count on you showing up. All of you. You are loyal and would never intentionally leave each other out in the cold, so to speak. Your problem is, however, that you don't know when to quit. That's why you're where you are."

"Oh, and you're drinking from the cup of sanity," said Sophie.

"My sanity isn't the issue. I believe it's yours, particularly Manny's."

"Why would you say that?" asked Manny.

Keep him talking, Williams. Keep him talking.

"Because you're obsessed with your life as a profiler."

"How so?"

Mike laughed. "Let me explain. From the moment I pulled that body out of the ground and had it brought out here, you thought Argyle alive."

Mike was right. Manny *had* believed that.

"You see, you're not the only one who can study habits of the rich and psycho. It took me a year, but I learned everything about him, even how to speak the way he did from that damn DVD he'd left on the cruise ship. Then I started playing games with you. The couple in the casket, the text, the phone call to my worthless father, the woman in the hotel room, the dead agent driving you from the airport—all of it was thrown out there for you to follow a hidden trail."

"We knew you weren't Argyle hours ago," said Manny.

Mike shook his head. "It didn't matter. You thought it was possible, and you came here, to Vegas. That's what was important. You needed to be in this town of good times to suffer horribly. And you will. The best way to get you here was for you to think that the Good Doctor had somehow tricked you. Obviously that worked. The only thing I really wanted you to sort out was the meaning of the Canopic jars. Everything else was a diversion, well almost. You see, Argyle *is* here."

With a swipe of his hand, Mike pulled the tarp from the hidden object.

Manny blinked as he stared into the casket. Mike had angled it away from the others and the only way to see who was inside was to be near where Manny sat.

His eyes refocused to the head of the box causing his heart to jump. The mostly decayed body of Fredrick Argyle lay in state. He was almost unrecognizable, except for one major part of his condition. The right side of his skull was partly missing. The bullet Manny had killed him with had also displaced much of his facial structure, causing that side of his skull to pattern in an unnatural arch.

Mixed emotions flooded him. Argyle was dead, no question. Manny knew deep down, finally, that it was him. He felt a final surge of relief. But that wasn't all he felt. He was suddenly angry at himself. He'd let his emotions run away with him. His fear and hatred had led him to the obsession Mike had described. He'd taken his unit from the pan into the fire.

"Is it him?" asked Alex, his voice higher than normal.

Manny nodded. "It's him. The same man I killed in Galway."

"Oh. I can tell you're angry and upset, Agent. Don't be too hard on yourself, yet. Argyle or not, eventually the BAU would have come to Las Vegas looking for me. This way, however, you got here sooner."

He was right about that. Somehow that didn't make Manny feel any better.

Mike stepped toward him. Bending close to Manny's face, he spoke softly. He was losing his focus on reality again. This wasn't just a psychotic episode. His friend was in another world.

"Did you get the rest of this setup, Agent Williams? Did you get it?"

Exhaling, Manny shifted to the moment. "You tell me. Dean and Alex are represented by the liver and stomach because they process and sort out details, then break them down into details we can understand. Josh is parallel with the intestines because he's the leader and the backbone, the guts of the unit. Sophie represents the lungs because she's the most vocal, our real voice at times. How am I doing?"

Manny watched Mike's face break into a crooked smile. "Well. You're doing well. What of you?"

"You believe that I'm the brains in the outfit, so you made a fifth jar and put that poor woman's brain inside. You think the unit revolves around me, as evidenced by this setup. But you're wrong. We work as one. We always have. It's the only way to accomplish what we need."

"Congratulations. You've solved that part of the task. And you might be right about doing everything together. You're going to die together. I guarantee that. So what's next, Agent?"

Taking another quick look over his shoulder at Josh, he saw the blood dripping on the floor from his left arm and Josh was losing his color. He wasn't going to last much longer.

Here we go. He turned toward Mike.

"I have a question. Why here? Why Vegas?"

He shrugged. "Why not here? It suited me. And, like I said, I wanted you to suffer in a place where you wouldn't expect to suffer. I want your families to have to deal with the pain of getting your bodies home. Above all, I wanted you out of your element and into mine to complete your task, so to speak."

Manny kept at him. "Why a task at all, Mike? Why do we have to worry about what's next? You're not a killer. You've been a good cop. Now this? Are you nuts or just a spoiled little punk who always got his way? Tell me."

The degree of rage surprised even Manny. But he'd pissed Mike off and that was what he wanted.

Mike grabbed his shirt and backhanded Manny again. His head jerked to the left, as another eyeful of colorful stars came and went. He vaguely noticed Sophie working on her wrist binding. She needed to hurry.

"Because of you, Williams. Because of you. You not only let the women in my life die, but you robbed me of everything else. My happiness, my family, my job, and even my father. He cares for you more than me."

"Not true, Mike. Not true. You're suffering from delusions. Come on, man, get your shit together."

Mike raised his hand again and Manny braced for another strike, but it didn't happen. Instead, Mike began to laugh. "Almost got me again, Williams. Almost. As much as I like hitting you, it's time to get to the reason we're here."

"The cell phone in my hand controls the power grid running from your throne to the others. Each set of cables is controlled by a number. There is enough voltage running through those cables to fry ten people."

Mike waved the phone under his nose. "Technology does work, yes? Now I need you to do something for me."

Manny felt sick. He knew what was next.

Mike put his hand on Manny's shoulder. "You, Agent Williams, must now pick a number from one to four to get this party rolling."

"Mike," he pleaded, "stop this madness. You're not a killer."

Standing straight up, Mike exhaled, raising the cell phone. "You also know nothing of my past. I've killed before Vegas, before Lansing. A long time ago, someone tried to take what was mine. Lexy became my wife and it didn't end well for him. Just like it won't for all of you. But enough of the past you know nothing of."

"But I do, son, I do."

The voice coming from the direction of the doors caused everyone in the room to turn in that direction. For the second time in fifteen minutes, Manny's mind struggled to understand what he was seeing.

Gavin Crosby stood mere feet away, his gun pointed directly at his son.

CHAPTER-62

The two men, father and son, locked eyes, neither moving. The silent communication going on between them welcomed an interpretation, but Manny didn't think it possible to fully understand what that meant.

He didn't have to wait long for it to be revealed.

"I don't know how you found me, Father, but what are you doing here?"

"Technology works, Mike. I agree. And you know why I'm here. I turned Alan Gordon's murder file over to Chloe, and she figured out that I was hiding something. That I was hiding you," said Gavin.

His voice was calm. He appeared not to be surprised by what he was seeing. Manny wondered if he knew that Mike was going to snap at some point.

"So you knew I killed him?"

"Yes. Over time, I'd put most of the pieces together. The motorcycle, the lame excuse as to where you were, the way your other friends covered for you, and how Lexy used to tear up when we talked about Alan. I knew they were lying. But the biggest thing was the screwdrivers. I remembered buying you some like that for Christmas the year before. I searched for them in the garage and never found them."

"Well, well, well. You are a bit of a cop after all. Too bad you were never a dad," said Mike, his anger showing.

"Maybe not, but I did my best. I regret many things, Mike. I should have put you away after Lexy and your Mom died. I knew what kind of man you could become. But none of that matters now. I'm here to take you home and get you help."

"Help?" Mike laughed and held the cell phone higher. "You know I can kill all of them with a touch of this phone screen."

"I heard. I won't let that happen, son. Just drop the phone and the gun. We can walk out of here alive, all of us."

"He's right, Mike. Listen to him," said Manny softly.

The younger Crosby hesitated and seemed to mull over what he'd heard. For the first time since they'd reached this building, Manny's hope rose.

It shouldn't have.

Mike Crosby looked at the floor, lifted his head, and then moved quickly. He raised his gun and fired, hitting Gavin in the thigh. Gavin returned a wild shot as he was going down. Mike ducked as the bullet whizzed over his head, his momentum forcing him to within inches of Manny.

Reaching out with his left leg, he kicked at Mike's feet and felt Mike's ankle give way.

He shrieked and the gun flew from his hand as he rumpled to the floor. Unfortunately, Mike still maintained possession of the phone.

Manny tried to kick him again, but he was just out of reach. He strained against the metal bindings on his arms and felt the one on the left give, but not enough. He couldn't pull his arm through. He needed more time, time he didn't have.

Mike had recovered.

"You're all dead," he screamed. "I'll fry all of your asses."

"I don't think so," said Sophie.

The next sound Manny heard was the subtle, familiar whisper of a throwing star cutting through the air.

Mike screamed again as the pink star buried deep into his hand, sending the phone flying across the cement floor. The next star hit him in the side of the head, then bounced to the floor. He was dazed, but not out.

Sophie swore. She'd missed by an inch of stopping him in his tracks.

Glancing her way, he saw that she had one hand and one leg free, working on the others. The hard-plastic versions of her stars hidden under each sleeve had not been detected by whatever technology Mike had used to make sure they were unarmed. Dean and Alex began to yell in Mike's direction hoping to confuse and distract him so that Sophie could finish freeing herself.

No such luck. After a few seconds, he got to his hands and knees, pulled Sophie's star from his right hand, then scrambled toward the gun located just a few feet away, muttering to himself.

Manny quickly looked in Gavin's direction and saw his friend struggle to a seated position. He was sitting in a pool of blood that made Josh's look like a drop. Manny felt his heart sink.

Mike's bullet must have hit the femoral artery in Gavin's thigh. He was quickly bleeding out.

"Mike, sto-stop, stop, now," Gavin's voice was weak, but it was still his.

Ignoring his father, he reached for the gun, grasped the handle, and began to turn in his dad's direction.

"MIKE, DON'T!" hollered Manny.

He hesitated, glanced at Manny, then pointed the gun.

The sound of the next shot rumbled through the warehouse. Then all was quiet.

His friend, his pseudo little brother, his would-be killer, blinked twice, and then reached down to his chest. He never made it. Mike Crosby fell over dead, the bullet from Gavin's gun striking him directly in the heart.

Manny had time to look at Gavin to see him fall back, groaning.

Somewhere, Manny gathered more strength and pulled against the brace with all that he had. It gave completely away from the armrest. In a few seconds he was free, running to Gavin's side.

His substitute father, the man who had trained him and had him over for all of those meals before he'd married Louise. The one who'd helped him become the man and cop that he was, lay on the cement, pale as his white shirt, eyes closed.

A man should never be in this situation once, let alone twice. He'd watched Louise die in his home, bleeding to death from a stray bullet, and now, in this lonely warehouse thousands of miles from home, he was watching it again.

Gavin's eyes opened as Manny grasped his hand. They were clear, at least for the moment.

"There's a letter in my pocket for you and Chloe."

He sounded so far away.

"We're getting help. Just hold on," said Manny, tears forcing their way down his cheeks.

"Too late. Just know I'm sorry about . . . about Mike. I should have . . . t-tell Haley Rose—"

His mentor and friend never finished the sentence.

His eyes fluttered shut and Gavin Crosby died.

CHAPTER-63

Chloe's hand slipped into his as she and Manny stood to the left of the chapel's small alter. He kissed her then put his hand on the ever-growing baby bump.

"You need to put that girl on a diet," said Alex.

He laughed as he turned to Alex and Barb standing on the other side of the aisle.

"She's going to hurt you, you know?" said Manny.

"I am, but I'll wait for a few more months," agreed Chloe, her eyes sparkling.

"I could do it now, Uncle Alex," said Jen, grinning as she and Haley Rose moved up to stand by Chloe.

He laughed. It felt good. It had been too long.

Four months too long.

Gavin and Mike had been gone that long, and he missed them, at least the old Mike. He was still besieged with *whys* and *whats* and *hows*, and he guessed that would always be.

Gavin's letter and the long text he'd sent Chloe before he died had helped, but Manny was trying to reconcile why Mike had been a killer at such a young age, and why Gavin had hid it. Gavin's letter spoke of anger within his son. He and Stella had even taken him in for counseling. Mike refused to talk to the therapist, only saying he was fine and wanted to talk to his dad. But Gavin was busy working and building a career, leaving the everyday routine of raising a child to his wife. The last line in his letter said he regretted that now. Mike's state of mind was his fault, and he was sorry.

The text to Chloe stated that he knew Mike had killed Alan a few years after it happened. His jealousy for Lexy the trigger for killing Alan. But he didn't see the point in ruining another young man's life over something that no one could change anyway. Besides, Mike had changed. He wasn't the same angry kid—and he was his son.

In the end, Gavin had done the right thing by trying to bring Mike in. Manny was sure killing him wasn't in the plan, but he knew Gavin had been prepared to do what was necessary.

Still, Manny tried to imagine what it was like to pull your weapon and kill your own child.

He glanced at Jen and shivered. Hell on earth.

To top off everything, he had to tell Haley Rose that Gavin had been thinking of her when he died. Her tears were few, but it took her months after the funeral to get out and around. Jen had helped with that. His little girl had been Haley Rose's rock. Much like she'd been for him.

Help had arrived at the warehouse, and while it had been a tough few days for Josh, he came through the ordeal with flying colors.

That wasn't the extent of Josh's next step in life, however. John Dickman, the assistant director, had sent out a special agent to retrieve Josh and bring him back to Quantico. He'd interviewed and tested three main candidates and, much to Josh's surprise, offered the leader of the BAU the job of assistant director upon Dickman's retirement. Dickman told Josh that even though his disregard for some rules made him a risk, his other leadership traits, and concern for his staff made him a perfect choice. Dickman also admitted that he'd always done what was necessary and right, ignoring a few regulations along the way himself.

In the end, Josh had turned down the AD job. He told Dickman he wasn't ready, and if the Bureau wanted to cut him loose, he understood, but he was staying at the BAU for as long as his team wanted him there. End of story. Dickman had laughed and told Josh "maybe next time around" and to keep up the good work. Josh had thanked him, and then went home, kissed his boys, put them into bed, and in his words, made love to his wife all night.

Something had happened because his wife was now pregnant. Maybe the all-night thing wasn't an exaggeration.

The night Josh had confided all this to the BAU, they all went out for a drink to celebrate.

Sophie asked him if he knew what caused that baby-making situation. He told her he was pretty sure but still doing research.

What a night that had been. Dean and Sophie got to make an announcement of their own.

He recalled talking to her the night before.

"Do you remember that night in North Carolina when I said I want to have what you had with Chloe someday?" she'd asked.

"I do. I said you would, right?" She'd nodded. "That day in Las Vegas when I thought I might lose Dean forever was the worst day of my life. I wasn't just pissed. I was terrified that I wouldn't be able to touch him, talk to him, or hear him say my name again. I sat in that damn chair Mike put me in and made myself a promise that if God got us out, I'd give us a chance."

"And?"

"And I'm going in for the third time. Besides, I want to have sex with someone who wants me more than I want them, ya know?"

She'd winked. He'd laughed. He did know.

So here they were. Back in Vegas.

Just then, Josh walked into the chapel, hung up his phone, and stood beside Barb and Alex. He smiled at Manny and winked.

He wasn't sure how Josh was going to handle the fact that Dean and Sophie were going to be on the BAU as a married couple. The Bureau frowned on such things. Something about being against regulations. Josh told his superiors to trust him, that he would figure it out. It looked like, at least for now, he'd done just that.

Life was nothing if not ever-changing, and his boss understood that too.

The next moment, the wedding march blared through the small, powerful speakers.

Sophie, wearing the same short red dress, hat, shoes, and handbag she'd worn in the Egyptian months ago, and Dean, in a red paisley tux with matching driver's hat and a trimmed beard, walked down the aisle arm in arm, giggling.

Manny was flooded with an abrupt visual of Gavin's face, smiling. The man would have loved this. Who knew? Maybe he was watching.

They reached the altar, and the man conducting the ceremony, dressed in a white Elvis jumpsuit, began.

"We make this here kind of thing brief in Vegas. I have just three questions, plus the one you want me to ask. Are you ready?"

They nodded in sync.

"Is anyone giving away the bride?"

Manny stepped forward. "Yes. Manny Williams, her family, and her friends from the BAU."

"That's a first for me, but thank you, thank you very much."

Elvis paused. "Okay. Dean, do you love this woman and are you going to take care of her?"

"I do and I will," he answered, his voice suddenly quiet. "She's my Princess and the answer to my dreams."

Manny wasn't the only one to feel the groom's elation. Chloe, Jen, Haley Rose, Barb, and Alex had joined him in wiping at tears.

"Sophie, how about you? Do you love this man and will you watch his back?"

"I do and already have," she said, letting her own tears flow.

"Okay then. Last question. I got to say, we don't get this one a lot out here."

The Elvis look-alike glanced down to the sheet of paper in his hand.

"Will you both do your best to honor God with this union?"

"We will," they answered in unison.

Manny felt his chest rise. Sophie and Dean had come to him and asked him if they thought God would mind since they weren't exactly believers, but they both believed that not mentioning Him wouldn't be quite right.

He'd agreed and was pretty sure God was on board as well.

"Okay y'all, get yer behinds out there and celebrate. By the authority given to me by the state of Nevada, you are now man and wife. You can kiss the bride."

Kiss they did. After a few seconds, Jen started to yell for them to get a room. The laughter rang through the tiny chapel.

"Y'all need to hurry out to your limo or you're going to get hit with one of those rare rains during a Vegas summer," said Elvis.

The group followed Sophie and Dean as they hurried out the door and down the steps, ducking rice and laughing.

They piled into the car as Manny helped Chloe into the fourth door.

He was bending to get into the limo, when he felt something wet on his hand. He looked up into a dark cloud and felt two drops hit his face, and then more.

Elvis had been right. Rain in Vegas was indeed rare.

He smiled.

This time, the Vegas rain was a good omen.

Thank you so much for reading Vegas Rain! I'd love to hear what you think, as always. You can reach me at rickmurcer@gmail.com or come visit our website at www.rickmurcer.com.

Next up is **Caribbean Fire**.

After Baby Williams is born, Manny and Chloe head to Cozumel for a long-awaited honeymoon.

Sun, sand, warmth, the Mayan culture, and murder. You won't want to miss this one.

Due out in late spring...I promise! ☺

Perfect Sinners, the next Ellen Harper Psycho-thriller is in line after that.

Ellen, Big Harv, Brice, and Bella will all be back for at least one more.

Celtic Fire--The eighth Manny Williams Thriller is in my thoughts, as well.

Then a collaboration I'll be doing with another writer, but more on that later.

As you see, I have a few more projects in line for next year. If you e-mail me, I'll be able to add you to the Newsletter List and keep you apprised on how things are progressing.

Again, thank you all for helping me on this journey. I'm grateful for this writing gig and you've all made it possible. God bless and live like you mean it.

Rick

CPSIA information can be obtained
at www.ICGtesting.com
Printed in the USA
LVOW07s1614260617
539414LV00012B/762/P